Cath ....wright
and t.. .....starring
Carol ....ks have
been short-listed for the Crime Writers Association (CWA)
Best First Novel award and for the Dagger in the Library. In
°012 Cath was joint winner of the CWA Short Story Dagger
ʾr Laptop, sharing the prize with Margaret Murphy. Cath
. also the author of the *Scott and Bailey* novels based
cn the popular ITV series. Cath lives with her family in
Manchester.

www.cathstaincliffe.co.uk

Follow Cath on Twitter @CathStaincliffe

Also by Cath Staincliffe

Witness
The Kindest Thing
Split Second
Blink of an Eye

The Sal Kilkenny Mysteries

Looking For Trouble
Go Not Gently
Dead Wrong
Stone Cold Red Hot
Towers of Silence

Short stories

In the Heart of the City
Violation

TOWERS
OF
SILENCE

CATH STAINCLIFFE

Constable & Robinson Ltd
55–56 Russell Square
London WC1B 4HP
www.constablerobinson.com

First published by Allison & Busby, Ltd, 2003

This paperback edition published in the UK by C&R Crime
an imprint of Constable & Robinson Ltd, 2013

A copy of the British Library Cataloguing in
Publication Data is available from the British Library.

ISBN: 978-1-47210-111-2 (paperback)

Typeset by TW Typesetting, Plymouth, Devon

Printed in the UK

1 3 5 7 9 10 8 6 4 2

Towers of silence: the small towers on which Parsees and Zoroastrians place their dead to be consumed by birds of prey.

Brewer's Concise Dictionary of Phrase and Fable

For Fay, Julia, Maggie and Polly – partners in crime

CHAPTER ONE

It was the festive season. Less than three weeks till Christmas but we'd all been smothered with tinsel, fake snow, holly and Santa Claus since they'd whipped the Hallowe'en stuff away at the beginning of November. We were on the home run. Three weeks and counting, nineteen shopping days. Well, every day was a shopping day and half the nights an' all. The Manchester stores were busy, tills a-bleeping in the steady chant of commerce, shop windows ablaze with all the sparkling ingredients for that magical celebration, the city festooned with luxury. Samaritans signing up for extra duty on the phone lines. Festive season, restive season.

I had three bags full of stuff and a creeping headache from the combination of over warm shops, desperate concentration and the noxious fumes of the perfume departments which were strategically placed inside the entrances to most of the big shops. I'd still got nothing for Ray, my housemate, nor Laura, his girlfriend. What did you get a thirty-something of Italian ancestry whose sole interests are carpentry and computing? A chisel? A mouse mat? On a par with treating your mother to a duster, I reckon.

I knew it was time to cut my losses and get the bus back. If I spent any more money it would be ill spent on poor choices. I knew; I'd been here before.

I clambered onto the bus, got my ticket and sat down, easing the bags onto my knees with a sigh of relief. I rubbed at the deep welts the carriers had carved in my fingers. The bus trundled along Cross Street and swung round by Albert Square. I craned my neck to look at the inflatable Santa suspended halfway up the Town Hall. The comic blow-up doll hardly complemented the Victorian splendour of the building. The place boasted a clock tower and a soaring style that celebrated the civic pride of nineteenth-century Manchester; it was a testament to the time when Manchester ruled the world, and not just in football and music.

You'd think they could have got someone to design a Victorian-style Father Christmas, like in the old picture books, chubby cheeks, curling beard and moustache, twinkling eyes, instead of this paddling pool monstrosity. Maddie, Tom and presumably all the other children thought it was great but I reckon it was the idea they liked (as did I) rather than the thing itself.

Barring hold-ups I would just have time to get the two of them back from school and get round the corner to the office for my four o'clock appointment with the Johnstones. Transforming myself from Sal Kilkenny, single parent, to Sal Kilkenny, private eye. New clients and I'd yet to find out what they wanted from me. But whatever it was, the money would come in handy for Christmas. I didn't know then that I was going to turn them away. I didn't know a lot of things then. Let's just say I've had better Christmases.

CHAPTER TWO

'Everybody had decided it was suicide but it just didn't make sense.'

'You weren't happy with the coroner's verdict?'

She assessed me. 'No.' Connie Johnstone, a black woman in her mid-twenties, was doing the talking. Her teenage sister, Martina, nodded in agreement now and again or scowled at my questions, their brother Roland, the youngest of the three at fourteen, kept his arms folded and his eyes averted. Connie's boyfriend, a white man who had introduced himself in a strong Irish accent as Patrick Dowley, watched me silently.

I'd not expected four of them and had to bring down chairs from the kitchen to the cellar so they could all sit down.

'What weren't you happy about?'

She held my gaze for a moment, eyes the colour of hazelnut shells, her skin a shade or two darker. Her black hair was braided in corn rows. There was an edge of pain in her expression then she blinked slowly and took a breath.

'Ma was scared of heights. Petrified. She would never have gone up there. Not in a million years.'

'Even if she were distressed?'

'Particularly then. Like I said she had periods of depression and at times she'd get anxious, start getting paranoid about things but she wasn't mad,' she snapped the word defiantly, 'she never lost it completely. If she had started feeling down she would never have gone there, she'd not have gone out.'

Martina nodded slowly. Patrick shifted his weight on the chair. Roland swallowed.

'You told the coroner this?'

'Yes. But it didn't make any difference. He'd made up his mind, they all had. Once they knew she'd been treated for depression, that she'd spent time in hospital, then that was it. Case closed. Mentally ill – chucks herself off a building,' she said harshly. 'That explained it for them but not for us. It didn't make sense. If she had wanted to kill herself she'd have done it some other way.'

'She wasn't even depressed,' Patrick put in quickly. His hair was cropped close to his skull, he wore small wire glasses. He was thin-faced and blue veins showed through his milky complexion. 'We saw her on the Wednesday and she was okay then. She hadn't been bad for months.'

Connie nodded. 'She was fine,' she said to me.

'And you told the coroner that as well?'

'Yes.'

What were they saying? If Miriam Johnstone hadn't jumped then what? She'd been pushed? My stomach tightened and I asked her outright.

'You think her death was suspicious? That someone else was involved?'

She drew in her cheeks, nodded.

'Or maybe an accident,' Patrick added, catching my frown.

'Is there anything, anything at all, to suggest that someone else was there?'

No one spoke for a moment.

'That's what we want you to find out,' Connie said.

A tall order. I sighed. 'Were there any witnesses?'

'No,' she said quietly.

'Any forensic evidence, anything at the inquest to suggest she was with someone?'

'No.'

'Any evidence of a struggle or an attack?'

'No.'

4

'Do you suspect somebody?'

'No,' even quieter.

I could sense the mist of despair seep into the atmosphere.

'Couldn't you just make some enquiries though? The police hardly talked to anybody,' Connie said urgently.

Because there was no need to, I thought. I carried on trying to establish whether there were any grounds for an enquiry. I could do with the work but I need to believe that there's something I can usefully do for my clients.

'Did Miriam have any enemies?'

'No,' Connie said.

'Feuds?' A shake of the head. 'Was she involved in any business dealings?'

'No.'

'Did she have any money or property that someone outside the family stood to inherit?'

'No.' A sullen burn in her eyes. She knew my game.

'Any insurance policies payable on her death?'

'No.'

'Was she seeing anyone, romantically?'

Roland wriggled with resentment.

'No.'

I sighed. No reason for anyone to harm her. I didn't need to say it aloud.

'I told you it would be a waste of time,' Martina burst out. 'She's just like the rest of them.'

Connie looked down at her hands resting on the folder on her knees. Her head bowing. Patrick put out his hand and clasped her arm.

Martina sighed theatrically and glared at me sidelong, Roland studied his shoes.

'We read about you in the paper,' Patrick told me. 'About the racial harassment case. We thought you'd . . . have an open mind.'

'What's the point?' Martina repeated.

'You think there could be some racial element?'

5

'She was a black woman,' Connie said.

'Had anyone been causing her any trouble?'

She shook her head again.

'Nothing? Threats, damage to property, hate mail?'

'No. What I mean is the police, that's why they didn't do much, didn't listen to us. Because she was black.'

I nodded. It was plausible. Senior officers had recently acknowledged that there was institutionalized racism in the force. Black and Asian communities had known it for years and had little faith in the police. They didn't trust them and there'd been a sorry stream of cases, including that of Stephen Lawrence, which demonstrated police failure and incompetence in serving black citizens.

'Look, I'm sorry,' I said. 'I'm sorry about your mother's death. Maybe the police could have done more but I don't think it would have changed the verdict. If you could give me any stronger reason for investigating it I'd be happy to help but everything points to suicide.'

Connie rolled her eyes in impatience and inhaled. 'She was fine when we last saw her,' she looked straight at me, spoke slowly to emphasize her points, 'and she had a phobia of heights, high buildings. She even used to swap her duties with the other orderlies at the hospital so she wouldn't have to do the higher floors.' She looked away sharply, I could see the tears of frustration glittering in her eyes.

'When she did get depressed, how quickly did it come on?'

'A few days.'

'Is it impossible that she was okay on the Wednesday and became ill on the Thursday?'

'It's not likely.'

'Had she tried to harm herself before.'

I waited for her reply. 'No.'

'We just want to know what happened,' Patrick tried.

'I think the coroner's verdict is the closest you're going to get. I'm sorry if that sounds hard but I don't think I can do anything for you. If there was anything more concrete to go on . . . but as it is . . .'

'Think about it,' Patrick said, his face flushing lightly. 'Don't decide now, take a little time, maybe.'

'What's the point?' Martina stood. I guessed she was about seventeen, tall and skinny. She was like her sister but she wore her hair pulled back in a bun. 'She's only going to say no again.'

Roland rose too, stuffing his large hands into his pockets, staring resolutely at the wall. He wore school uniform and had the awkward look of a boy growing into his body. His hair was twisted into small tufts.

'Look, in all honesty, the police saw nothing suspicious, found nothing. And from what you've told me I agree with them.'

'They didn't even bother. They didn't care. How did she get there? They never explained that.' Connie blurted out. 'She didn't drive. If she was depressed – and I don't buy that – then she'd stay home. She'd retreat, not go off into town. She wouldn't have been up to getting on a bus. And she would never, never, never have gone up to the fifth floor of a building and thrown herself off.' Her words reverberated round the small room.

I waited a beat. I wanted to help if I could, but all I was hearing was her insistence that it couldn't be suicide. She was grieving, maybe in denial. It didn't make sense, she claimed, she wanted to know why. What if there was no reason? No logical explanation? 'Hiring someone like me isn't necessarily going to answer those questions. I could launch an investigation and find nothing and you'd be wasting your money.'

'It's not about money,' Connie said, a frown furrowing her brow, 'it's about . . .' she broke off, wrestling her emotions.

'I want to be straight with you,' I said. 'It sounds like you want me to prove something suspicious about your mother's death but from my point of view there's really nothing to back that up and I wouldn't be happy working for you with that expectation there. I'd be just as likely to confirm the inquest verdict. But I don't think that's what you want, is it?'

No one spoke.

'I'm sorry. There are other agencies, obviously, but can I suggest if you do approach anyone that you agree on a fixed number of hours and a fixed rate.'

There were plenty of rip-off merchants about who would milk the Johnstones for all they had.

Connie rose, avoiding eye contact. Patrick took the folder from her. The four of them walked up the steps and along the hall to the front door. Their shoulders were set and the air stiff with tension.

The teenagers walked down the path, Connie muttered a goodbye and followed. Patrick hung back. When they were out of earshot he turned to me.

'Will you not think this over, give us an answer tomorrow.'

I opened my mouth to refuse but he barged on.

'Connie had to identify her mother. She had to do it by looking at her hands. Things were that bad.'

Oh God. I didn't need to hear this.

'Connie can't accept it. The police did nothing. If we just knew more about those missing hours. Even if all you could do was fill in some of that last day, that would really help. It wouldn't explain everything but it might tell us something of what Miriam was doing. We'd have a bit more of the picture. Surely, you could do that?'

That wasn't what Connie had asked. I shook my head slowly.

'Aw, Jesus,' he cried out, his voice strained. 'Where's the bloody harm in it?' He pinched the top of his nose near the glasses. Blew out. 'Look, we'll ring tomorrow. Think about it.' He pushed the folder at me. I took it. To refuse that would have been heartless.

'We'll ring tomorrow,' he said again and turned away. He walked down the path pulling up his collar against the cold, his shoulders rounded, head thrust forward.

'Where's the bloody harm in it?'

CHAPTER THREE

It's only a few minutes' walk home from the office. I rent the basement room from the Dobson family who occupy the rest of the house. When I first set up as a private investigator I wanted to have some separation between home and work; a cheap room to meet my clients in and store my paperwork. When I knocked on doors looking for a space, the Dobsons liked the idea of having a sleuth in the cellar. Not only did I pay them for that, I also regularly used their older daughters for babysitting when Ray wasn't home to look after the children. Selina Dobson was obliging me that night. I found her on the sofa, between Tom and Maddie transfixed by a Pokemon cartoon. I thanked and paid her, once the programme finished, and set about making tea. Tagliatelle and tuna sauce. Just for the three of us; I knew Ray would be late back.

It was a blustery evening, the wind whipping the trees and shrubs about. A clatter from the back garden sent me out to investigate. Light spilt out from the lounge and the kitchen, illuminating an empty plant pot skipping over the grass. I caught it soon enough. A small maple I had in a pot had been blown over too. I moved that to the corner between the house and the fence we share with next door, to give it more shelter.

One or two stars glimmered dimly above but that was it. Starry nights are rare in the city. Not just because of the frequent cloud cover – Manchester AKA Rainy City – but also because of the bright lights that illuminate the streets, the clubs and the buildings and drench the heavens. As I headed

9

for the door at the side of the house I could hear more clatter-ing, from above. I peered up at the house. It was hard to tell in the dark, but it seemed to be the wood that ran along the edge of the roof. Another job for the list. The old Victorian semi boasts big rooms, a big garden and big bills. To be fair, the owner who lectures in Australia pays for all the mainte-nance but it can take several weeks to come through and my overdraft suffers.

Ray and I have shared the house since Maddie was a tod-dler. Ray was a single parent trying to find accommodation for himself and baby Tom, and I'd just got the tenancy of the house and needed someone to help fill it. We've become a sort of alternative family over time and people often mistak-enly assume that Ray and I are living together in the Biblical rather than the practical sense. We sublet the attic flat and we've had a series of lodgers. Sheila, a mature student and divorcee, has been with us for a couple of years and we all get on very well. Ray's mum, Nana Costello, a small, fierce Ital-ian woman, lives nearby and is a frequent visitor to the house. She is a vociferous critic of some of our lifestyle choices. I've learnt to take her in my stride – just about.

During tea, Maddie and Tom re-enacted for me all the adverts for absolutely brilliant, must-have toys that were dominating the telly.

'And you can cut her hair off and make it grow,' Maddie said. For £29.99, I thought sourly. And then what? It hardly seemed the basis for hours of creative play.

'I want to do another list,' said Maddie.

'And me,' Tom echoed her.

'I'll get you pens and paper.'

'You have to help us, though, with the spelling.'

'Or you could do a picture list – draw what you want.'

'Nah,' she said.

'You might only get one thing on the list,' I reminded them later. We were sat on the floor in their playroom, the fabulous gluttonous lists before us. 'Or even nothing.'

'Or for my birthday,' Tom, ever the optimist. 'When I'm six. Like Maddie.'

'I'll be seven by then, dumbo.'

'Maddie,' I complained.

'Will Laura buy us presents?' She asked, still in infant school but already a fervent materialist.

'I don't know,' I replied.

'She is,' Tom said. 'She told me.' Tom was passionately fond of his dad's new girlfriend.

'When are we getting the tree?' Maddie demanded. 'You said soon.'

'Maybe next weekend. We'll have it up for a couple of weeks before.'

'Why can't we get it now?'

'We don't want it up too long.'

'Yes we do,' she said.

'I don't – it feels more special if it's only up for a couple of weeks. If we get it sooner it'll be bald for Christmas.' I knew you could get trees that didn't drop as much but they didn't smell the same. And for my money the tree was the best bit of all.

After they were in bed I soaked in the bath then watched ER on the telly. They had Christmas every couple of months. Plenty of drama, families forced together or apart, nativity scenes, snow and loneliness. Families.

I looked briefly at the folder Patrick Dowley had left with me. It included official documents, the death certificate, the bill for the funeral, papers from the coroner's office. There was a cutting from the *Manchester Evening News* – the announcement in the paper.

Johnstone, Miriam. Suddenly on 6th October. Beloved mother of Constance, Martina and Roland. She has gone home, bathed in love, rocked in the warm and gentle waters, and her soul is bright with joy. Arrangements to follow.

A further clipping gave the funeral announcement and asked for family flowers only and donations to MIND, the mental health charity. The rest of the papers were notes that the Johnstones must have made. Names and addresses of people to notify, questions to ask the coroner, practical lists for the funeral. There was a photograph too, Miriam Johnstone, head and shoulders, smiling, her eyes bright, crinkles at the corners. Holding a glass. A party? A happy, attractive woman. A fuller face than her children but a clear resemblance. I turned it over. It was dated the previous year. The picture was a million miles away from the image I had formed of a scared, depressed woman climbing the stairs to her death.

If she'd been like this on the Wednesday when her family last saw her I could understand more easily their refusal to accept the suicide verdict. Though it was the only plausible explanation. I'd sleep on it. Decide in the morning. This would be their first Christmas without her. A matter of endurance rather than celebration. Every aspect made poignant by her absence. One of the milestones of the grieving process. And would it be any easier to bear if I could tell them more about how she had passed her last day?

CHAPTER FOUR

Ray was taking the children to school so I was at my office for nine. I switched on the convector heater to take the chill from the place and made coffee. The aroma of the drink replacing the faint smell of damp brick. There was no hint of Christmas here apart from the temperature and the utterly natural frosting on the narrow basement window. I liked to keep it uncluttered; practical and functional though I painted it in bright colours and hung one of my friend Diane's abstract pictures on the wall. I suppose my office is the only space I have complete control over, even my room at home bears witness to Maddie who always seems to come into it carrying something and leave without it.

I looked again at the file on Miriam Johnstone. If I still said no what would they do? Try another agency? What could I offer? I sipped my coffee and thought. By the time my drink was finished I had made my decision and rehearsed what I would say.

I turned my attention to my intray. I'd two invoices to send out and a report to spellcheck and send off. I'd managed to get a reconditioned computer cheap from a contact on Ray's IT course. I was gradually transferring my work from the machine at home which Ray had let me share. I switched on and waited for it to boot up. Then got going. Invoices and report done, I busied myself signing up for e-mail and Internet access with one of the companies offering free calls. No one else had grabbed *salk* as a user name and I gave myself

13

the same thing reversed as a password. Easier to remember. I updated my address book and set up folders for my inbox. I emailed Ray at home as a test, as well as my friends to let them know my new address.

At eleven the phone rang.

'Sal Kilkenny Investigations.'

'Oh, hello.'

I didn't recognize the voice.

'I got your name from the Yellow Pages. It says you do tracing and matrimonial work but I don't know whether you could do what we require . . . it's not very straightforward.' She sounded quite businesslike though a little breathy. I wondered whether the 'we' was a firm or something else. I didn't ask her name. Some people want a bit of confidential advice before committing themselves. Some want to remain anonymous until you'd agreed a contract.

'Tell me what sort of work you were thinking of and I'll have an idea of whether we can take it on.' I was a 'we' too. Gave people the impression that I was part of an organization, not a lone operative. Safer all round.

'I have a son,' she said. 'He's seventeen now and we've been having a lot of problems with him. He's missing classes at college and he's been disappearing for hours on end. Sometimes he doesn't come back until the early hours. We've ended up having to drive round in the middle of the night looking for him. It's an awful strain and the worst thing is that he won't talk about it.'

Sounded like fairly common teenage behaviour. Did she want someone to act as a truancy officer or a counsellor? I listened.

'It's affecting us all. We've other children too and it's not fair on them. If you could find out where he goes, what he's doing?'

'Report on his activities for you?'

'Yes. And find him when he goes off like that.'

'You say he won't talk to you? Have you told him you might involve someone else?'

14

'Oh, no.'

I told her what I always tell people who want to investigate a family member, spouse or otherwise. 'Try and talk to him again. Tell him what you're worried about and see if he'll confide in you. Ask specific questions – start with the easiest – *where did you go on Tuesday* is easier than asking him what's wrong. Perhaps find out if there's anyone else he would rather talk to: a friend or a teacher.'

'We've tried that,' she sighed.

'Okay. I ought to warn you that there is a risk that this could backfire – bringing me in. If your son thinks he's being spied on it may drive him further away. He'll see it as a breach of trust. Have you thought about that?'

'Not really,' she admitted.

'Don't get me wrong, I can definitely take the job on but you might want to have another go at talking first. You could even tell him that you're thinking of getting help from someone else because you're so worried – that's up to you. Then if we go ahead I'd report his movements to you and you choose whether or not to confront him with what we find.'

'Yes.'

'Has there been any trouble with the police?'

'No, nothing like that.'

'Any drug use?'

'I don't think so, nothing we're aware of.'

'What do his teachers say?'

'That he's very quiet, withdrawn. His work is sporadic.'

'Is there someone at the college with responsibility for pastoral care?'

'Yes and I've seen them. They said they'd try and have a quiet word with him but nothing's come of it. They say unless Adam goes to them they can't interfere. Although if his attendance drops too low he'll be asked to consider whether to retain his college place.'

'Okay,' I leant back in my chair, 'going on what you've told me we could keep tabs on your son for a set period of time

15

and give you a report – verbal and written – on his activities. We cost the job at an hourly or daily rate. Is there any pattern to his disappearances?'

'No. Sometimes he skips college but he's back for tea, other times he's gone all hours. The first couple of times Ken drove round trying to find him but now he refuses to go, we just lie awake worrying.'

'Might he be with friends . . . have any other parents said anything?'

'He hasn't really got any friends. No one we see. He moved to the college in September and he doesn't seem to have made any friends.'

So this wasn't just a teenager getting drunk with his mates every so often and not making it home.

'And when you ask him where he's been he refuses to talk?'

'He's monosyllabic at the best of times but he just clams up and digs his heels in. He always was stubborn. I just can't see why he won't tell us. It seems so petty.'

'Where do you think he goes?'

I poised my pen to write. People often have suspicions that they don't voice for fear of sounding silly or paranoid or because they might be wrong. Or because they might be right and they don't want their fears to come true. It's always worth asking.

'I don't know. I don't think there's anywhere in particular but I really don't know. He just goes.' She sounded tearful and I brought things back to the practical again. I established that he never left during the night which got me out of overnight surveillance. She agreed to try talking to him again and would come back to me if she wanted. At that point I would begin to follow her son. Tracking him from home to college or wherever. I told her my rates and warned her that it would soon mount up. There was silence.

'I'll leave it with you,' I said.

'Yes,' she sounded subdued.

'Sometimes,' I suggested, 'families can do the work themselves. Though of course the emotional impact can be difficult if you find out something upsetting first hand. But you could always try it yourselves.'

'No,' she said. 'It'd be hard. I'm partially sighted so I don't drive. Just getting about is tricky enough. And Ken has to travel with his work. He's a rep and he covers the north-east as well so he's up there half the week. When he is here he's out every day at work.'

'I see. Well, think it over and see how you get on. Get back to me if you decide you want to go ahead. I'm sure we can help.'

'Thank you. I think we'll need it.'

She had little faith that her son would open up. It looked like another job was winging my way.

17

CHAPTER FIVE

The room was stuffy. I turned the heater off. I filed the notes I'd made from the phone call and returned to work at the screen. After another hour I felt as though cement was seeping into the muscles that run from my neck to my shoulder. It's always been a weak spot. Driving aggravates it too. And no matter how clear I am about the need for good posture at the computer; wrists relaxed, and level with the keyboard, one foot ahead of the other, knees lower than hips, back comfortably supported, when it comes to real life I end up hunched over the keyboard, head thrust towards the screen, neck horizontal, legs tangled, shoulders high with concentration, back rigid like some myopic emu.

I stood and swung my arms a bit, managed to bash the paper shade on the light. Cellars have low ceilings. I swung my head about more gently but nearly dislocated it when there was a sudden loud knocking from upstairs.

Through the spy hole I made out a distorted version of a face I knew. Close-cropped grey hair, slate-coloured eyes, generous mouth. I flung open the door.

'Stuart, you're back.'

Observant, aren't I?

He grinned. 'Last night.' Stepped forward to hug me. Then stood back.

'I thought if you hadn't had lunch . . .'

I rounded my eyes. Cheeky sod. Lunch was a euphemism.

Oh, sure, there'd be something to eat but eating would be the hors d'œuvre or maybe the afters. I glanced at my watch.

'All over by three,' he said. He had children himself and was well-versed in the school run.

'I'll turn things off.'

He waited in the car while I closed up. I felt like a kid playing truant. As I climbed in the passenger seat I recognized the thrill of excitement and the lurch of uncertainty that accompanied teenage dates. I hadn't been going out with Stuart very long – just a couple of months. My friend Diane had introduced us; she had decided we would be a good match and engineered it so we met at Stuart's cafe-bar without telling me first. It was my first relationship for longer than I care to remember and I felt as though I was entering unfamiliar territory where the ground might shift under my feet at any moment.

I snapped my seat belt shut, turned and smiled at him. He leant closer and kissed me very, very softly. He ran the tip of his tongue along the edge of my top lip. My stomach rippled and my breasts tingled. The ache in my shoulder seemed completely irrelevant. I was starving. Mmmm. Love in the afternoon.

In between sorting laundry and refereeing the children who were in squabbling mode I rang and collected my answerphone messages. Patrick Dowley had rung, he gave a phone number. I wrote it down.

'You pig, you evil smelly pig.'

'Get off me! Sa-a-al,' Tom roared for help.

I marched into the lounge where the pair of them were glowering at each other. 'He turned it over,' Maddie said, pointing at the telly. 'I was watching it.'

'I didn't. She hit me.'

'I didn't.'

'Leave the telly alone,' I told Tom, 'and you don't hit people,' I said to Maddie. 'If there's a problem, get me. And if there's any more messing about, it goes off.' Maddie pulled a smirky 'see' face at Tom.

'Maddie,' I scolded her. 'I need to make some phone calls for work and I can't do it if you two are screaming and shouting.'

'It's finished now anyway,' she said.

'Would you like a video then?'

They finally agreed on Winnie The Pooh and I went back to the phone and returned the Johnstones' call.

It was Connie who answered.

'I've had a look at the file you left and a chance to think about it. I'm afraid I still agree with the official version of events, going on the evidence available. And if I did do any work for you I'd want that to be understood.'

'Oh,' she said cautiously.

'Mr Dowley suggested I could try and establish more about your mother's movements during the Thursday. Try to fill in some of the gaps in the police account. There's quite a lot of time unaccounted for when no one knows where she was, is that right?'

'Yes, nothing after lunchtime. After she left the community centre. The police asked her neighbours if they'd seen her and I think that's all. I don't think they spoke to anyone else.'

There was no reason to. Suicide isn't a crime. And once it was clearly a suicide then there would be no need for the police to look any further.

'They wouldn't have,' I said. 'But if further information about those missing hours is what you want then I can take the case on that basis but only on that basis. You may want to discuss it with the family?'

'No, we all agree. We talked about it last night after we'd seen you. Patrick told us what he'd said.'

'And you'd be happy with that?'

'Yes.'

'Okay. I have a basic contract which I use and we'll need

20

to agree on an initial number of hours and fee. And I should make it clear that I can't guarantee I'll find any information. All I can do is look and use my professional skills to try and find out where she was, how she got to town and so on but I might not get anywhere. There's always that risk. I'll explore all the leads I can but at the end of the day you might not know any more.'

'Yeah, but we'll have tried and anything would help,' she said flatly.

We agreed that I would call the following evening, when they would all be at home.

Connie and Patrick had a house on one of the streets tucked away behind Wilmslow Road in Rusholme – the famous curry mile. That December evening the place was awash with neon, fragrant with the mouth-watering smell of pungent spices, crammed with traffic and already busy with the first wave of customers, some of them big groups obviously out for the work's Christmas party; it was the fake antlers and pointy red hats with white trim that gave it away. It would get busier still when the pubs emptied later and the streets would be thronging with revellers after that final part of the night-out ritual – the curry that followed the last drink. After the clubs there would be another influx of people ravenous for Rogan Josh, Chicken Korma and King Prawn Madras.

In amongst the curry houses were the other Asian shops, windows shimmering with saris in vibrant shades: coral, emerald, vermilion and royal blue; displays of glittering gold and silver jewellery, travel shops and banks, video and music outlets, sweet houses with windows piled high with pastel coloured treats like sculptures in coconut, sugar and dough, grocers with tables full of coriander, lady's fingers and sweet potatoes, mangoes and passion fruits.

At each restaurant, a man stood in the doorway, enticing customers in, giving them the low-down on the superiority of the chef, the awards the place had won, the specials on the menu. Smiling, beckoning, talking up the food. Competition was fierce but there always seemed enough customers to go around.

Maddie loved coming here for a curry, enchanted by everything from the glittering lights and the after-dinner cachou sweets to the pretty multicoloured rice and the elephant-shaped cocktail stirrer in the drinks. She liked the food too.

I found the house but there was no parking space nearby. I drove a little until I found a gap on an adjoining street. The terraced houses were quite large, many had the signs of multiple occupancy – a row of bells, several wheelie bins, neglected gardens, grubby windows with torn or badly hung curtains. In among these were smarter lets where the landlords had kept up the maintenance and a neat plaque advertised the management company and then there were the private family houses not adapted into flats or bedsits, looking settled and usually well looked after.

Connie Johnstone's home was one of these. The windows weren't new PVC but had recently been painted, and a winter window box with conifers, pansies and heathers provided a splash of colour at the bay window.

Patrick let me in. I left my coat on the pegs in the hallway and then went on through to the back room with him. They were all there. Martina and Roland sat on a large russet-coloured sofa opposite the television, Connie at a beech dining table in the first part of the room. I could smell coffee and a sweeter smell – fabric conditioner from a blanket drying on a rack by the radiator. The walls were painted pale terracotta with cream above the picture rail and on the ceiling. Thick curtains in a darker terracotta covered the window at the rear. Pale wood shelves beside the television held large church candles, a large piece of driftwood, some pebbles. A painting hung opposite the door, blocks of cream, gold and apricot, abstract but it made me think of buildings on a hillside. There was an air of tension in the atmosphere and I wondered whether I had interrupted a family row.

I put the folder down along with my own file and took a chair next to Connie.

'You can go do your homework,' she said to the other two. 'We'll call you if we need you.' They seemed glad to escape and the atmosphere certainly lightened once they'd gone.

Over the next hour I worked through all the known facts about Miriam Johnstone: her friends, routines, contacts, the places she visited, where she shopped and worshipped, her doctor, hairdresser and dentist. Connie gave me her mother's address and phone book and her small appointments diary. I confirmed that the photo of Miriam was dated correctly and that she hadn't changed her appearance substantially since it was taken. I would need to make copies of it to show to people.

I wrote down a potted history of her life and made a sketch of the known and close family tree; it was quite a small family. Miriam had no brothers or sisters though there were cousins still in Jamaica. She was fifty years old when she died. Mr Johnstone had left them while Miriam was carrying Roland.

Miriam had stopped working at St Mary's after her last time in psychiatric hospital, two years previously. She led a frugal life. Connie could help out with unforseen expenses. Martina had a Saturday job at British Home Stores. Martina and Roland had moved in with Connie and Patrick the night of their mother's death.

'It was awful,' Connie closed her eyes at the memory.

I asked them to tell me about their last visit to Miriam.

'There was nothing out of the ordinary,' said Patrick.

'She was fine,' said Connie. 'She'd made a big meal and we cleared the plates. We all watched *Coronation Street* with her and then we left.'

'What did you talk about?'

'Just stuff,' she said, 'someone she knew, their son was auditioning for a part in Coronation Street, so she was full of that.'

23

'And her feet,' Patrick said.

Connie smiled. 'In-growing toenails. She would moan about them but she loved her fancy shoes. She hated flat shoes, anything wide and sensible reminded her of working at the hospital, she always wanted to look smart and she had a pair of shoes for every outfit.'

'Anything else, any news, any worries?'

'Nothing,' she sighed and ran both hands over the rows in her hair, 'we've gone over it so many times.'

I nodded. 'Martina and Roland would have seen her the next day?'

'Yes, before school. Martina's at sixth form college and Roland's doing GCSEs. They both left around eight o'clock.'

'And she was okay then?'

'Yes.'

'No upset, no signs of anxiety?'

Connie shook her head.

'Would she try to hide it from them?'

'Well, yes. If she was a bit down then yes she would. But if it was worse then she wouldn't have the strength to do that. But she was managing it all fine. It had been two years since her last bad spell and she hadn't needed tablets for the last six months.'

I made more notes. 'So, we know she went to the community centre that morning.'

'Her craft club.'

'Tell me about that.'

'She loved it. They had a project, it was aimed at people who maybe needed a little support, people like Ma or people who were on their own. It was quite a mix, some unemployed, some pensioners. The worker there, Eddie, he's built it up, got them some Lottery funding so they can do more things. He spoke at the service for her.'

'He was as shocked as we were,' Patrick said.

'Yes, talk to him. He'll tell you she was perfectly all right.'

'Right. And she left there about midday?'

24

'Yes.'

'That was the last anyone saw of her?'

Connie nodded. One hand tightened over the other.

I gave them the contract and we agreed I'd do two days work and then prepare a report.

'Before I go, could I have a word with Martina and Roland?'

Connie went to fetch them and Patrick nodded at the mass of papers on the table. 'Where will you start?'

'The obvious places, talk to people at the craft club, her neighbours, contact friends and people on the list and in her book. No one at the funeral said they'd seen her?'

'No, we weren't going round asking people but I think they'd have said, don't you?'

'We might want to try an advert in the paper; that can sometimes bring people forward.'

'Like *Crimestoppers*?'

'Yes,' I smiled, 'without the crime.'

Martina and Roland came in and hovered by the table.

'I won't keep you long, your sister's told me all she can. Is there anything either of you've thought of, anything that might be useful for me to know?'

Roland shook his head, blinked at me, looked away, sad.

'No,' said Martina.

'What about the Thursday morning, you both saw her before school?'

They both nodded.

'And she seemed fine then?'

'Yeah,' Martina said, 'she was.'

'That day or the days before, was there anything unusual, anything a bit off-key?'

Roland shook his head.

'There wasn't anything like that,' said Martina.

I turned back to Connie. 'Your father left. Has there been any contact since?'

I knew he wasn't on the list they'd given me.

Her face hardened, Patrick stiffened. Roland actually looked shocked as though I'd said something obscene. His eyes widened with alarm and his face blanched. Then he blinked and blanked his expression. I'd obviously put my foot right in it.

'He made her ill,' Connie said, 'leaving when he did, leaving like that. We don't talk about him.'

'And you don't know where he is?'

'No.'

That was that then. Mr Johnstone was taboo. But their reaction was so hostile I wondered whether there was any more to it? Had he just abandoned them – or was there anything else?

'Okay. Thank you.' I began to gather my notes. Roland ducked out of the room followed by his sister.

Patrick and Connie saw me out. It was freezing, black ice glinted dangerously on the pavement. I walked as briskly as I dared to the car. I couldn't guess whether I'd find anything or not but I'd do my best. Would anyone remember seeing Miriam? It's easy to get lost in the city if you want to. Easy to move unnoticed through the crowds. Though I hadn't said so to the Johnstones I would go there first, put myself at the scene where Miriam died. I'd try to figure out how she got there, imagine the final stages of her bleak journey, the last steps she took before her fall to oblivion. It wasn't an attractive prospect and I might not learn anything from it but it was part of the job and I wouldn't be behaving professionally if I only did the easy bits. Being thorough, checking and rechecking, attention to details – it's often the mundane that brings illumination rather than the dramatic. Some trails start at the beginning and others begin at the end.

CHAPTER SIX

'Poor woman.' My friend and confidante Diane generally got to hear about my cases and could be trusted never to breathe a word to anyone else. 'Imagine jumping. I'd take pills if I ever got to that point.'

'How do you know, though? If you're so distressed that all you want to do is stop the pain.'

'But you'd do whatever was easier, near at hand.'

Farmers cradling shotguns, men sitting in fume-filled cars, lads hanging by a belt. *'Time for tea, Gary . . .'* I shuddered.

She changed the subject. 'Stuart?' Reached out and poured herself some more wine.

'Is back from Fuerteventura.'

'Tanned?'

'Mmm. All over.'

She giggled. 'Are you going to thank me now, Sal?'

'Thank you? No way! I still haven't forgiven you. You should have asked before doing your matchmaking number.'

'But it's obviously a great match.'

'It's still so new. Strange. It's nice but who knows . . .' I took a drink, Tempranillo, savoured the berry rich taste.

'Did you miss him, though?' she probed.

Did I? 'He was only gone a week. Sometimes we don't see each other from one week to the next. He has his kids every weekend and then he has to go into the bar some nights and sort things out, if there's any problems or staff off. It's a long, slow process. I don't know if we're right for each other.'

27

She tilted her head, narrowed her eyes.

'You can't rush these things,' I protested. 'I like him but . . .'

'What?'

'Just but . . . there shouldn't be a but, should there?'

'– but there is.'

'When I work it out I'll let you know.'

'What are his kids like?'

'Still not met them. Feels too soon. I've not told Maddie about him either. We agreed at the start that we'd keep the families to one side until we knew whether things would develop. I can imagine it being quite hard for Maddie, me having a boyfriend, she's not exactly had to share me before, I didn't want to involve her when it might just be a short-term thing.'

'You said Tom's all right with Laura.'

'Tom's not Maddie.' The children were opposites. In everything from colouring to character. 'And I'm not Ray.'

As if on cue we heard Ray come in the front door and peer round into the lounge, his dark curly hair glistened with raindrops. He'd grown a neat goatee in the last few weeks, along with his moustache it made him looked like some spaghetti western bandit. 'Hiya, Diane. Everything okay?' he asked me.

'Yep. Your mum rang. I told her you'd be late.'

'Ta.'

'And Digger's been out in the front garden.'

'Oh, great. It's like a monsoon out there without the heat.' Diane groaned. She'd come on her bike.

'See you later.' Ray left us.

'I'd better make tracks.' She stood up and stretched, filling the space in front of the fireplace. Diane was a big woman with a flamboyant dress sense, an artist who experimented with colour and shape on her clothing and her hair as well as in her work.

'I won't see you till New Year, will I?' I said.

'That's ages.'

'Well, you're off to Ireland tomorrow . . .'

28

'Back Thursday, then Bristol, there's a couple of nights after that, I don't go to Iceland till the 20th.'

She survived by combining her own art work with commissions and running workshops and courses. She'd had a burst of success in the last eighteen months and was enjoying the chance to exhibit more widely and to develop new projects. The Iceland work sounded wonderful, a winter school entitled Ice, Glass and Ink. People were to spend Christmas week in the land of reindeers working on sculptures, stained and etched glass, print and paint with several European tutors. Diane was the Ink woman. In between classes there'd be the northern lights, skating and sleigh rides, and a traditional Icelandic feast for Christmas. Certainly sounded more fun than turkey and tinsel.

'I'll ring you,' she said, 'we'll do one of those nights.'

In the hall she wriggled into a cycling cape and switched her bike lights on. Digger hovered nearby on the off-chance that a walk was coming. Futile hope. I could see he knew this too by the half-hearted thump of his tail. Ray equalled walkies, no one else. I held him back while Diane manoeuvred her bike out and down the steps. It was truly wet. Manchester does rain in a thousand varieties; this was the heavy sort, large, fat, plopping drops, drenching everything. Filling the potholes in the road, the gutters and the drains, saturating the grass and the gardens, drumming incessantly on the roofs and windows, making the red brick and slate slick and shiny, raising the level in the canals, swelling the banks of the River Mersey.

You can't live in Manchester and not know rain.

I listened to it in bed. Heard the board by the roof rattling too. Tried to imagine living somewhere dry; East Anglia, the Sierra Madre, Nevada. Parched. Day after day. Clear skies. Wind and sand and dust, cracking and bleaching and desiccating everything. Wouldn't you long for rain, crave a sky of leaden cloud, the deluge, the fresh scents after the rain had been? The cleansing power. Wouldn't you pray for rain? Well, maybe.

29

CHAPTER SEVEN

First thing Monday morning my potential client, worried mother, rang back.

'I've tried to talk to him,' she said. 'It was hopeless. "I'm all right", that's all he would say, "don't worry". She sighed. 'How can I not worry? I just can't get through to him. I want you to find out what he's up to.'

'Fine. I'll need some more details.' I remembered she didn't drive. 'Is it easier if I come to you?'

'Yes.'

'This morning? Tomorrow?'

'This morning, yes.' Relief in her reply

'I didn't take your name before.'

'Susan, Susan Reeve.'

'And the address?'

I recognized the street name. It was in Burnage, only a few minutes' drive away. We agreed to meet in an hour's time.

I packed my bag so I could go from my meeting with Mrs Reeve on into town. To the car park where Miriam had died. As well as paper, pens, copies of a contract, money and keys, I put in my mobile, the photograph of Miriam Johnstone, a camera and a small cassette recorder. I checked that I had plenty of my business cards on me too.

I drove up the road to the centre of Withington where my local shops are, parked behind Somerfield and went to get photocopies done of the picture. Every window shouted Christmas and even the pet shop was in on the act with a display of gifts for dogs, cats, rabbits and hamsters. The shops teeter on the edge of survival, partly due to the plethora of big supermarkets within a couple of miles but Withington, though it has its share of students who come and go, is a long-established community and there always seems to be just enough trade to keep the modest high street from closing down completely. The library sits at one end of the main drag and what used to be the local cinema at the other – until competition from the multi-screen complexes put it out of business. There's a popular swimming baths nearby which the council are always trying to rationalize by shutting one of the pools and which the people of the area fight for fiercely. With a couple of parks in the neighbourhood and reasonable schools Withington has enough basic facilities to make it a good place to be with small children. Not much going for the older ones though and consequently there was always a lot of youth crime reported on the Old Moat estate, near to the village.

Adam Reeve's home was in Burnage, another area with a rough reputation and the place where Oasis brothers Noel and Liam Gallagher grew up. A half a mile or so west of Withington and across Kingsway, the large dual carriageway, most of Burnage is a large traditional council house estate with pockets of privately built semis. Burnside Drive was private housing, the houses were an unusual design, chalet-style roofs reminiscent of gingerbread cottages swept right down to either side of the ground floor bay window. The bottom half of the house was brick, the top rendered in cream and black, the roof red tiles. I parked outside the house and rang the bell. It echoed ding-dong inside.

Susan Reeve answered the door. Short and slim, long brown hair streaked with grey. She wore thick glasses which magnified her grey eyes. She had a long face, a sharp nose, a thin mouth with a cold sore on her upper lip.

'Come in. Would you like a drink?'

'Coffee, please. No sugar.'

31

'You don't mind the kitchen,' she asked, 'only it's warmer in here at this time of day.'

It was. Warm and cheerful and shabby round the edges. A country feel with lime-washed wooden units, yellow walls with paper peeling in places, and apples and pears on the curtains. I sat at the circular pine table while she made our drinks. The only indication that she was partially sighted was in the fluid movements her hands made as she found and used mugs, coffee and milk. She had biscuits too. Home-made.

'The twins made them,' she said. 'Rachel and Rebecca. They're seven and baking is this month's fad.'

'Great.'

'I think it's the mess they like,' she said, 'plus the chance to eat biscuits all day.'

'So you've three children?'

'Four. Penny is eleven. We're a bit cramped. You can only just get a bed in the little bedroom, that's Adam's. And Penny gets sick of sharing with the twins. If we could only build an extension but . . .' She shrugged.

I sorted out my pen and paper and told her I'd brought a contract along. Would she be able to read it?

She had a magnifying glass and scanned the print, nodding when she'd finished. It wasn't a complicated document but it served to establish that someone had hired me and would pay me the set rate. It also included a confidentiality clause and a disclaimer. So no one could start throwing lawsuits my way if my investigations opened up a Pandora's box. It happens. God, it happens.

'I sign here?'

'And here.'

Formalities over, I turned my attention to her problem.

She'd told me most of the situation over the phone. I checked further details and established that Adam was at Parrs Wood Sixth Form College taking A levels in Geology, Geography, Spanish and English. His school career had started brightly and he'd been doing well on transfer to High School. He'd attended Burnage Boys but a prolonged bout of bullying had seen him move to Parrs Wood High for his GCSE years. He'd worked hard and achieved respectable grades. Things had deteriorated rapidly in the time he'd been in the Sixth Form.

'I've even asked him if he wants to leave. Get a job instead but he just shook his head.'

'I can follow him to college.' I was thinking aloud and trying to decide how best to allocate my time. 'But presumably they can come and go as they please. I could be waiting there all day.'

I tried a biscuit. Crunchy and intensely sweet.

'I was wondering about that last night, about the money,' she said apologetically.' When we went to college about this they looked at his attendance record and the days that he went missing he hadn't even been into registration.'

'So if he gets to college he stays there.'

'Seems so.'

'That helps. And these times when he's not come home? Does that happen after skipping college?'

She nodded. 'Yes, he just doesn't come home for tea. And once or twice he's gone off after tea. Won't say where he's going and stays out all hours.'

'Are there any problems at home?'

'No,' she said.

'Is your husband worried as well?'

'Oh, yes. He gets wound up about it. He tends to shout but that doesn't get us anywhere.'

'He shouts at Adam?'

'Has done, but don't get me wrong, he's a very caring father. He's tried talking to him but he gets the same response as I do. Of course he's not here as much as I am so he doesn't have to deal with it day after day.' Worry pulled her mouth down at the corners and she blinked a couple of times.

'He works away, you said?'

33

'Monday to Thursday, occasional weekends. He's got an enormous area to cover. He'd like to be home more but it goes with the job.'

'What about the bullying, at Burnage High.'

'That was awful. There were three of them and they just picked on Adam. We still don't know why. We were in and out of school, meetings and letters. The school kept telling us it was sorted and then I'd find Adam in tears and they'd have got at him again. It was ridiculous. In the end we got him transferred. We should have done it sooner. Mind you he didn't tell us for long enough. Him being the eldest, he's always been very responsible, self-reliant, and I think he was trying to protect me, not that I need protecting.' She gave a sad smile.

'It must have been awful.' I imagined my Maddie being persecuted by bullies. How fiercely I'd want to protect her and how sick I'd feel if I failed.

'And now . . .' She shook her head. 'It really is out of character. I think that's what makes it so difficult. If it was Penny I could understand it. But Adam.'

'Okay. Time and money. I'll leave you my mobile number and you ring me if Adam goes off after tea. In addition I'll arrange my schedule so I can follow him from home some mornings and see if he goes into college. We'll take it from there and we've agreed a ceiling of eight hours for now.'

She winced. Obviously the money was going to be hard to find.

'You can pay in weekly instalments if that helps.'

'It might,' she acknowledged, 'thank you. I realize you might find out things that are . . . awkward for us, but at least now I feel I'm doing something about it instead of driving myself mad with worry.'

'He may be just testing you, taking risks, pushing the limits, trying to break away a bit. Being a teenager.'

'Yes. And I can deal with that, if that's all it is. It'd be easier if he was slamming doors and coming in plastered and refusing to clean his room but . . .' she broke off and turned to me again, her eyes brimmed with tears. 'It's the secrecy I can't bear, the secrecy and the silence.'

CHAPTER EIGHT

On 6 October at five o'clock at the start of the rush hour Miriam Johnstone had flung herself from the top level of the Arndale Centre car park and fallen to her death.

I peered down, looking at the traffic on Cannon Street and the pedestrians dotted along the pavements. She had landed on the road side. It had been busy but she had not hit anyone or anything – only the ground. *Connie had to identify her mother. She had to do it by looking at her hands.*

I swallowed. Tried to imagine the strength of purpose or the level of desolation that drove her to come here, to pull herself up the concrete wall, to climb over the railings, lean forward, release her grip. Did she look down that moment before she plummeted? Or up to the skies? Did she think of her children? Of her God? Did she cry out or was she mute? I shuddered, felt dizzy, a swirl of unease circled in my stomach. She had to do it by looking at her hands. Things were that bad.

I took a step back, tightened my scarf against the wind, there was a churlish sky threatening more bad weather. I looked carefully at the structure. There wasn't that much space between the top of the railings and the low concrete ceiling. Enough for the average person to climb through but it would have been an awkward manoeuvre.

Why here? Did this place have some significance for Miriam? It was near the bus station so perhaps that's how she had travelled to town. Had they found a bus ticket in her coat or handbag?

I turned and surveyed the car park. It was full of vehicles but there was a feeling of desertion here. The low concrete roof, the smell of oil, the dim light, the ranks of cars, silent, waiting. Not a place to linger. In one corner I spotted the CCTV camera. Had that been checked? Surely the police would have looked at it. I couldn't recall any reference to it in the papers I'd had from Connie. Wasn't it likely that at that time of day the place would be busier, people returning to their cars after work? But no one had seen her jump. Had she been controlled enough to wait until the coast was clear? Determined that no one should try and stop her?

I moved close to the parapet again. Leant on the railings and looked down, watched the people sliding past each other without contact. Strangers in the city. My mouth was dry. I stared at the ground, five storeys below, my head swam. When Miriam had let go, on the cusp of her descent, had she felt a flicker of relief? Felt peace approaching or terror thrilling in her veins? Or nothing? Save the wind on her face and the pulse in her ears?

A shout and a whoop of laughter made my nerves start and my heart leap. Down on Cannon Street two young women clutched each other giggling helplessly. All the world to live for. I turned away.

CHAPTER NINE

The man in the booth at the car park entrance pulled a face when I asked about CCTV footage.

'Hang on,' he rasped, he struggled to his feet and gestured to the side of the booth. 'Come in,' he said irritably. He opened the door and waved me into the room. An ashtray full of fag ends sat on the table beside the console of screens. He sat and leant forward, pressed the switch for the microphone, his fingers were the colour of mustard. 'Tony, to the office please.'

He twisted round to me. 'Tony has more to do with the cameras.'

I nodded, leant back against the door of the boxy little office and prayed that Tony would arrive before I contracted lung cancer.

'Alright?' Tony opened the door and introduced himself in a Mancunian swagger: part question, part greeting. I moved to let him in.

'Young lady's got some questions about CCTV tapes,' his colleague wheezed.

Tony tutted. 'Confidential love, can't help you.' He was a barrel of a man with a bald head.

'She's a private detective,' the other said.

'Are you? Well, you'd know all about that then, wouldn't you? Electronic surveillance, rules they have.'

'I'm working for the family of the woman who jumped from here back in October.'

His face flattened, eyes hardened. He didn't enjoy the recollection.

'Horrible that was,' Wheezy chipped in.

'Doing what exactly?' Tony stared at me, folded his arms defensively.

'The family have found it very hard to come to terms with what happened. They've asked me to try and find out what Mrs Johnstone was doing here, trace her last hours, that's all. But I realized there's nothing in the coroner's report as far as I can see about the CCTV. There is a camera up there.'

Irritation flared in Tony's eyes then he let it go, sighed. 'Wasn't working,' he said flatly.

'It was broken?'

'We'd no idea. Screens here looked fine, course no one here saw anything but you're not watching every single minute. You've problems with the barrier, or people can't remember where they were parked, out of petrol, always some crisis or other. The police asked to view the tape and then they find the camera's faulty, or the tape was.'

'Head office weren't best pleased,' Wheezy observed.

'They get the cheapest bloody equipment and then expect perfect bloody results.' It was obviously a bone of contention. Had Tony had an earful because of it? Not checking the cameras adequately?

Whatever, it meant there was no record of Level 5 for that day. I pictured Miriam arriving, had she used the lift, the stairs?

'I think maybe she came here on the bus. She hadn't got a car, she didn't drive. You've a camera at the pedestrian entrance, too.' I could see it on the screens and people queuing to pay before claiming their cars.

'Yeah,' Tony said.

'But they didn't find anything on that?'

Tony shot an uncomfortable glance at Wheezy who promptly lit a cigarette and began to cough ferociously. Tony sighed, shook his head slightly.

'What?' I said.

'They never asked,' Tony replied.

'What?'

'They only asked us about the tape from Level 5.'

'But,' it was my turn to sigh. 'Didn't anyone think . . .' It seemed so obvious to me. Why on earth hadn't the police asked to see all the tapes? 'Didn't you . . .'

It was the wrong thing to say. 'What?' Tony challenged. 'Not down to me, was it?'

A pause. I felt uncomfortable. 'How long do you keep the tapes?'

'Four weeks and then we record over them.'

That was that then. I exhaled.

A loud squawk blurted from the intercom, making me jump. I caught a trace of amusement in Tony's eyes. Someone with a faulty ticket. Wheezy looked at the screen, flicked a switch and lifted the barrier.

'Were you here, that day?'

Both men nodded.

'Can you tell me the sequence of events after it had happened?'

Tony shifted, shirty still at my implied criticism.

Wheezy coughed. 'First we knew, a police officer comes in and tells us not to let anyone else in and they want to talk to all cars leaving the place. Was him that told us, that she'd jumped, like. By then the ambulance had come and there were police all over, looking round the place. They found her shoe, that's how they knew it was level 5, because no one had actually seen her jump.' He blew smoke into the fuggy air. I tried to breathe as shallowly as possible.

'Place was shut for a couple of hours. They took the CCTV tape away, see if it would play back on their machines.' Tony shrugged. 'That was more or less it.'

Wheezy cleared his throat in agreement.

End of story. Closed for two hours then business as usual.

'Horrible way to go,' Tony shook his head.

40

'Makes you wonder,' Wheezy added, 'what she was thinking of. If you're going to top yourself least you could keep it clean. For the family and that.'

Tony pulled a pack of cigarettes from his pocket. Cue my exit.

So, no tapes. One broken, the other taped over. The police hadn't even bothered to watch it. Why not? I knew there was no reason for extensive enquiries but surely establishing when Miriam Johnstone arrived at the car park and determining what state she was in would have been pertinent to the inquest. Those observations could have helped the coroner rule on the cause of death and help Miriam's family comprehend her suicide. I thought it was reasonable to expect the investigation to include attempts to find out the state of mind of the deceased, especially in a suspected suicide. And now I'd seen the physical layout of the place I could see that the possibility of accidental death was a non-starter. No way could anyone slip and fall from up there. She hadn't slipped, she'd jumped. It had been intentional.

I understood some of Connie Johnstone's grievances now; the police had barely done the basics. An approach to the police complaints authority might be on the cards if I found more evidence of sloppy work or corners cut. Was it just par for the course? A matter of too few resources stretched far too thinly coupled with the pressure to improve the clear-up rates for crime in general? Would any suicide get the same half-hearted attention? Or was there indeed a racial element? Had Miriam Johnstone received less than equal treatment because she was black?

CHAPTER TEN

The community centre was on Moss Lane East, near the Rusholme junction and opposite Whitworth Park. It was a new-built single storey block with all the paraphernalia of inner-city security; chain link fencing round the car park topped with razor wire and more wire on the roof, steel shutters available to roll over all the windows. A large sign mounted beside the door announced Whitworth Community Centre and gave a phone number. I pulled into a space in the car park and locked the car up.

Just inside the door there was a small vestibule with notice boards cluttered with posters, messages, leaflets and adverts. Everything was there from Tai Chi classes to second-hand baby buggies. One board listed the regular groups: Craft Club, Mums and Tots, Luncheon Club, Yoga and Aerobics and the times they met. The Craft Club that Miriam attended met on Tuesdays, Thursdays and Fridays.

The entrance hall led into a larger hallway with several doors off. A reception booth was in the corner to my left. The place smelt of new carpets, a strong chemical tang. Around the room more posters were displayed along with a patchwork banner, showing the centre's name and depicting the activities that took place, and two beautiful large ceramic panels made from broken tile and mirror. One showed a tree by a stream and the other a bowl of fruit. There was no one at reception. I peered in through the reinforced glass.

'Hiya,' a voice came from the far end of the hall. A young

woman carrying a cup headed towards me. 'Just getting a drink,' she smiled and made her way to her post; there was a small door into the booth which she had to open with a key. 'Have to keep it all locked round here,' she said. 'When we first opened they'd come in off the street and walk off with stuff. Phones, computer, the lot. Can I help?'

'Eddie Cliff, is he in?'

'I think so. Can I just ask you to sign in?' She swivelled a book with lined paper round my way. I filled in the columns.

'Thanks. You want to go through the bottom door,' she pointed to the right-hand side to the lower of two doors. 'That's the craft room. If he's not there try the hall,' she gestured over to the left. 'They were talking about putting some decorations up in there earlier.'

The craft room was empty. The walls were awash with pictures and models and a central working area had been made by putting tables together. The room was well lit by a run of windows which looked out of the back. Evergreen shrubs grew there and a small cherry tree hung with bird feeders.

I crossed to the hall door. I looked in. It was a riot of streamers and lanterns in garish reds and golds, silver and green. A large Christmas tree stood at the far end beside the front window and at the back of the room sat a giant Christmas pudding. At the window two women held a tall step ladder as a man stretched up to attach more streamers above the glass. The trio turned as I came in.

'Hello,' I crossed the hall, my boots squeaking on the wooden surface.

'Eddie Cliff?'

'That's me,' the man replied. 'Nearly done.' He grunted as he reached to hammer-tack the streamer in place. 'There we go.' He came down the ladder.

He looked at me enquiringly, held out his hand. He had a bushy beard and moustache, grey and brown, like his hair which reached his shoulders and didn't look as though it ever saw a brush. He had a furrowed, friendly face, a patch of broken veins making each cheek rosy, bright seaside-blue eyes, a generous smile. With a plaid shirt, denims and cowboy boots he looked like a country and western fan. We shook hands. 'Sal Kilkenny. If you could spare a few minutes, I'd like to talk to you about someone who used to come to the centre?'

'Sure.' He turned to the women. 'Can you start the windows?'

The small dark-haired woman nodded quickly. 'Yeah.' The girl beside her, dramatically overweight and with a shy demeanour said nothing.

'Spray a border right along the bottom. Up and down, like mountains. About this high,' he showed them. 'We can go in the craft room,' he said to me.

Once seated he listened while I explained the reason for my visit. When I mentioned Miriam Johnstone his eyes softened and he nodded in recognition.

'It was completely out of the blue,' he said when I'd finished. 'She was here that morning, smiling and joking, next thing . . .' He stroked his beard. 'It's hard for those left behind,' he had a soft edge to his voice, a west country lilt, like someone from the Archers. 'I've worked for most of my life with vulnerable people and sometimes there's no warning, nothing.'

'And Miriam had been well for some time?'

He nodded. 'That's right. Her death didn't make sense then, still doesn't now. I don't think we'll ever know what prompted her.'

I murmured my agreement. 'I'm trying to find out where she went when she left here. Have you any ideas?'

'No. She usually went home for her lunch, she'd stay here on Tuesdays for the luncheon club. That's a pensioners group, they have a hot meal in the hall. I could ask around at the Craft Club, you could come and talk to them yourself but it might be easier if I broached it first. It upset everybody

44

and there are some people in the group who might find it very difficult to be reminded of it again.'

I asked him to do that and gave him my card. 'I can pop back in, if you could ring me and let me know who I can talk to.'

'Will do.'

He accompanied me back into the foyer.

'Lovely ceramics,' I pointed to the still life.

He smiled, creases fanned the outside of each eye. 'Craft Club's own work. We get an artist in every so often for special projects.'

'Connie said you'd got Lottery money.'

'That's what built this place. Before we had an old prefab. Leaked like a sieve, break-ins twice a week. All the money went into shoring the place up. And it wasn't very attractive. Now we can concentrate on the activities.'

'You run the centre?'

'In effect but there's a management committee of users and funders, they're officially in charge. They employ me and we've Sharon half-time.' He nodded at the woman at reception. 'This area was crying out for a decent place where people could meet. You can't talk about community if there's nowhere for people to gather.'

He was obviously passionate about the place.

'It's great.'

'Have you signed our petition?'

'No.'

'The council are talking about cutting back on our core funding, just as we're getting sorted out, we're asking them to reconsider . . . if you . . .'

'Yes.'

He gestured towards Sharon. 'Over here.'

I followed him across, read the text of the petition to make sure I agreed and then added my name and address to the list.

'Withington,' he noted. 'I was there for a bit when I first moved here. Do you know Lausanne Road?'

'By the library?'

'Yep. But the lads next door were up all hours, drugs I reckon. I've got a nice place in Cheadle now.'

'Quieter,' I smiled.

There was a commotion at the entrance.

'That'll be the Tai Chi group. Villains the lot of them.'

'I'll leave you to it,' I smiled.

I made my way out against the flow of elderly people who were streaming into the hall and joshing each other in loud voices. Outside I waited while the two minibuses that had brought them turned and left, before I could drive out.

Had Miriam gone home for lunch that day? Her house in Heald Place was a few minutes from the centre. According to the police her neighbours hadn't seen her that lunchtime but it was part of my job to double-check the facts. It wouldn't be the first time that a second look revealed new information.

CHAPTER ELEVEN

'No, I bloody well didn't,' Mr Jones, Miriam's neighbour, was emphatic and obviously disgruntled at being interrupted. He wore a stained sky-blue pullover stretched tight over a large round belly and tweed trousers. He had several badly drawn tattoos on his fingers and forearms. He smelt rank.

'Did you know Mrs Johnstone?'

'Not to speak to.'

'Can you remember when you last saw her?'

'No, I bloody can't.'

I was relieved to get away and took a couple of gulps of cold, damp air to replace the nauseating smell.

I tried the neighbour on the far side.

Mrs Boscoe invited me in and made me tea. Miriam had been a good neighbour 'God rest her soul'. She hadn't seen her that Thursday, she'd told the others, she'd seen her the day before, the Wednesday, just to say hello. Both getting home at the same time, coming down in stair rods so they didn't linger. She missed her. Missed them all. Roland used to help her, anything heavy to move. Always polite. Brought them up so nice, Miriam did, not like some these days.

I left her my card in case anything else occurred. At the doorway she asked, 'What is it you're actually doing? Is it for the insurance?'

'No, for the family. I'm just trying to find out where she was that afternoon.'

'Oh. Well, if she had been home Roland would have seen her, wouldn't he?'

'Roland?'

'I think it was Roland. He plays the music loud, rap music he calls it, but if it's not late I don't bother, you've got to get along with people haven't you.'

'That Thursday, you heard it?'

'I think so,' she looked uncertain. Pulled a face in concentration. 'It wouldn't have been after then,' she rationalized, 'what with . . .' she let the sentence hang.

'What time?'

She thought again. 'The news was on, the lunchtime news. Because I had to turn the sound up. I remember that,' she dipped her chin decisively.

'But it could have been another day? The Tuesday or Wednesday?'

'You've got me thinking now. I couldn't put my hand on the Bible and swear to it.' She looked anxious.

'Don't worry. If you remember anything else just give me a ring.'

She promised she would.

'You never mentioned this before?' I asked her.

'It never occurred to me. It's not important is it?'

'No,' I reassured her.

But I had the impression that Martina and Roland had been out all day. Had I just leapt to conclusions? And like Mrs Boscoe said, it wasn't important. Or was it?

CHAPTER TWELVE

Next to the loathsome Mr Jones was a classic Manchester corner shop. Grills on the windows, plastered with adverts for cigarettes and the *Evening News*. Open eight till late. Prices might be higher but if all you wanted was a pint of milk, a loo roll, a can of dog food or ten Bensons then it beat the nearest huge supermarket hands down.

I introduced myself to the middle-aged Asian man at the counter and told him my business. 'Very nice lady,' he said. 'She got her papers here and my daughters are at school with Martina. We were very sad. Terrible thing.'

I repeated the questions that I'd asked the neighbours but he hadn't seen her that lunchtime either. 'Someone else was asking,' he said.

'The police?'

'No, asking if she'd be home for lunch, the day . . . you know.'

My neck prickled.

'I said I had no idea. They say the shop is part of the community but I don't know everybody's goings on.' He raised his eyebrows.

'Did you tell the police?'

'Oh, yes. But I'd no name. It was a gentleman from her church, passing and wanted to say hello.'

My prickling subsided. 'What time was it?'

'Late morning.'

'Before midday?'

49

'Yes.'

Miriam would still have been at the Whitworth Centre.

'I said she sometimes went down to the community centre and he could try there.'

The bell on the shop door announced two teenage girls. I waited while he served them with cigarettes. If Miriam's visitor had gone to the Centre first instead of calling at her home, how differently might that day have gone? But how was he to know her daily schedule? Who was this man from the church? Wasn't it more common to ring and see if someone was going to be in before calling on them? I waited till the shop keeper was free and got a description of the caller. Middle-aged black man, grey hair, maybe had a moustache; that was as much as he could tell me. It niggled though, just the fact of him being there the day of her suicide. I needed to check him out, contact the church and see if they could help me identify him.

So I had established that none of the near neighbours had actually seen Miriam return home. That didn't mean she hadn't eaten lunch there. But there was a more straightforward way to establish that; by asking Martina and Roland what they had found on their return from school. In doing so I could also find out whether Roland was at home playing his music that day or whether Mrs Boscoe had got it wrong.

CHAPTER THIRTEEN

'I've invited my mother again,' Ray said as he cleared the table.

'And?'

'*I don't know Raymundo, lottsa people, lottsa fuss. I don't wanna be in the way,*' Ray mimicked his mother's martyr act.

'She wouldn't miss it,' I said. 'As long as she's home for the Boxing Day races.'

'She made seventy pounds last Saturday.'

'Blimey.'

'Mind you, she only tells me when she wins. We'll have to do turkey though.'

'You do the turkey and I'll make a veggie alternative.'

'Just for you?'

'I suppose. Something luxurious that I'd never normally eat.'

He moved the salt and pepper and wiped the big pine table down.

'So you don't mind?'

'I'm fine. It's Laura you should check with.' The acid remarks and general disapproval that Nana 'Tello had once directed my way now seemed to be reserved for Laura. I couldn't fathom it. She'd spent the last years wanting to see Ray fixed up, wanting the prospect of a 'normal' family for Tom and now it was on the horizon (well, not beyond the bounds of possibility) she was daggers drawn about it. 'You can't not invite your mother.' I added. 'The secret is to have no expectations, or only realistic ones. No nice presents, no delicious meal, no relaxed hours in front of the telly or playing games. Think of Christmas as a chore to be got through.'

'Who rattled your cage?'

'I'm not rattled, just resigned.'

'Cynical.'

'Pragmatic. It's for the children, who will have consumed enough chocolate by breakfast to sink the Titanic and who'll then be hyperactive and feverish till bedtime.'

I wondered what sort of Christmas Stuart and his family would have? We hadn't talked about it, silently acknowledging that we weren't established enough to be a part of each other's seasonal plans. Would he have his kids for Christmas or would his ex? Would he be on his own or off to visit other relatives? I ought to find out. With Ray and Laura off work and able to look after Maddie there might be a chance of doing something special, a night at a country inn in the Peak District; long walks and home cooking.

'What do you want for Christmas anyway?' I asked Ray.

'Oh,' he groaned and began to load the dishwasher. 'You don't need to bother. We could just give the children things.'

I didn't know whether to be relieved or disappointed. 'That's the spirit.'

'Only . . .'

'You've got me something?'

He looked sheepish. 'Get me a CD then.'

'Who?'

'Surprise me.'

'Okay.' What on earth had he got me? And why so soon. I was curious and I felt a hint of excitement. Maybe it was something good, something perfect for me. There I was, letting my expectations get the better of me.

The doorbell rang and I went to get it, Maddie and Tom came out of the playroom to see who it was. A shaky, giggly version of 'We Wish You A Merry Christmas' came from outside. I opened the door to two small boys, both with close cropped hair and tatty clothes. The smaller was missing his front teeth.

'Wait there,' I said.

I gave them fifty pence each.

'Fifty pence!' Maddie observed, when they'd gone. 'They weren't very good. Can we go carol singing?'

Oh, please no. Trailing round knocking on doors with Maddie coming all over shy. I knew who'd end up doing the singing. 'Maybe when you're bigger.'

'You keep the money, don't you?' she checked.

'Some people do it for charity, to help other people.'

She thought about this. 'You could give half of it to charity.'

'You could.'

'Look,' Tom interrupted to show me his wobbly tooth. 'I 'an do 'is,' he spoke with his mouth open and one finger pulling said tooth forward to expose the hole in his gum.

'Gross,' said Maddie.

He turned to give her a better look.

She covered her eyes.

'I bet it'll come out soon,' I told him, 'and you can put it under your pillow.'

'For the tooth fairy.'

'Yep.'

He waggled it a bit more.

'Do you remember losing your first one?' I asked Maddie. 'You walked around for weeks with it just hanging by a thread and you wouldn't eat or brush your teeth or do anything that might bring it out.'

She grinned at me. 'Mummy,' she looked serious again. 'Who's Noel?'

'Noel? Which Noel?'

'Is it Jesus? It's on this card at school.'

'No-el,' I smiled. 'It means Christmas, about the nativity when Jesus was born. Now, it's nearly bedtime, you've got another half hour and then it'll be time to get ready.'

They ambled back to play.

There was a scream and whispering from outside and then a ragged chorus of 'Away In A Manger' started up. The lads must have told their mates.

CHAPTER FOURTEEN

On Tuesday morning I was up for seven and on my way to spy on Adam Reeve by seven forty-five. The traffic was building up already. I parked a few doors down from the house and waited for him to emerge. It was just getting light when he appeared, a bulky rucksack slung over one shoulder. He was taller than his mother with blond hair cut short all over. I noted the time and when he'd reached the end of the avenue in a quick loping stride I got out of the car and locked it and set off after him.

There was a steady stream of pupils walking down Kingsway, the dual carriageway, in the direction of the school and college. Some were clustered at bus stops. Adam kept up a brisk pace. He never looked back. The walking made me warm and I unzipped my coat. It was a dry day, cooler with a fresh blue sky. Most of the route was lined with houses, red-brick council houses with privet hedging or fences round the front gardens. I amused myself by comparing the plots with the Christmas decorations in the window. Was there any correlation between horticultural and festive style?

The college was behind the large multiplex cinema, bowling alley and bingo hall and opposite Tescos. The place had been rebuilt as part of a private finance initiative. The city council sold off the prime site land in return for a new state-of-the-art school and sixth form centre. The Millennium school they called it. Adam's transfer from Burnage Boys would have been before the rebuild. These days he wouldn't get a look in. It was way oversubscribed and there'd been ructions about who would get to go there. A lot of the other city high schools had poor reputations or they were single sex schools which some parents didn't want (myself included.) It was still five years before Maddie would move up and I hoped by then there'd be a real choice of where to send her.

I made sure that Adam actually entered the college building and then retraced my walk to the car. I reckoned I'd done three miles there and back. I could notch it up as good exercise but I can't deny that I was disappointed that Adam Reeve hadn't done a bunk with me hot on his heels.

CHAPTER FIFTEEN

Back at the office I logged my time and turned my attention back to Miriam Johnstone. I was calling round to see Martina and Roland at four thirty. In the meantime there were plenty of names on my list to talk to. I settled down with coffee and the phone. I got through to Reverend Day at Miriam's church on the first attempt. We went through the preliminaries then I talked to him about the mystery man who I wanted to trace. When he'd heard me out his response was lukewarm. 'I don't recognize the description, it's very vague. I don't see how we can help, it's hardly the sort of thing that we'd read out at the ten o'clock service with the notices.'

'Perhaps you have a newsletter?' I suggested, 'a bulletin that I could place a small advert in?'

'Saying?'

I thought on my feet. 'That Miriam Johnstone's family wished to find out more about their mother's final day and would welcome any information from the congregation.'

'I thought you wanted to identify this man?' he grumbled.

'Well, yes. I might need to add something about that but I'd like to hear from anyone else too.'

'What makes you think any of our members have something to tell you?'

I was beginning to feel like a schoolgirl whose essay was not adequately reasoned. 'I don't think that but I'm trying every avenue.' I'd only know later which were dead ends.

'The bulletin for December is already out and we don't do another until late January.'

He wasn't going to help. Was he like this with everyone? No matter what he thought of me he should have been bending over backwards to support Connie and her family. 'That's a real shame,' I said crisply. 'I'm sure you know how devastated the family have been and this is their way of trying to accept what has happened.' I was hoping to shame him into action but all I got was a grunt. He was a waste of space. 'Did Miriam belong to any church groups?'

'The sewing group,' he said. 'Mrs Thomas runs it.'

'Oh yes, I have her details. Thank you.' I made it sound like an insult.

Hopefully Mrs Thomas would be a little more accommodating than Reverend Day.

'She was an angel,' Mrs Thomas proclaimed. 'Truly, an angel.'

Murmurs of agreement rose from the women around. As they spoke about Miriam the older ones slipped in and out of a patois that I couldn't follow but the overall sentiment was positive. Miriam had been well-liked by her peers.

'It mek me very sad,' one said, 'that she all alone. She can't call on we to ease her pain.'

'The family find it very hard,' I said.

We were seated around two long trestle tables pushed together. There were half a dozen women each working on their own sewing projects. Three sewing machines sat along the far side of the table and a cornucopia of scraps, silks and ribbons littered the centre. I could see from the red, green and gold colours and the holly and fir tree patterns that Christmas gifts were amongst the creations.

'The last time anyone saw Miriam was when she left the Craft Club at the Whitworth Centre.'

'Melody, you went there,' one of the older women, who'd been introduced to me as Mrs Michaels, addressed a younger one.

Melody looked guilty. 'I don't go any more,' she said to me hurriedly.

'She likes the sewing better, don't you, Melody?'

Melody nodded. She had a graceful face, large almond-shaped eyes, her skin the colour of milky coffee. Her hair was cut close to her head, like a neat black cap. She trembled constantly giving the impression of frailty and ill health. I didn't want to add to her problems but I did ask her if Miriam had said anything about her plans for that afternoon.

Melody shook her head, eyes lowered.

I asked the rest of them if anyone had seen Miriam.

Nobody had.

'I have found out that someone from the church called to see her, around lunchtime. An grey-haired gentleman, middle-aged or elderly. I'd like to find out who it was. Can you think of anyone who fits that description?'

'Albert Fanu,' ventured Mrs Thompson.

'And Mrs Beatty,' said one of the women, 'her husband has grey hair.'

'It's white,' Mrs Thompson said.

'Grey.'

'Mr Beatty,' I said. Writing it down to forestall argument.

'Who else? Grey hair.' said Mrs Thompson.

'There's a lot more ladies in the congregation,' Mrs Michaels said.

'Nicholas Bell.'

'And Trudeau.'

'Trudeau – has he still got some hair? He having it stitched on?' Mrs Michaels said disdainfully.

'Extensions!' someone hooted.

The place erupted in laughter. The joke was so hilarious that Mrs Thompson had to wipe her eyes and one of her friends slapped at the table.

I smiled inanely and waited for the paroxysms to subside.

With the group's help I listed the men and their addresses

or in one case a description of the house as no one could remember the house number.

'Were any of them friends of Miriam, likely to visit?'

Shrugs all round.

At the doorway Mrs Thompson leant close and put her hand on my arm. 'Have you thought that maybe this gentleman caller was a secret?'

'Yes and I will be very discreet.'

She nodded solemnly and patted my arm.

As far as the Johnstones knew, Miriam hadn't been involved with anyone but maybe she just hadn't told them. Until I had more information I had to keep an open mind on all counts. The man who'd called for Miriam and missed her could simply have been a friend. If he was her lover and he'd kept the relationship quiet even in the wake of her death the burden must have been horrendous.

Hopefully he was among the four names on my list and would soon be able to tell me himself what the state of affairs had been.

CHAPTER SIXTEEN

After a quick swim at the baths in Withington I called home for lunch; chunks of courgette, fried with olive oil and garlic, topped with grated cheddar and accompanied by a chunk of homemade bread. Not mine. Sheila, who rented the attic flat, loved to bake. Since she'd joined the household we were regularly treated to the smell of cakes and bread rising from the shared kitchen. I couldn't get enough of the Greek olive bread she did and added the ingredients to my shopping list so we'd always have them in the next time Sheila got the urge.

We'd be without her for Christmas; she was travelling in connection with the geology degree course she was doing and going on to visit her student son up at St Andrew's in Scotland. I'd never had the inclination to bake. Or the time. But Susan Reeve managed, didn't she? Even with four children and her husband away half the week. Her twins liked it, she'd said. Maybe I'd have summoned up some interest if Maddie had been keen when she was younger. But there's never been any inkling of it until Sheila moved in and now it had become their particular thing. Fine by me. Meant I could go and play in the garden.

I consulted the A–Z and reordered my list of churchgoers according to location. Then I began my mission. Albert Fanu, who lived near Brook's Bar, the big junction in Whalley Range, was my first port of call. A woman answered the door.

'Good afternoon. I'm a private investigator – my name's Sal Kilkenny. I'm carrying out some confidential enquiries and I'd like to speak to your husband, is he in?'

She looked intrigued. 'Yes, wait a minute.' She fetched Mr Fanu and then disappeared back into the house.

'Hello. My name's Sal Kilkenny, I'm a private investigator. I'm carrying out some confidential enquiries for Miriam Johnstone's daughter, Constance?' He nodded in recognition. 'We're trying to contact someone who called on Miriam the day she died – a gentleman from the church. I'm calling on people to try and find out who her caller was.'

He pulled his lips down, a facial shrug. 'Not me. Pearl does all our visiting.'

I had the same sort of response from Trudeau Collins in Old Trafford. (He came across as a right flirt, vain into the bargain, that gave me some notion of why the sewing circle had made him the butt of their jokes.) Mr Beatty, who had a flat over the shops on Mauldeth Road, needed me to go over my story twice before asserting that he definitely hadn't called round on Miriam Johnstone. 'I didn't know her well,' he said. 'Don't know where she lived.'

And I agreed with Mrs Thompson – his hair was white.

Nicholas Bell, who lived off Ladybarn Lane was out at work at Ringway. His wife told me he'd be home at four unless there were any delays on the trains from the airport.

I promised to return later. 'About five, I think.'

And if he said no, too? I could sense the lead turning into a cul-de-sac.

CHAPTER SEVENTEEN

At school Maddie and Tom each had a batch of letters reminding us about the school play, the school Christmas Fair and the holiday timetable. Tom also had a painting of a Christmas Tree, the powder paint layered on in thick green lumps. It must have taken days to dry. I could feel the weight of the paint as I took it from him.

'That's lovely, Tom.'

'It looks like snot,' Maddie observed.

'Hey,' I shot her a warning glance. She was never at her best after six hours in the classroom.

'We'll put it up in the playroom,' I promised Tom.

'When can we have our real tree?' Maddie said, her voice dripping with impatience.

'I told you, next weekend.'

A blast of wind whipped the papers back and forth in my hand.

'Zip up,' I said, 'it's cold.'

No reaction.

Fine. The kids had internal temperature control systems that didn't seem to bear any relation to external conditions. If they felt cold they'd do their coats up. Tom practically never felt the cold while Maddie veered from one extreme to the other. Boiling or freezing, usually at odds with other people's responses. She'd once worn a thick Arran sweater all summer, even on the exciting three-day heat wave, insisting she was cold.

'Come on, then.'

There was an oyster sky, the setting sun licking clouds salmon and silver and grey. The street lights were coming on as we reached home. The dark and the wind setting off the warm glow of windows and the pretty twinkle of fairy lights. One particularly brash display that we passed had ribbons of lights in several colours including some very bright white ones which flashed around the windows like strobes spelling out NOEL and a neon centrepiece of a sleigh and Father Christmas.

'Wow!' Tom breathed.

'Sick,' Maddie said. It was the latest slang for approval. No longer bad or wicked or cool, this year everything was sick. And really 'sick' things were psychosomatic. I ask you.

As we reached home I could hear the board on the roof clattering again and once I was inside I scribbled a reminder on a post-it note, to tell Ray.

The house was warm and I didn't feel much like setting out again but Rusholme wasn't far and I'd be driving against the early rush hour traffic.

Ray was in the cellar. The place smelt delicious, the tang of wood and sawdust. He'd taken on three Christmas orders; two chests of drawers and a set of dining chairs. He was planing the drawers and a pile of curly shavings covered his feet. There was a fine wood dust over everything including Ray. It made him look older.

'How's it going?'

'Oh, don't ask.'

'Ah.'

'It'll be a bloody miracle if I get any of this finished by Christmas.'

I made a noise to show sympathy but I knew he'd do the jobs. It might mean he was down here till the early hours every night but he'd get it done. He only ever completed things under pressure of a deadline and this panic was par for the course. If things didn't have a deadline he'd work on them for months, constantly refining. Once I'd cottoned onto this I always made a point of telling my friends to give him a completion date. That way they got their stuff.

'I'm off now. Be about half five when I'm back. Maybe sooner. Don't wait though. Feed them before.'

'Save you some?'

'What is it?'

'Haven't a clue, yet.'

'No, don't bother.' It might be something that didn't reheat well. I'd rather look forward to something I could rely on and make it myself. Or seeing I'd be in Rusholme, to visit the Johnstones, I could maybe treat myself to a vegetable bhuna or a prawn biriyani. I brightened at the thought and made sure I'd got a bit of money on me.

CHAPTER EIGHTEEN

Connie Johnstone flung open the door, her face divided by a frown, opened her mouth to speak then, seeing me, slumped and shook her head.

'Come in. I thought it might be Roland. He's not back.'

Martina, coming out of the back room, also looked anxious.

'I could come back tomorrow,' I suggested. 'Do you think he's forgotten?'

'No. He knows you're coming. I reminded him this morning.' Her brow creased sharply again. 'He may have got held up somewhere,' she said feebly and I could tell she didn't believe it for a moment. So, what was really going on with Roland? I couldn't work it out.

'If you want to talk to Martina?'

'Okay. It shouldn't take long.'

We went into the back room and Martina used the remote to turn off the television. She sat down with me at the table, Connie leant against the door.

'I've been back to Heald Place,' I told them both, 'asking the neighbours if anyone saw your mother come home for lunch. The police had already done that, as you know, and no one saw her. Then I realized that Martina and Roland were the obvious people to double-check with. You'd be able to say if there were signs of your mother being in that afternoon or home for lunch.'

Martina exhaled. 'Right,' she said quietly. She closed her eyes. 'I can't remember anything.'

'You can't remember?' I wasn't clear what she meant. Was it all lost to her given the trauma that had followed or couldn't she remember seeing any sign of Miriam's presence?

'I don't remember any dishes in the sink. The paper wasn't there. She usually read the paper with her lunch.'

'What time did you get home?'

'About four,' she smoothed her hair back towards her bun.

'And Roland?'

'Same,' she told me.

'Who was home first?'

'Me.'

'Was it unusual for your mother to be out at that time?'

'Not really. I thought she'd be home soon to start . . .' She stopped abruptly, misery making her suck in her cheeks and clamp her lips tight against the quivering.

'Okay,' I said. My heart went out to her as she tried to compose herself. To lose a parent was painful enough. I still mourned the loss of my father who'd been dead for eight years but at least I'd been able to blame a disease for his death, it wasn't at his own hand. With suicide what did you blame? Mental illness? The person who left you behind? Yourself for not being able to prevent it?

Connie stepped closer and put her hands on Martina's shoulders, rubbed her upper arms. 'Martina rang me at six,' she said, 'the police about half an hour later.'

I was relieved I didn't need to ask Martina anything else. She'd told me all I needed to know; Miriam had stayed out that day and Roland had been home last.

'Thanks, that's all I need for now.' I said.

Martina took my cue and nodded. Connie released her and she went upstairs.

'I'm sorry – it's upsetting.'

She sighed and nodded, sat in the chair Martina had left.

'Do you have a list anywhere of her possessions, things she had with her, clothes, bag and so on?'

'I don't remember a list. Why?'

'I thought she might have got the bus to town. If there'd been a ticket, I could try and trace the driver, the passengers.'

Connie nodded her understanding. 'They just gave us a plastic bag, with her rings and her handbag,' she swallowed. 'We didn't get her clothes.'

I nodded fast. They'd have been bloodied, torn.

'Her bag?'

'Yes.'

I thought of Miriam Johnstone falling, clutching her bag. There was pathos in the image.

We heard the front door open. Connie sprang up and out of the room. I heard Patrick's voice mingle with Connie's. Someone running downstairs.

The pair of them came in followed by Martina.

'And he's run off?' Patrick asked, unzipping his jacket.

'Run off? Is this because I was coming?' I asked Connie.

'I think so,' her face was drawn. 'He's only fifteen. When Ma died . . . he couldn't talk about it, still can't really. The only way he could cope was to retreat.' She paused. Her caramel eyes glistened. I could tell she was on the verge of tears but determined to hold them back while she explained. 'He didn't want to know. He never asked a single thing, not one question. He was like a block of wood at the funeral. Never spoke to anyone, never said a word . . . I don't know how to help him. He's a child really. I think this, asking him to talk to you, maybe it was too much. Pushing him too far.' Guilt clouded her eyes and she turned to Patrick.

I wished she had said something sooner. I recalled his silence when they had come to my office; he hadn't said a thing.

'Where is he?' Patrick said. 'Where will he have gone?'

'Maybe Wayne's,' Martina said, 'or Jordan's?'

'I'll ring them.' Connie used the phone but Roland wasn't at either place.

'Has this happened before?' I asked, conscious of the atmosphere of crisis that prickled in the room.

'The day of the inquest,' Connie said. 'Roland didn't come, that was fine, it was his choice. But we came home and . . . no Roland. He came in later, went straight upstairs. He didn't want to know, he didn't even want to hear the verdict.' Her face was twisted with confusion.

'Connie, it's hard,' said Patrick, 'at his age, at any age. Men don't find it easy to show their feelings.'

'I don't need him to be a man,' she said fiercely. 'If that's what being a man is. I need him to be my little . . .' she pressed a hand to her mouth.

'This isn't about what you need,' Patrick said softly.

Martina studied her knees, sat very still on the sofa.

'If Roland's avoiding me,' I said, 'then he'll probably be back in a little while. He won't expect me to stay all evening. Martina's answered the questions I had. I won't have to trouble him.'

'He'll be back,' Patrick reassured Connie.

'Will you do me a favour?' I said. 'Ring and let me know when he gets in. If I'd realized he was so upset . . .'

'We think he's upset,' Connie said, 'but even that's guesswork.'

'Of course he's upset,' Patrick chided her, 'he can't handle it, Con, this is his way of telling us.'

'Yeah,' she rubbed at her face. 'I know.'

'I'd better go now.' I stood up. 'Do let me know, won't you. I hope he's all right.'

Mrs Boscoe must have mixed her days up. And as I thought about it more I decided that if Roland had skipped school he'd have picked a day when he was unlikely to run into his mother who, from what I'd heard about her, would have been less than happy at him playing truant.

It was just after five and I was early for my last doorstep call so I walked through to Wilmslow Road and treated myself to a vegetable biriyani with naan bread and all the trimmings. It was warm in the restaurant and pretty quiet.

I watched the world go by through the plate glass windows strung with fairy light and lanterns. People were coming home from work, traffic heavy from the direction of town. Buses chugged past, plastered with advertising slogans. I watched two students window-shop, arms wrapped about each other. Both had startling hairstyles; his was closely shaved and striped black and white, while she had hair to her waist, cobalt blue. I smiled. Diane would approve. A man selling the *Big Issue* got rid of his last copy and walked off.

I paid my bill, accepted some scented cachou sweets to suck and drove back to Ladybarn. Mrs Bell answered the door. She remembered me and called out, 'Nicholas, it's the lady I told you about.'

He came downstairs slowly as though age was stiffening his joints. I waited for his wife to withdraw before I made my enquiry. 'Hello. I'm Sal Kilkenny, I'm a private investigator working for Miriam Johnstone's family. We're trying to trace someone who called on Miriam the day she died – a gentleman from the church. I wonder whether you can help?'

He glared through his spectacles at my question and unceremoniously shut the door in my face.

I dealt with my hot sense of rejection by speculating on the reasons for his action. Was he the grey-haired caller panicking at being traced? Or simply outraged at the implication that he, or another churchgoer, may have visited Miriam with less than platonic intentions. But I hadn't said anything like that, I'd kept it innocent enough. Suppose he was seeing Miriam – wouldn't slamming the door on me have aroused his wife's curiosity? A discrete denial, or even admission, would have been a cannier response. Mind you, sudden discovery doesn't always lead to logical or considered reactions. Then again, maybe one of the amenable denials of the other three men concealed a secret relationship. I was getting nowhere fast with the identity of that caller and it may have been completely insignificant. The man hadn't found Miriam at home, and there was nothing to suggest that he'd seen her

70

later that day. I wasn't sure that there was much point in pursuing that line of enquiry at this stage. I could always come back to it.

And I did.

Oh, boy, I did.

I'd been home an hour when Patrick rang to tell me Roland was back. They had not pressed him for an explanation of his absence but told him Martina had answered all my questions.

'Have you thought about bereavement counselling for him?'

'We're working on it,' he said. 'There's a teacher at school who Roland gets on really well with. He knows someone who's done a lot of work with teenagers. Roland's not taken him up on it yet but there's also a book he's recommended. Connie's got it on order. I think Roland might find it easier to read something first of all. Talking to people . . . well . . .'

'Yes. Thanks for letting me know anyway. I'll be in touch.'

I was glad that the lad had come back and was okay but a small crumb of doubt tickled away at me. Was it just grief that drove him away at the prospect of talking to me or was there anything else? I needed that edge of scepticism to do my work but I hated the taste it left in my mouth. I wanted to think the best of people, to find the good in them, to see that triumph. But I'd learnt enough to know that life wasn't like a fairy tale, that people go wrong – some people. They make mistakes and mess things up; they hide and cheat and choke themselves with secrets and guilt. Suddenly, like missing a step in a dream, their world changes. And it can happen to anyone. It had happened to Miriam through her illness. That lunge for destruction, annihilation. Her act, her loss had created a tidal wave of change for her children. I wasn't sure how Martina was dealing with it, though her tears seemed healthy enough. Connie was searching for facts, a schedule, sightings, details, anything to throw into the yawning 'why'? She was still at the stage of anger, disbelief, almost denial.

And Roland? Was Roland drowning? I would leave him be for now but I wouldn't forget that sliver of uncertainty I had. I'd learnt to trust my intuition; it is a skill I use in the work, it's imprecise, shadowy even, but when I get that tug in my gut and the tightening sensation on my skin then I know something's going on. I hadn't felt it when I'd been so rudely banished from Nicholas Bell's doorstep but I had when Roland Johnstone stood me up.

File under pending.

CHAPTER NINETEEN

My world seemed full of teenage boys. Unhappy teenage boys. On the second morning that I trailed Adam Reeve he wagged college. He set off in the same direction as before but as soon as he reached Kingsway he crossed the road and walked to the bus stop that was served by buses running into town.

I followed on. There was a cluster of people waiting and although I didn't expect Adam to notice me, the extra numbers would help. I watched him now and again out of the corner of my eye. He had a sleepy look, created in part by the way his eyes turned down at the corners. A crop of spots had erupted over his nose. He was slightly stooped and his hands in pocket and head down stance made it clear to all that he was not up for any idle chit chat.

The two women next to me were. They talked in a desultory way about the appalling bus service and tried to cap each other's stories of nightmare journeys. I was glad it wasn't raining. The wind had dropped and the temperature too. The sky was airbrushed with touches of breathy cloud. A nip of frost threatened. Gloves and hat weather. I had both. Adam had neither. Was he hunched partly against the cold?

At long last two buses careered into view. We all piled onto the first as the second swooped past. Playing leapfrog all the way to town. Adam went upstairs and I sat down, the better to maintain my status as the invisible woman.

The journey to town was excruciating. Roadworks were a

permanent feature of life in Manchester. The place had mush-roomed in Victorian times, the centre of the cotton trade and a mercantile capital. Now a hundred and fifty years on things were crumbling, repairs went hand in hand with renovation to create a constantly changing city. The sewers had been dug up and shored up, new Metro Link lines installed for the successful light rapid transport system, old warehouses were converted into swanky apartments overlooking tarted-up canals, city living was in vogue. Cafe-bars and restaurants sprang up along the canal sides and under the railway arches where once goods had been lifted on and off the barges, carts had been repaired, paint mixed or candles made.

The latest transformations were in honour of the Commonwealth Games. There were new roads being made and stadia built. The journey would have been slow at the best of times, commuters streaming into work in their cars but with lane closures along Birchfields Road and work on Upper Brook Street I could have walked there in the time it took the bus. I thanked my lucky stars that this wasn't part of my daily routine.

Adam got off at the bus terminus in Piccadilly Gardens. They were rebuilding here too, in the square which lay between the old parade of buildings on Piccadilly and the shabby, stolid concrete, sixties-built Plaza Tower opposite. It was a controversial scheme to relandscape the site and take part of the gardens for a new building. Planning had been approved in spite of protests about green space and parks in the city, and work was cracking on apace.

The sun was shining and had climbed high enough to reach over the buildings. It spread golden light but little warmth. Adam set off away from the shopping centre and along to Portland Street. His loping gait was easy to see and I could keep some distance between us without losing him. Where was he going? Chinatown? The gay village? Neither as it turned out. He went into Chorlton Street coach station, into the ticket office.

Were we going on a coach? I got in the queue, next but one to Adam. There were two clerks behind the counter. Their turnover seemed painfully slow. I could feel the tension in the queue as our wait ground on, hear muttered complaints and regular heartfelt sighs.

My mobile startled me. It was Susan Reeve. 'Adam's not in college. They've phoned.'

'I'm dealing with it,' I said, 'I'll get back to you later.'

'Oh, good.' She said with relief. 'Right. Thank you.'

I closed my phone put it away.

At last it was Adam's turn.

I strained to hear what he asked for from my place near the head of the queue but couldn't catch a word. I began to feel panicky. How could I buy my ticket if I didn't know where he was going? Would they let me pay on the coach? My dilemma was resolved by the clerk dealing with him who said in ringing tones, 'Return to York, ten pounds fifty.'

Adam muttered something.

'On the hour, change at Leeds.'

Adam nodded and stepped away. No ticket, nothing. Was he paying on the coach? I didn't want to lose him nor attract his attention. I waited until he'd left the office before sighing in supposed frustration and abandoning the queue. Given I was now next in line they must have thought I'd lost my marbles – or maybe missed my bus.

I scoured the lanes in the depot for Adam, my eyes flicking fast in search of the boy with a bag on his back, stooping a little, gangly stride. No sign. I ran out onto Bloom Street. Nothing. I went up and round the corner. There he was, heading back towards Piccadilly. I let my heart settle back in my chest.

I followed him across the tram lines and down to Market Street. The pedestrianized area beside the Arndale Centre was always busy. A stall in the centre of the thoroughfare was selling cheap socks, inflatable reindeers and Santa hats. There were Christmas lights slung between the shops. The patterned paving was littered with chewing gum like urban lichen. A pair of buskers, accordion and sax were playing carols in a jazzy style. Two middle-aged women hovered with clipboards, out to recruit new takers for a mail order catalogue.

Adam went into the Arndale Centre. The next three hours were a prime example of the numbing boredom of most surveillance work. Adam Reeve mooched. I followed. He never bought anything, not even a drink or a sandwich, never tried anything on or spoke to anyone. He wandered in and out of the shops though I noticed he avoided the women's fashion shops where he'd look out of place. Occasionally he'd pick something up, examine it for a bit, then replace it. I wondered if he was building up to shoplifting but nothing transpired. I trailed behind him, increasingly hot, tired and thirsty. I loathe the Arndale centre; I would nominate it for a sick building award – sick in the old-fashioned sense of the word – along with every other shopping mall I've ever been dragged into and I'd count Ikea as one too. I just can't hack it. I am not a mall rat. Not even a mall mouse and I pride myself on never having set foot in the massive out of town Trafford Centre. Maddie is always pestering me to take her.

At one point he sat on a bench. For a whole half hour. Killing time. I pretended to browse my way through discount books and children's clothes in the front section of nearby stores. The beginnings of a headache cupped my forehead and I was desperate for the toilet. The toilets were tucked away in a corner of the lower mall about a million miles away from our present spot. If I built a mall there'd be a toilet on every corner, and somewhere to rest. And I'd arrange all the shops in a row with a street between them open to unlimited daylight and fresh air. I mean, what is it with all this emphasis on everything being under the same roof. Can't we cope with a spot of rain or a gust of wind? We were designed to be weatherproof when all's said and done.

I resolutely ignored the dull pain in my bladder and

hung on. Hordes of people circulated through the building. I watched one young woman pushing a buggy laden with boxes and bags. She had a toddler as well as a baby. He was beside himself, screaming and red-faced. His mother looked exhausted. 'Shurrup,' she screamed at him, yanking the hood of his coat and dragging him up close. 'Shut yer bleeding noise,' she released his hood and slapped him across his head.

I felt sick. And sorry. I knew how she felt. There were times when I'd come so close with Maddie. Times I had to leave the room, go and vent my inept rage on a pillow or let it out in scalding tears. I counted myself lucky, I'd had the resources to hold back, to walk away, to count to ten or fifty or whatever. Managing to stay one side of the line. Just. How did the child feel? Did that shouting face and the swipe of her hand make him angry inside, did it hurt still or was he learning not to feel it? And what about her? Did she feel guilty? Justified? Too strung out to care? Depression is a common side-effect of motherhood. Comes with the territory. I thought about Miriam. She had to raise three children, most of the time on her own. She wouldn't have earned much as a cleaner at the hospital and the break with her husband had been irreparable. He wouldn't have helped with maintenance. No child support agency back then tracking down absent fathers. His leaving had made her ill. Had she had any help with the children? Connie was ten years older than Roland. Had she played mother when Miriam was too sick?

The tape loop was on its third rendition of 'The Holly and the Ivy' when Adam got up and wandered back to the bus. I held my pelvic floor muscles very tight as we lurched and bumped our way south to Burnage. As I expected he got off near home and went straight back there.

I was released.

Back at mine, once I'd answered the deafening call of nature (oh bliss, oh bliss), I made myself a bowl of carrot and coriander soup and soaked it up with a slab of bread. I felt my blood sugar levels climb back to a reassuring level. I get cranky as anything when they're low. There was some fruitcake too so I cut a large piece of that and had it with a chunk of Wensleydale cheese; an old Yorkshire tradition that I'd acquired from my father.

Appetites sated – well, some of them anyway – I rang Stuart. He runs a cafe-bar in Didsbury but he's often at home doing paperwork in the daytime. Not today though. I was disappointed. It would be nice to see him soon. I wondered why he hadn't rung me, I knew it was a really busy time at work for him plus he'd had his children all weekend but it was Wednesday already. I left a message suggesting we fix up a drink or something. I was most interested in the something.

I rang Susan Reeve. I could hear the clamour of family life in the background and kept my call short. Told her there wasn't much to report, Adam had hung around town all day but there was something I wanted to follow up with her and I arranged to pop round in the morning.

Adam's enquiry about travel to York was the only item of any interest. Why York? Friends? Relations? A girlfriend? I'd see if Susan knew. But he'd obviously not been there on previous jaunts, not by coach anyway. Had he just been sitting round the Arndale? They didn't stay open that late. Even for Christmas shopping it was shut by ten.

I pictured Adam sat on the bench, chin practically on his chest, arms crossed, gaze faraway. What was he doing? One word sprang to mind. Brooding. That's what it looked like. Miserable, introspective, lonely. Adolescent angst? A lonely boy with nowhere to go. Except York? Why York? Was there something there to give him hope?

CHAPTER TWENTY

I was in the middle of mopping the kitchen floor when my mobile rang. It was Eddie Cliff from the Whitworth Centre. He had spoken to the Craft Club the previous day and he thought tomorrow would be all right if I still wanted to talk to them. Some people were a little edgy about it but he could be there and give me the nod if he felt anyone was getting uncomfortable.

'I know the signs,' he explained. 'It's not always obvious.'

It was short notice but fitted in with my plans to do anything other than spend another day bored rigid watching Adam Reeve brood at the Arndale Centre.

Digger slunk in while I was finishing the call. I shooed him away with my foot. He shot me a doleful look, resentful that he couldn't occupy his favourite spot beside the old armchair by the bay window in the kitchen. Originally I thought he liked it there because it was handy for any food dropping events but it's actually just where the central heating pipes run under the wooden floor to the radiator. Warmth plus the prospect of table scraps.

Mopping complete, I shut the door on it and plugged the hoover in the hall socket. First I needed to sweep the stairs with a stiff brush. I don't enjoy housework but I try and do it as energetically as possible and consider it exercise. Well, I try. I duly swapped the little brush from hand to hand and went down the stairs like the clappers. Digger was now stretched out alongside the radiator in the hall. When

I switched the hoover on I swear he rolled his eyes at me before getting to his feet with an air of resignation and padding off into the playroom.

I had been responsible for arriving home unannounced with Digger. But my role in his care stopped there. Digger adores Ray and sees me as a bit of an irritant. It's mutual, every which way. Oh, he's a pleasant enough dog but I am not a doggy person.

Looking in the playroom there was precious little carpet visible beneath the tide of bright plastic bits that reached from wall to wall. I couldn't face the sort and tidy ordeal required to excavate the carpet for hoovering and I didn't have the time anyway. It was ten to three. The lounge was okay. I wheeled the hoover in there.

The garden looked glum at this time of year, even though there were plenty of evergreen shrubs. I'd left most of the herbaceous perennials as they were, hoping that a coating of frost would redeem them and preferring old stalks to bare earth. However we hadn't had such low temperatures yet and they all had that sodden, battered look. Half-dead and neglected. A hardy fuchsia still sporting tiny deep pink flowers, hanging like delicate lanterns and a snowberry bush heavy with masses of small white balls were the only bright colours in among the muddy browns and straw shades. Oh, of course the grass was green. The grass was drenched. I could have grown rice out there. Or farmed trout. Well – almost.

A squirrel dug in the lawn, stashing some nuts or seeds. Another month or so, maybe six weeks and the snowdrops would be starting. The days would get a little longer. Everything would start to grow again. I couldn't wait.

CHAPTER TWENTY-ONE

'Does Adam know anyone in York?' I asked Susan Reeve the following morning.

'York? No.'

'No family or friends there?'

'No. Why?'

'Adam went into town yesterday. He spent most of the time just hanging around the Arndale Centre. But he went to the coach station and asked for information on services to York.'

'How peculiar,' she frowned. 'Do you think I should ask him about it?'

'Not yet, not unless you want to tell him you've hired me. I haven't put in two days yet and we don't know if this is a pattern – if he always goes into town when he skips college. I'd like to give it another go.'

'Oh, yes.' She was quick to agree. 'And he just hung round the shops?'

'Yes, didn't look like he was waiting for anyone either. Just filling in time.'

She sighed. 'I wish I knew what was going on. I'd like him to see the doctor but the last time I suggested it he was anti the idea. Said there was nothing wrong with him. It's so hard to weigh up when to intervene and when to let them get on with it.'

'What does your husband think?'

'Says I'm overreacting. Says Adam will settle again, that we need to give him time. Have you got children?'

'One.'

'How old?'

'Six.'

'You've got all this to come then.'

I grimaced. 'I hope not. Do you think your husband might have any ideas about York?'

'I doubt it.'

'Can you ask him?'

'Yes, I'll let you know.'

'I better go then. You'll get all this in my written report as well.'

The hall was bitterly cold and I realized that the kitchen was the only room that had any heating on.

I zipped my coat up as Susan Reeve opened the door. She shivered.

'Cold,' I said. Not sure whether I meant the conditions or how she felt.

'Economy measures,' she said ruefully. She didn't elaborate. She didn't need to. It must have been a struggle keeping six people on one wage. They'd be scrimping to make ends meet, countless tiny economies; putting off buying shoes, cancelling the window cleaner, being careful with the phone, only shopping at the cheapest supermarkets. I'd been there, done that, still had the t-shirt. The last few months I had brought in more money than in any previous year and I was able to relax slightly, reduce my credit card debts and treat myself and Maddie to things that were usually out of bounds. But I could only relax slightly. I was only slightly better off, after all. Plus it was a precarious existence; a drop in income or an unexpected outlay and I'd be catapulted back to the tedious strain of trying to make ends meet.

I got a resoundingly warm welcome from the members of the Craft Club and a cup of tea and a biscuit too. There were eight people there and Eddie told me when I arrived that seven of them had been coming some time and knew Miriam Johnstone. He introduced everybody.

I recognized the two women who had been helping to decorate the hall. Tracey, the slim, dark-haired woman and Sandy, the overweight teenager, who barely spoke. Then there were two women wearing the same purple sweatshirts and shared similar husky smoker's voices, though one, Carla, had a Manchester accent and the other, Dolly, had a thick Glaswegian brogue.

A young black woman with lurid green-framed spectacles was introduced as Pauline. She said little but scowled a lot. Joe, shaky, shy and stammering and thin as a whippet, looked to be in his fifties and beside him sat Charlie, a heavy-set man with brown teeth and badly cut hair.

Then there was Jane. Jane talked all the time, oblivious as to whether anyone was listening or whether anyone else was trying to speak. She had bubbly blonde hair and a heart-shaped face with small features and virulent eczema. Periodically Carla leaned across the table and told her to shut up. It worked for a few seconds then she'd start again. No one else bothered and I soon adapted to two streams of conversation.

'Jane,' Eddie said, 'Sal's come here today to ask us all about Miriam.'

'Oh,' Jane said flatly and shut up.

'Yes,' I said, 'you remember back in October, the last session Miriam came to?'

'We were starting the batik,' Eddie said.

'Burnt my fingers,' said Jane. 'It's very hot, the wax gets very hot. That's so it melts but you've got to be very careful. It's got to be hot, smoking hot and then when . . .'

I realized I'd have to talk across her. I raised my voice a little and addressed the others.

'I want to find out which way Miriam went after the session. Did anyone go out with her?'

A chorus of no and shaking heads.

'She cleared up,' Jane said.

'That's right,' said Eddie.

83

'I should've cleared up but I burnt my fingers. I was going to do it. Me and Melody.'

I recalled the pretty young woman I'd met at the sewing circle, the one who trembled like a leaf. She didn't come any more, preferred sewing.

'We were on the rota. I had to put some cream on. Thought I'd have to go to Casualty.'

'It was a small burn,' Eddie smiled.

'Hurt a lot, hurt more than you think. If you'd . . .'

'Shut up,' said Carla.

'So Miriam was one of the last to leave?' I checked.

'Melody was crying,' said Jane.

'She wasn't,' Carla said scornfully.

'She was, in the toilets,' said Jane.

'Melody was upset,' Eddie intervened, 'I think there'd been a bit of a row at home.'

'No one told me,' Carla said defensively.

'What are we doing today?' Charlie asked.

'The presents,' said Eddie. A ripple of excitement ran round the group. His eyes twinkled. 'But we'll finish talking to Sal first. She wants to know if anyone saw Miriam after the session.' He glanced at me to see if that was right.

I nodded. 'Yes, that afternoon, or perhaps on her way home?'

'I go in the minibus,' Jane began. 'So I couldn't see her. She never gets the minibus. She walks doesn't she. Me and Pauline we go back to the centre. Everyone else . . .'

'We made a lovely wreath for her,' said Dolly.

Jane fell quiet. There was a pause. Sandy began to rock in her chair ever so slightly.

'No one saw her?' Eddie tried again.

Shaking heads.

'Did she talk to anyone about her plans that afternoon?'

More shakes.

'I burnt my finger. It's that hot,' said Jane.

'Thank you,' I said and made to leave.

I could feel the relief and people shuffled in their seats.

Eddie took me through to the foyer. 'It makes some of them anxious,' he said. 'Suicide. A couple of them will have already attempted it.'

I must have looked shocked.

He shrugged. 'Comes with the territory. Not with Jane and Pauline, they have learning difficulties. But those with a history of mental health problems, depression, well . . .'

'So not everybody's been ill?'

'No. We're open access. Anyone's welcome, literally. We do get referrals, other professionals ring up and ask if their clients can come and give it a go but I wanted it to be about breaking down the labels and the barriers not reinforcing them. You don't have to be mad to come here,' he grinned. 'Take Charlie. He's lonely. His wife died last year, world fell apart. All he's looking for is some friendship, some focus. And that's what we offer.'

'Not therapy?'

He laughed. 'Only with a small "t". I'm not qualified to do that sort of thing. I wouldn't want to. I'm much more interested in making things, using arts and crafts as a way of people building up their self-esteem.'

'They've made some great stuff.' I gestured to the huge banner on the wall.

'Oh, yeah. Miriam did a lot of that, the figures.'

I waited a moment. 'When she was clearing up with you, she didn't say what her plans were.'

'Nope. I didn't see her go either, or I could tell you which way she went. I assumed she was going home, she usually did. I was pretty occupied, we'd a visit from the Central Grants people, they were due at half twelve so Sharon and I were busy getting everything ready for that.'

'Did anyone call here asking for Miriam? A black man, middle-aged maybe older, with grey hair?'

'No.' He looked curious.

'No one ever met her after the sessions?'

'Not as far as I know. You think there might have been someone?'

'I'm not sure.' And the information I was gathering was confidential, for Connie's family only.

'I'm sorry it's been a wasted journey,' he said as we reached the outside door.

'Not at all. Nothing's ever wasted; even if it just confirms what I've heard, it's still progress. All part of the job.'

I had followed in the footsteps of the police; talking to Miriam's family, her neighbours and to Eddie Cliff. I'd found that the police had not been particularly thorough in their actions immediately after Miriam's death – at a time when it was deemed suspicious and before it became obvious it was suicide.

I had visited the scene of her death and talked to her friends from church. I'd discovered that she'd had a mystery caller but had no way of knowing whether that contributed to her decision to take her own life. I'd a funny feeling about Roland but nowhere to go with it. Any progress I was making to fill in Miriam's missing hours was painfully slow. But investigations are like that – you can't hurry things along. There were still several names on my list of contacts, people I would speak to before giving up. But I was aware I might have nothing to tell Connie at the end of the day. Just a big *don't know*.

CHAPTER TWENTY-TWO

O ne of the things I love about my work is the freedom it
gives me to manage my own time. No clocking on, no
set hours, no annual leave allocation. That flexibility meant
I could go along to the school show at two o'clock that afternoon without having to fill in any forms or ask anyone's
permission.

Maddie was a kiwi fruit and Tom was a cactus. From this
you can probably deduce that this was not your traditional
Christmas nativity play. No. This was winter celebrations
round the world; an opportunity for each class to be a different country and enact the rituals (very broadly interpreted)
for winter feasts and pageants.

Maddie had been practising her song all week but as I
craned my neck I could see her face was set in a mask of
abject terror. Last year she had burst into tears and had to
be led from the hall. Tom, in contrast, waved a spiky paw at
me, beaming all over his face. I looked round but couldn't
see Ray yet.

A quick check of the programme told me that Maddie's
class would be second. It couldn't be soon enough for me. I
tried to ignore the seething tension in my stomach and smile
at her encouragingly. She refused to catch my eye.

The Swedish lot, done up as candles with flame hats, kicked
off with a story about the feast of Santa Lucia. I couldn't
see Maddie for the duration and hoped she was still compos
mentis. Riotous applause from the packed hall greeted the

end of scene one. A baby began to wail. Those parents with video cameras vied for a good position.

I remembered to breathe as the classes changed places. The Maori chant began. Maddie stood between her friends Kim and Ayesha, her lips barely moved. A group of children with feathered hats began to dance. Jacob, another of Maddie's friends, was among them. His hat slid down over his eyes causing helpless hilarity among the audience and some of the performers. He soldiered on. Every time he pulled it up he had to let go to perform the handclaps and at that point it slid inexorably down again. There was an extra burst of applause for the laugh factor. New Zealand was over. I felt my shoulders settle back. I could relax. Maddie shot me a shy smile. I grinned back and gave her the thumbs up sign.

The other high point of the show was a number of cactus jokes from Tom's lot followed by an off key but extremely enthusiastic rendering of 'La Cucaracha' and a sort of Mexican clog dance. They had obviously been well drilled in the steps but it only needed one boy out of step to create perfect slapstick. The woman beside me laughed so hard she cried. And I bet all the people shooting videos were thinking of the cheque from You've Been Framed.

Ray had watched the show from the back as he'd cut it close time wise. The four of us walked back together; a most unusual occurrence which made the children even more giddy. I told Ray about the loose board near the roof.

'I'll ask Barry to take a look,' he said. 'He wouldn't do it himself but one of the lads might. I'm seeing him next week about some work in the New Year, says he's drowning in conversions and one of his joiners has left. Don't know if I can fit it in. If I don't get these orders done.'

'Will it cost much to fix?'

'Nah. Good man could do it with a ladder. Cost of the timber if the wood needs replacing, labour. Barry'll give us a fair price.'

I looked at Tom running ahead. He was a lovely child.

My dealings with him seemed more straightforward than those with Maddie. I didn't know whether that was because I wasn't his mother or because he was a boy or because of his personality. He was so good natured. Would he stay that way? Would adolescence turn him into a sulky young man or a truculent one?

'What were you like as a teenager?' I asked Ray.

'Gorgeous.'

'Sod off.' Ray is incorrigibly vain. 'Seriously.'

He shrugged. 'Dunno.'

'Well, did you cause your mother grief or not?'

'Not much. I went through a druggy patch,' he looked ahead, made sure the children couldn't hear. 'Magic mushrooms, grass, cough medicine.'

'Cough medicine – yeuch.'

'It was. And booze of course. The trick was to get in and say goodnight in the gap between getting hammered and either being sick or passing out.'

'Were you happy?'

He tutted.

'Depressed?'

He shrugged again. His shrugs can be quite eloquent, especially when read with his facial expression. This was a stop-talking-about-it-I-don't-like-it sort of a shrug.

'Confused?'

'Probably. Why?'

'Oh, something I'm working on. I can remember feeling desolate as a teenager, and misunderstood. Craving everything but it was all just out of reach. I wanted to be somewhere else, doing something else. And wanting to escape. Awful time. The world was a mess, people were cruel or stupid, life wasn't fair. Grinding dissatisfaction. But I don't know what boys think about.'

'Sex,' he said.

I looked at him.

'Yeah, there was that.'

89

'And fitting in . . . having mates, spots. But mainly sex.'

I raised my eyebrows.

I thought of Adam Reeve, sitting on the bench. No mates, plenty of spots. Was he brooding about sex? I wasn't convinced.

CHAPTER TWENTY-THREE

Hattie Baker had known Miriam for years.
'We met back in 1987,' she said. 'In hospital.'

'You worked at Saint Mary's too?'

'No, no. We were patients. Mental patients.' She said it gently as if she was taking the sting out of it for me, followed it with a small smile.

She was a tiny, birdlike woman, with an enormous beaky nose, warm brown eyes and a scrawny frame. She wore lurid orange lipstick which more or less matched her tousled dyed hair. I guessed that she was in her sixties.

We were in Hattie's lounge, a real fire blazed in the hearth and I suspected that the central heating was on too, as the room was incredibly hot. The decor and furniture was a complete mismatch of styles; a traditional richly patterned carpet, Turkish style, the main colour was burgundy, a black leather three piece suite, an Indian rosewood coffee table, ornately carved, an incongruous computer station in one corner and garish geometric wallpaper in brown, orange and beige. Thankfully most of the latter was covered with a plethora of prints and paintings, mainly landscapes and street scenes.

There was the tang of satsumas in the air, a bowlful sat beside Hattie and the peel from several lay on the occasional table.

'Miriam wasn't there long. She responded well to the shock treatments. But she'd come back and visit me, you see.

And when they finally let me come home, she'd come here. Funny, really. Most of the people you meet in hospital . . . well, it's not a happy time, you don't want reminding. You never see them again. We just clicked. I do miss her.' She gave a sigh, turned the ring on her finger. 'Oh, I do miss her. I could rely on Miriam. She always came, without fail. Didn't mind that it was always here.'

I must have looked puzzled because she leant towards me to explain. 'I don't go out. Agoraphobic. So she always came to me. And the fun we'd have,' she smiled. 'I manage. But there are times, like the funeral,' she winced, 'if only I could have been there. I sent a letter of course. Times like that, it makes me think what a stupid, scared, silly woman I am. But I can't . . .' She stopped talking.

I waited.

'She seemed to be so well. I never imagined . . . You never really know anybody do you?' She turned her gaze on the fire. 'Just the surface. We barely know ourselves. I do miss her. And those lovely children,' she looked at me, 'how are they bearing up?'

'It's hard.'

She nodded.

'When did you last see Miriam?'

'September the thirtieth. My birthday. She brought me that.' She pointed to a watercolour above the fireplace. It was a Manchester scene, St Ann's Square looking towards the church. Springtime. Trees in blossom, shoppers, a fire-eater entertaining the crowd. 'Someone in her art club did it.' I stood to peer at the signature. Dolly B.

'These are my substitutes,' she waved at the pictures, 'for the real world. Of course now with the Internet, I go all over the place, marvellous,' she beamed. Then pulled herself back to my question. 'So, Miriam. She came on the thirtieth but I spoke to her after that. She rang me.' Her eyes watered. 'I'm sorry,' she said. She pulled a tissue from the box beside her. 'I do miss her. It was the day she died.'

I felt a squirt of adrenalin tighten my concentration, speed up my pulse.

'She was in a bad way, panicky, raving. I couldn't do anything. All I could do was listen. I felt so . . . bloody useless,' she said bitterly.

'What time was this?'

'About two o'clock.'

'What did she say?'

'Nothing that made any sense. Something about being put in hospital again, if she told them.'

'Told them what?'

'I don't know. And she said it was awful and he'd punish her.'

'Who would?'

'God. I thought that's what she meant. Miriam spoke about God as if he was a real person, like he was in the same room, really there. She'd often talk about Him and mean God.'

'What else?'

'I tried to calm her down. She just kept on, a lot of it was garbled but she kept saying she couldn't hide from him and she didn't know what to do.'

God? Or the grey-haired man? Could it have been him?

'What did you think she meant when she said she didn't know what to do?'

'About the state she was in, about getting help. I told her to go to the hospital, that they'd make her feel safe but she wouldn't listen. But I was only guessing. It was hard to understand her. And I told her to get a taxi and come here. I'd pay the fare.'

'Do you know where she was ringing from?'

'No. I assumed she was at home. Then she rang off. I tried ringing but there was no answer. I even tried to ring Connie but I couldn't remember which school she taught at. If only she'd have come here, I could have got help and then . . .'

'You never told the family about this call?'

'No. I thought about it. When I wrote with my condolences.

But I couldn't see what good it would do, to hear that she'd been so distressed. They knew that anyway, given what happened. Do you think I should have?'

'I don't know. I'll be telling them now. It tells us quite a lot more about how she was.'

Connie Johnstone had found it impossible to accept that her mother had become so dramatically unstable. Now I had testimony from one of her oldest and closest friends that she was suffering from delusions by the early afternoon and was incoherent. It was the first evidence I'd found of her changing state of mind. The decline had been rapid. By the end of the afternoon she'd reached the point of no return. I wondered what would trigger that sort of episode. Something external or was it just part of Miriam's make-up, the black dog of depression poised to rear up with no good reason to devour her?

'If only she'd come here,' Hattie repeated, the firelight flickering in her tear-filled eyes.

If only.

CHAPTER TWENTY-FOUR

Over the years I've built up a network of contacts, some friends, some acquaintances, who I can ask for help in the course of my work. People who have their own expertise and don't mind giving me a little time.

Moira, our GP is one, and also a friend. I hadn't seen her for some time but that didn't matter. I rang and asked her who she knew that I could talk to about women and mental health; she referred me to Zoe Roberts and gave me a number.

'She's involved with MIND, and various community mental health schemes,' Moira said, 'but she's also done a good few years in hospital so she's a good all-rounder. And she's still publishing research.'

We left it at that.

Zoe Roberts was happy to talk but not available till later in the day. 'Ring me at home,' she suggested.

'Are you sure?'

'Yes, it's fine.'

I rang back as arranged and described to her what I knew of Miriam's mental health history and explained that the family were resistant to the scenario that she'd gone from being apparently well to suicidal in a matter of hours. Could it happen like that?

'Well, it did in this case, didn't it?' Zoe pointed out. 'Medicine is as much an art as it is a science. Changes in mood, response to drugs, social context, cultural mores; they all impinge on our health and they are all impossible to measure in neat scientific units. How we feel is hard to quantify, it's subjective, it has to be. We can point to statistics or patterns or probabilities but there are always exceptions, lots of exceptions. What you've described isn't the most common story but nor is it unheard of. And it is definitely possible. Everything's possible.'

'And can you usually find something to explain why someone becomes suicidal one day when they've not been before?'

She laughed. 'No, no, no. Health is a process. So is disease or lack of health. It's a continuum too. Even when we talk with people who are failed suicides they can't often articulate what precipitated the attempt. I'm sorry, I'm not deliberately being vague but we're talking about complex human conditions and decisions and chance and everything else you can think of.'

I thanked Zoe, appreciating her honesty but disappointed that I had nothing more clear-cut to take back to Connie. Though Hattie's information was a plus. Proof positive of Connie's mounting fears and increasing dislocation.

CHAPTER TWENTY-FIVE

Friday night was self-defence. I'd promised Ray, and myself, that I would learn to look after my precious body after a particularly nasty attack. Are any attacks not nasty? The course was being taught by an instructor who used to work for the police. She had set up in business to answer the growing demands from people such as healthcare workers, teachers and housing officers who were seeing an increase of violent behaviour among the public they were there to help.

I'd been casting about for something that wouldn't involve a lifelong dedication to a martial art, and then Stuart told me about the course. He used to own a nightclub in town and one of the bouncers had raved about Ursula's self-defence classes. It sounded just up my street.

I hated dragging myself out on a cold, dark night to the shabby church hall in Chorlton where we met but I knew it was important. Once I got there, I worked hard, determined to get my money's worth and to emerge at the end better equipped to deal with the aggro that occasionally comes my way. It wasn't all chucking each other around either, the course also looked at diffusing difficult situations, using role play to practise techniques for minimizing the risk of escalation.

We went through the warm-up. The heating was on in the hall and it took the edge off the cold but the place was draughty. It had a highly varnished wooden floor the colour of toffee and thick, navy gloss paint on the tall sash window frames, the skirting board and the wide, rounded old-fashioned radiators. The ceiling was high and grimy, draped with cobwebs, flaking cream paint peeled off the beams. At one end dull green velvet curtains concealed a small stage, beneath this our mats and equipment belonging to other groups was stored. The place reeked of old varnish and trainers and mildew.

'Right,' Ursula announced as we finished the warm-up, 'someone comes at you with a knife . . .'

A fist of fear clenched at my bowels. I hate knives. Although I'd been threatened and even attacked with various weapons it was knives that haunted me. I'd had flashbacks for years after an incident with a knife but the episodes had become less and less frequent. Still, I didn't like to contemplate knives but I ignored the queasy churning in my stomach and paid fulsome attention as Ursula took us through several scenarios and moves to disarm or escape from an attacker.

I was partnered with Brian, a big lad who was working security for the Co-op. We went through the moves, taking turns to defend ourselves. Brian was much stronger which made the exercises reassuringly realistic for me. It always took him a while to relax into the session, I think he felt awkward lunging at a woman. Quite often Ursula told him to stop pussyfooting around. Now and again she took him on herself, tipping him to the floor or rendering him helpless with speed and grace.

I came away from the session feeling grimy but gratified; there were no showers at the church hall. Driving back, I considered the fact that Stuart hadn't returned my call. I felt the first flickering of dissatisfaction. We were still weighing each other up, surely he realized that I might read all sorts into his failure to get back to me quickly. Or was it intentional? Should I assume his interest was waning? What if he hadn't got the message?

I resented the way that even the simple business of arranging to meet was taking up my energy and awakening anxieties that I'd rather stayed dormant. I would not sit around waiting for him to call – sod that for a game of soldiers.

I rang as soon as I got in. The answerphone was on at his house so I rang the bar. He was there, a wall of sound in the background.

'Sal, hi. I've been meaning to ring you.'

So, why didn't you?

'I've got the kids all weekend, I'm here Monday but how about Tuesday?'

'Evening or lunchtime?' I quipped.

There was an awkward pause. I felt my skin crawl. What? Only he could suggest lunch, not me?

'Erm, I don't think I could do lunch. Jonny's wife's being induced on Monday and he'll be off for the week at least, new staff in.'

'Tuesday night then.'

'What do you fancy?'

Daft question, or it had been till I started feeling wrong-footed. 'I'll come to yours, bring a bottle.'

'Just bring yourself. I'll get the wine.' He could get nice stuff from work.

'Half eight?'

'Fine, see you then.'

My hand was aching from gripping the receiver and a blush had made my cheeks burn. We'd arranged a date, mission accomplished, so why did I feel so awkward? I was a grown-up now. I could do without the roller-coaster emotions of teenage dating, without all the mind games and the lurches into self-doubt.

I ran myself a bath. I'd see how Tuesday went. But if seeing Stuart was going to mean spending half my life worrying about it, getting cranky because he hadn't rung me, then I wondered whether it was really worth it. He was a nice man and the sex was great, really great, but I was not hopelessly in love with him. Not in love at all. I liked him; he was attractive, friendly. I liked the attention, I liked the idea of a relationship but I wasn't so sure about the reality. I wasn't in too far. Still able to feel the ground beneath my feet and wade out of it if I chose. I sighed, stepped into the bath and slid under the water. Let my worries float away.

CHAPTER TWENTY-SIX

I generally avoid working weekends so I can be around with Maddie, but it was easier to snatch an hour on Saturday to call in on the Johnstones and let them know how things were going than it was to arrange something later in the week and use up part of an evening.

The traffic was ridiculous going up Wilmslow Road; everybody off Christmas shopping. I would come back down Kingsway, it might not be so bad. It was the first time I'd been to the house in daylight. It was a cold, foggy day and the air was soaked with exhaust fumes. No Roland, but Martina was there with Connie and Patrick. I accepted a coffee and the four of us sat around the dining table. The curtains were drawn and I realized they had a patio door out into a small yard with blue painted walls and evergreen climbers and bushes in tubs. I pulled out my notes and began a resumé of who I had spoken to and what I had found out.

'I've not been able to identify the man who called on your mother and I'd suggest leaving that aside for now. As far as I can tell she was out, he then called at the corner shop but no one saw him at the Whitworth centre and he presumably gave up and went home.'

'But you can't be sure about that?' Connie checked.

'No.'

She looked disgruntled. I could tell she wanted everything to be cut and dried. 'Now, I also talked to Hattie Jacobs, an old friend of Miriam's who lives in Salford.'

Connie nodded.

'And I think what she told me is quite significant. She spoke to Miriam that afternoon.'

Connie drew breath in sharply. I saw Martina's hands tighten on the table and Patrick leant forward in his chair. 'It was about two o'clock. Hattie says that your mother was very distressed.'

Connie blinked and swallowed, her face screwed up as though she'd had a sour drink. Martina glanced away and out of the window.

'Hattie described her as panicking. Your mother was frightened. Kept saying that they'd put her back in hospital. Something awful had happened and she would be punished,' I cast a glance at Martina, was this too much? Patrick caught my meaning, gave a tiny nod. 'That He would punish her.'

'Oh,' Connie made a small sound in her throat and moved one hand to her forehead.

'It's not clear who she was talking about but Hattie thought she might have been referring to God.'

Patrick nodded, a sober expression on his face.

'We don't know where Miriam was when she made the call. But it does tell us that by that point in the day Miriam was already unwell.'

Connie maintained her position, expression obscured by the arm and hand covering her face. Martina looked my way, being brave. Patrick sighed.

'I know one of the things you found hard to understand was the fact that your mother had seemed so well when you last saw her. So I spoke to someone who specializes in women and mental health and asked her about it. She said it's not unheard of, such a rapid switch . . .'

'Something must have happened,' Connie said thickly. 'Surely something . . .'

'Not necessarily.'

'I don't believe it,' Connie moved her hand, swung her eyes up to the ceiling. 'I don't believe it,' she repeated slowly for emphasis. She looked across to me and sighed with exasperation, her eyes laced with pain.

'You don't believe Hattie?' I said.

'Yes, no. I don't know.'

'She'd have no reason to invent something like that.'

'Why didn't she tell us about it?' Connie demanded. 'Or the coroner, or someone?'

'No one ever asked her; she was never contacted by the police or anyone else. And she decided not to tell you about the phone call because she wanted to spare your feelings. At the time she couldn't see how it would help.'

'Salt in the wounds,' Patrick accepted. 'She wrote a lovely letter.'

I realized it wasn't what Connie had wanted to hear. In spite of all I'd said she was still nursing some hope that the coroner's verdict had been wrong; that something other than mental disintegration and suicide had caused Miriam's death.

'It wasn't what you expected,' I said, 'but it fits with all the facts.'

Connie looked gutted, face pinched, harrowed frown, mouth shrunken with misery, an ashy colour to her complexion.

I looked at Martina. She kept quiet; it was hard to know whether she shared her sister's sentiments or not. I didn't want to put her on the spot by asking her. Instead I sounded out Patrick. 'What do you think?'

He ran a hand over the stubble on his head. 'It's a surprise. Still taking it in. But like you say it fits . . .'

'Something happened,' Connie insisted. 'She didn't just leave her craft session and fall to pieces . . . something . . .'

Whatever she was going to say was lost when Roland barged into the room. I assumed he'd just got up. He wore an outsize t-shirt and jog pants, high top trainers. He took in the tableau, jerked his head and swore softly. 'Shit.'

'Roland!' Connie snapped at him.

He turned to leave.

'Roland, wait,' she said.

'Why?' Anger flashed in his eyes. 'What is the point?'

Connie flinched at the ferocity of his question.

'We found out more . . .'

'So?' He yelled. 'She's gone. Why can't you just leave it?' The words fell like blows, slow and heavy.

'Roland,' Patrick reasoned.

'It won't bring her back,' he shouted. 'Nothing . . .' his face crumpled. 'Fuck.' He slammed his fist into the door. Martina jumped at the violence.

I held my breath, watched his back heave, the muscles in his jaw pulsing.

Patrick put his hand on Connie's arm. She threw it off.

'I know that,' she said hotly, 'I know that nothing will bring her back. All I want is to understand what happened.'

Roland continued to face the door, fists clenched.

'Sal's told us things we didn't know, Ma rang a friend, we never knew that, and a man had been round to the house, asking for her and the police never even checked the . . .'

Roland flung the door open and ran out.

'Roland!' Connie shouted.

The slam of the front door answered.

There was a pause, a beat or two. I took a couple of slow breaths. My heart was galloping.

'Sal, I'm so sorry,' Connie began to apologize.

I waved it away. 'Don't worry. It might not be such a bad thing – getting angry.'

'He doesn't want all this,' Martina said, sniffing. I wondered whether she did. She had been as adamant for my involvement as Connie when we had first met. Now where did she stand? Was she desperate for any information or just supporting her sister? And if Roland was finding it so difficult, would she want to protect him? Was it really just Connie's quest? Were the others willing or reluctant travellers?

'We need to talk,' Patrick said to Connie and then looked

104

at me. The implication was clear. Should I continue? Should they back off for Roland's sake?

I left them to think it over.

Roland's outburst had made me feel shaky. Was Connie unreasonable? Should she have consulted them all more before coming to see me? But they'd all been there, hadn't they? Cramped in my office. And Martina had accused me of being like all the rest when I'd hesitated. I had assumed the whole family wanted the investigation. Wrong? Or had Roland only discovered later that probing into his mother's story would be so disturbing? I felt uneasy and knew that until I heard from the Johnstones I'd be worrying away at it like picking at a scab. I disliked the thought that my actions had added to Roland's misery. I tried to convince myself that in the long run his explosion would be a good thing – that he'd let out some of the feelings that he had been holding on to so tightly. But doubts chewed away at that logic. Had I let flattery at being sought out or vague liberal intentions get in the way of my professionalism? I usually have one client, in this case Connie who had signed the contract; should I have established more formally the rest of the family's attitude to hiring me?

And if they asked me to do any more? What would I say then? On what basis would I agree? Was it ethical to make any changes to the agreement we had?

I wiped the condensation from the windscreen and started the engine. The Johnstones weren't the only ones who had some thinking to do that weekend.

CHAPTER TWENTY-SEVEN

We were queuing up for Santa's Grotto. Santa was very obviously the caretaker in costume. Bernard was a stick-thin man with eyelashes to die for, bottle glasses and a thick Scouse accent.

'Aright den little fella,' he plumped Tom onto his bony knees. 'Whorrayawan' fer Christmas?'

Tom reeled off the first part of his list.

'Yer jokin' aren't yer?' exclaimed Bernard. ' 'Ow am I gonna get tha' lot in my sledge, eh? Think again, pal. I'll bring you a ball, how 'bout that, eh? A red, rubber ball?'

Tom squirmed and protested.

'Ey, go on then, lah. Have a lucky dip.'

Tom slid down and rummaged in the sack. Brought out a parcel.

'Next,' yelled Bernard.

Maddie had already been. We collected Tom who had ripped the paper off to find a stamp pad and animal stamps.

'They're all the same,' Maddie complained. 'You either get them or gel pens.'

We had nearly exhausted the delights of the upstairs school hall.

We made our way through the crush and down the stairs. There was a Tombola, a White Elephant stall, a place to make Christmas decorations out of pasta bows; lots of glue and glitter. I bought some handmade cards at the next stall. Maddie wanted her hair doing. If we queued long enough and paid 50p she could have brightly coloured cotton wound round some strands of hair. 'Last thing, then,' I told her.

Tom went into the playground with Jade from over our road. People had set up play equipment and a large trampoline out there. The rain had held off and it worked well to occupy the kids who were less than interested in the stalls.

The woman in the queue ahead of me turned round to survey the scene and we recognized each other.

'It's Sharon,' I said. The woman from the Whitworth Centre. 'Sal.'

'Hello.'

'I've not seen you at school before.'

'My niece,' she said, ducking her head towards the child beside her. 'Our Julie works Saturdays so I said I'd bring Chantelle.'

'Maddie,' I gestured. 'What year's Chantelle?'

'Year one.'

'Maddie's year two,' I said.

'It's our Fair at the centre next Saturday so I'll have to bring her to that as well. She likes it up there. She goes to all our dos, don't you Chantelle?' The child nodded.

'It's great for me,' Sharon confided. 'Working there. I'm only a few minutes away. When we were setting up the centre we all wanted jobs to go to local people. I was on the committee back then, something to do really.' She wrinkled her nose. 'I made a mess of school and I was out of work. I got one of these New Deals. Had to go through all the proper procedures and that but it's great. If we get the extra funding we want there should be another two part-time posts so it's creating local jobs and all.'

'Eddie's not local, is he?'

'No, he was in Hull before, place called Horizons, same sort of project. He's from Bath originally. But that post, there wasn't really anyone local with the right experience. And it's not brilliant money, not compared to similar jobs in other places. We did have a couple of applicants from Manchester but no one in Rusholme, and Eddie was head and shoulders above them. You should have seen his references from Hull. Sit down now Chantelle, that's it.' She bent to discuss what colours her niece wanted, then straightened up.

'You're working for Miriam Johnstone's family?' she asked me. I nodded, ready to deflect her curiosity by pointing out it was confidential.

'Such a shame,' she said.

I guided Maddie round near to the other chair where a tiny child, probably three years old, was protesting loudly at having to sit still and clearly wanted out. Her mother relented and moved her away. Maddie sat down. 'Silver, pink and purple,' she said.

'Did you see Miriam leaving that day?' I asked Sharon.

'No. It was chaos. Eddie had the people from the grants unit at the City Council coming. One of the Craft Club had burnt her fingers and you'd have thought she'd lost an arm all the palaver, there was. And Melody . . .' She stopped abruptly. 'You won't have met Melody, will you?'

'Yes, at the church sewing circle.' Shaking, fine-featured, her hair like a close-fitting cap.

'Did you hear about her?'

I shook my head.

'Suicide attempt. It was in the paper last night. Cut her wrists. She's all right, but . . .' Sharon tutted.

'Oh, God,' I murmured.

'It's not the first time,' said Sharon. 'But still.'

'How come it was in the paper?' Overdoses weren't routinely reported. Only if they were successful and had an angle to them; a particularly young person, a double suicide, that sort of thing.

'Fire brigade had to break in. She'd locked herself in the house. Her mother knew straight away. Good job and all. Can you imagine . . .' She shook her head sadly. 'Anyway, about Miriam. I saw her leave but not where she went. And she can't have been gone long when this chap comes in looking for her.'

I felt my heart squeeze. 'Who?'

'Middle-aged, grey hair. I told him if he hurried he might catch her. He can't have done, can he. More's the pity,' she shrugged.

A cold chill slithered the length of my spine.

Sharon bent to Chantelle. 'That is drop dead gorgeous.'

CHAPTER TWENTY-EIGHT

Sharon had no name for the mystery man. She confirmed he was clean shaven and she thought he had glasses but couldn't swear to it. He wasn't especially memorable, I could rule out Mr Beatty with his white hair and I thought she would have remembered Trudeau Collins with his mannered style. Albert Fanu, he had worn glasses, as had Nicholas Bell. One courteous to a fault, the other rude. Was it one of them? Or neither?

And did it matter?

Had that man caught up with Miriam? Had he upset her? Done something to trigger her breakdown? Or had he witnessed any of it, perplexed perhaps at her increasing paranoia or her withdrawal?

If I could get hold of photographs perhaps Sharon would be able to identify the man she'd seen. Reverend Day had referred to the ten o'clock service. The church was in Whalley Range. I could take the kids to Chorlton Water Park; Digger too. Call at the church for a few minutes en route. It might be a bit of a wild goose chase and I might be no longer working for the Johnstones but it was worth half an hour of my time if it led to identifying the grey-haired man. If I found that Albert Fanu or Nicholas Bell was lying I'd be very keen to talk to them again.

Sunday morning my lie-in stretched till 8.45. I had to get the children ready and get to the church in time to surreptitiously shoot pictures of the gathering congregation.

Maddie and Tom had eaten breakfast; on the kitchen table pools of milk and stray Cheerios bore witness. I sent them to get dressed while I made myself some porridge. My cold morning ritual. Once the temperature goes below freezing, out come the oats. I cook them with salt and water, Scottish style, and pour on golden syrup and cold milk. Heaven.

I dug out wellies and hats and gloves and found Digger's lead. Digger went demented, racing to the door and back and making an irritable whine like a faulty buzz saw. I parcelled children and dog in the car, scraped the ice off the windows and turned the heaters on. I needed my woolly gloves to drive – the steering wheel could have generated frostbite. It was a glorious morning. The sun hung low in the sky spreading molten silver rivers the length of the roads. Chorlton is west from Withington so I didn't have to drive blinded by the glare.

I told the kids I had to take a picture of the street for Diane so she could draw it. I don't like to give too much away about my work; it involves too many convoluted explanations for an endless sequence of 'whys', and often the cases I work on are sordid. They rarely reveal the best in human nature. It's not a view I want to share with the children.

Churchgoers began arriving in dribs and drabs, dressed in all their finery. I was parked some way down the cul-de-sac and facing the main road so everyone had to come past me. A digital camera was part of my recent upgrade. It was pretty foolproof and had a very good zoom. I could check immediately if the shot was usable.

It went like a dream. Mr Nicholas Bell and his wife drew up in a taxi which stopped nearby. I caught him getting out of the cab, his face clearly visible. To cover my tracks I immediately swung the camera round and snapped the kids in the back seat. No one even glanced my way.

A couple of minutes later I saw Mr Fanu turn in from the junction walking with a group of people, including his wife. I used the zoom and the job was done.

'Fasten your seat belts,' I told the kids. 'Time to go.'

* * *

A large flock of Canada Geese patrolled the landing stage at the nearest corner of the lake. Anyone with a bag of crisps or a satsuma was fair game. Maddie hung back as the geese waddled our way. Digger copied her, his tail lowered with apprehension.

'They're only after food,' I reassured her. 'Once they see we haven't got any they'll leave us alone.'

'I've got a biscuit,' Tom announced. And proudly retrieved a doughy mess from his pocket. The geese moved in with alacrity, practically obscuring him.

'Drop it,' I told him. 'Now.' I grabbed his hand and pulled him through the gang and up the grassy bank. We set off walking along the sandy path that circled the water park.

Several of the little jetties were occupied by anglers. They'd as much gear with them as Maddie and I take for a week's camping. Bell tents and umbrellas, flasks and iceboxes, chairs and blankets plus all the poles and maggots and stuff.

Out by one of the islands Tom spotted a swan and I pointed out the moorhens, with their red legs and beaks, nipping around the shallows.

'I'm freezing,' Maddie moaned.

'Walk faster then.'

'I'm tired.'

'Early night.'

'Just tired of walking.' I estimated that we were a sixth of the way round.

'I wish it was hot,' she said, 'then we could paddle.'

'Not here, it's not safe.'

'Why?'

'Sinking sand,' Tom pronounced.

'Yes, and stones, and old fish hooks and rubbish.'

'I'm a dragon,' Tom breathed clouds into the air.

I found a stick and we threw it for Digger. He's not exactly a retriever. He kept losing the stick and we had to search for a replacement.

The children ran ahead to ambush me. I walked along savouring the fresh air. The bare trees with their branches of brown and cream and grey made patterns against a pure blue sky smudged with wisps of golden cloud. Like a Christmas card scene minus snow. I ought to write my cards. Perhaps I could make a start after tea. I heard a giggle and saw Maddie's elbow protruding from the tree ahead. I prepared to be startled.

Near the end of the circuit we stopped at the small wooden playground. Tom leapt and swung over everything and made friends with another little boy. Maddie stuck to the swings. I called them away after a while. I had to get Tom back in time to go to Nana 'Tello's for Sunday lunch. It's a sporadic event which seems like a good way to do it to me. More of a treat than an obligation. It was her chance to stuff son and grandson to the gills.

'Men's food,' Ray said once.

'Meat?'

'You bet, piled high.'

She seemed to worry that my not eating meat and not cooking it for others meant we all lived on grass and that without her intervention severe malnutrition would result. I'd stopped trying to reason with her. I was even woman enough not to rub it in when the BSE scandal was in full spate.

'Chicken feed,' she'd say, when she looked at my plate. Did she know what they actually fed chickens these days?

CHAPTER TWENTY-NINE

Monday I went to York.
With Adam Reeve.

We took the bus to town again and there was an interlude of about an hour spent wandering round Lewis's and Debenhams and the top of Market Street. Susan Reeve rang; the college had called to check whether Adam had cause to be absent. I told her I was in town following her son and would keep her informed.

Adam set off for the coach station. He didn't go in the information office this time but to one of the stops. I watched from the news-stand. I bought a copy of the *Guardian* to hide behind. After a few minutes the coach came swinging round and drew up and disgorged its passengers. Adam got on followed by other travellers. When they were all on I went across and climbed up the steps. Asked for a return to York, which was the final destination. I was fairly sure he'd not recognized me but I had a different coat on due to the colder weather and a woolly hat in my bag that might come in handy to alter my appearance if I felt a little exposed.

I sat several seats in front of Adam and never looked back.

It was a three hour journey. The coach headed up the Oldham Road through the centre of the East Manchester redevelopment; a major site for the Commonwealth Games. We took the M62 towards Leeds. As we climbed away from the cities and up into the Pennines the view was spectacular; moors and hills rippled buff against a rich blue sky with a burnished sun. I could see for miles. Those parts of the ground where the sun hadn't reached were still dusted white. I enjoyed the landscape for a while but eventually I wanted distracting and turned to the book I'd brought with me.

We had to change in Leeds. A forty-five minute wait. I found a cafe a few minutes from the station, got a cup of tea which looked like washing-up liquid and tasted similar, and huddled in a corner with my book.

When it was time to go I got on the coach and sat near the front again. Adam was already on further back. I looked out as we swung through the streets. Leeds wasn't a city I knew well, though work has taken me there now and again. It has a similar Victorian feel to Manchester with some resplendent city centre buildings and arcades. The same sort of terraced streets that had sprung up to house the mill-workers and factory-hands spread outwards from the centre, but here they were mainly stone built instead of brick. And Leeds is hilly, unlike Manchester which sits on a plain surrounded by hills.

As we drove north the land became flatter. The vale of York. The buildings fell away to be replaced by grazing land, dotted with sheep and cows and enclosed by ancient drystone walls.

Fields grew winter crops or were shorn, bare stubble glistening with frost. The coach drove on, low easy-listening music faint on the tannoy. We passed a farmhouse with a huge tree in the yard strung with outdoor lights. Further along two barns were being converted, bright new sandstone walls and solar panels.

Where were we headed? Was Adam meeting someone? Perhaps there was a simple, utterly banal reason for our journey. A job interview, research for a college assignment. York was full of museums wasn't it? Dripping with history. As we got closer to the town there was much evidence of the dominant role of tourism here. Coach routes and stops were sign-posted, as well as scenic tours and heritage trails. Every other house had a B&B sign up. Presumably some people came up here in the winter. When the coach came to a halt I got off before Adam and walked across and into a phone box where I would still be able to see him alight.

He hesitated on the edge of the pavement as if he might change his mind and get back on. He certainly didn't look excited or happy to have arrived. Whatever awaited him here it was not something he was looking forward to.

He went into the Gents and then over to an inspector who was leaning against the information booth. Adam spoke and the inspector nodded and gestured across the bus station. A man came and waited outside the phone box.

I replaced the receiver and came out.

Adam went and sat on a seat at one of the bus stops. I consulted the schedule hanging on the wall and worked out that the buses there went to Ripon and the next would be in twenty minutes.

Adam had settled to wait. I took the chance to go to the Ladies and then got myself a tea and a cheese salad sandwich at the station shop. The tea tasted of melting plastic. I'd have been better with a cold drink but at least it served to warm my fingers up.

As we got further away from York and into unchartered territory it was more likely that Adam would recognize that I was the same woman who had got on the bus at home. Okay, at this particular point he didn't seem to know me from a hole in the ground but I must be pushing it. I had to stick with him but not stick out. I hovered in the shop as long as I felt comfortable and then went to the Ladies again. Wherever we were going it was not likely I'd be home to collect the children. I rang the Dobsons and spoke to Vicky. Yes, she'd take them home and stay until either Ray or I got back.

I also rang and told Adam's mother that I was still following him and that I would ring her later. I told her to try not to worry.

I put on my woolly hat. Mistress of disguise. I had some

116

sunglasses in my bag but they only made me look deranged with the hat in the middle of winter.

As it was, I was saved by a trio of middle-aged women laden with shopping bags waiting for the Ripon bus who engaged me in conversation. I chattered on with them about shopping and Christmas – or at least I asked all the open-ended questions and kept them going.

Their favourite topic was their individual shopping passions and foibles.

'Shoes get me.'

'She's twenty-eight pairs.'

'Imelda Marcos.'

'Twenty-nine. Not counting slippers.'

'I can never make my mind up. I come home empty-handed.'

'You need a personal shopper.'

'I can buy for anyone else, not myself.'

'That'd be a good job, personal shopper.'

'Ooh, no. I'd rather do it than watch others doing it.'

'She talking about shopping?'

'Hazel!'

To an outsider like Adam I hope I'd be one of the gang.

The bus was crowded which suited me. I bought a ticket all the way as I'd no idea of our destination.

I sat with my new friends who continued to tease each other as talk moved from shopping to fashions and nostalgia for the bygone styles. I nodded and smiled a lot.

We hadn't gone far and were still in the suburbs of York when the driver called out something unintelligible which drew Adam to his feet. I said loud goodbyes to my companions trying to make it sound like a weekly ritual. If Adam was going to clock me I reckoned it was going to be now.

I let him get off first then followed and immediately crossed the road looking purposeful. He was studying a piece of paper. We were on a suburban housing estate. Brick built semi-detached houses with small front gardens. A passing cat solicited my attention and gave me an excuse to loiter.

I bent to pet the cat, watching Adam out of the corner of my eye. He put the paper away and crossed the road. He was coming my way. The cat squirmed beneath my hand, purring and craning its neck. I waited for him to pass.

' 'Scuse me.'

Shit! My heart skittered around. I stood and braced myself.

'Can you tell me where Blandford Drive is?'

I pretended to consider. 'Sorry, no,' I smiled.

He nodded and walked off towards the bend in the road. I closed my eyes to steady myself. Swallowed hard. When he was out of sight and the prickling had gone from my arms I set off in pursuit. Mingled with the tension I felt a frisson of excitement. The same thrill I got from playing Cowboys and Indians and Cops and Robbers as a child. Though this wasn't a game and if Adam Reeve rumbled me it wouldn't be a case of 'now you're on'.

Blandford Drive was off to the left round the bend. It was a long gradual hill, lined with houses, and halfway down on the left was a parade of shops. Adam passed these, crossed the side road to the first house below the shops and stopped. He went up the path and rang the doorbell or knocked; I was too far away to see exactly. He waited. Meanwhile I made my way to the shops hoping for somewhere to lurk. There was a butcher's, a hardware shop, a baker's, a newsagents, a launderette and a Save the Children shop selling secondhand clothes. I went in the charity shop, said hello to the women at the counter, then looked at the items near the window so I could see the street. Adam had left the house and crossed the road. He walked up the hill until he reached a bus shelter where he sat down. It was a different route from the one we'd come on. Was he planning to catch another bus or was it simply somewhere to shelter? Almost immediately my question was answered as a bus climbed the hill, slowed but didn't stop and went past the stop. I could see Adam still there.

Adam had come all this way, yet there appeared to be no one in at the address he wanted. It looked like he was

118

sitting it out. I'd have to do the same. The old clothes shop was a heaven-sent opportunity to alter my appearance and also provided me with the means for hiding in the warmth while keeping Adam in sight. I found a long, camel-coloured raincoat and a dark wool hat with a brim which was suitably different to what I'd arrived in. I also bought two old candlewick bedspreads in the sale for a song. I put these and my own jacket and hat in a dustbin liner. 'Too big for the carriers,' the women agreed.

From outside the newsagents it was possible to read the number on the house. Twenty-one. Then I went next door to the launderette to do my washing. I got some soap from the dispenser, stuck the bedspreads in the machine, put in the money and found a seat near the window where I could alternate reading the paper with watching Adam. Regulars came in and swapped gossip with the woman who ran the launderette but they left me to my own devices.

It soon began to get dark and I transferred my load to the dryers. Parents and children were wandering back from school, the newsagents next door busy with people calling in for sweets and the evening paper.

I saw Adam stand up and walk down the hill. I left my seat and went outside in time to see a woman with two children, one about Tom's age and the other, a girl, about seven or eight, walk up the path and let them all into the house.

Adam didn't go over and knock again – he just stood there for a few moments. Then he went back to sit by the bus stop. Was it someone else he was waiting for? A girlfriend, still on her way home from high school? He must be freezing, and hungry. I was starving. I bought a Snickers bar and a can of lemonade in the newsagents and went back to the launderette. I really wanted something hot and wholesome like a creamy cheese and tomato lasagne or a bowl of thick soup and a hot roll but there was no chance of that.

Curtains were drawn and the lights went on in houses up and down the street, Christmas lights twinkled or flashed in windows. It was maybe another half an hour, and my candlewicks were virtually dry when I saw Adam move again; he stood up but stayed inside the shelter. I stepped outside, waited next to the newsagent's window where all the little cards bearing adverts were and we both watched a silver Mondeo with a buckled rear bumper enter the driveway of number twenty-one. A man got out, locked the car, and went in.

Adam went slowly down the hill and stopped opposite the house. He didn't approach it. What was this, some sort of vigil? Was he stalking these people or what? The orange street lights distorted his face, cast him in a sickly glow. My stomach flipped when I realized he was crying, his face was blurred, features screwed up, his head bobbing up and down as his shoulders rose and fell.

I moved away into the launderette and collected the bedspreads. Adam walked slowly up the road, past the bus shelter. I was ninety-nine percent certain he was headed for home but I would make sure. What I wasn't about to do was wait for any more buses or risk my cover. I used my phone to ring and check times for the trains to Manchester; if nothing was delayed I'd catch it and save myself an hour. Then I called a cab. I put the bag of bedspreads back on the step of the charity shop – which had already closed – along with the mac and hat. When the taxi arrived, I asked for the coach station. I found a corner to wait until I saw Adam arrive and wait by the Manchester stand. My hunch confirmed, I walked to the train station.

The picture of Adam standing in the sodium dark, staring across at the house, stayed with me. His face bleary and wrinkled and wet. Lost boy. Crying his heart out.

CHAPTER THIRTY

You cannot imagine how delighted I was when the train arrived on time to take me to Piccadilly. If only there'd been a buffet too. I was weak with hunger. How did Adam go without food so long? I thought teenagers were constantly grazing, needing vast amounts of food to fuel their rapidly growing bodies. Was he too lovesick to eat? Too disturbed? I rang Susan Reeve en route.

'I'm on the train,' I said and cringed at the cliché, though I had the carriage to myself so no one could hear me. 'I'm on the way back from York, Adam is getting the Manchester coach. He'll probably be another three hours at least.'

'What's he been up to?'

'I'm not sure, to be honest.' I described our afternoon without going into too much detail. I'd rather tell her in person, particularly about Adam becoming upset.

'It was just an ordinary house?'

'Yes.'

Adam's adopted. The thought dropped into my mind like a brick. It fit the scenario. Tracking down a name, an address. Turning up secretly. Unable to go ahead and make himself known. Absurd? Possible? Wouldn't Susan Reeve have told me though? Unless it was a big secret. I couldn't raise it on the phone.

'Can I call round in the morning and tell you all about it then?'

'Yes. I'll ask him where he's been,' she said, 'when he comes in. See what he has to say for himself.'

'Don't give anything away,' I warned her.

'Oh, no. I won't.'

'He'll be exhausted, too,' I said, wanting to protect the tearful boy from any more strain that day.

'I don't know what's going on; it doesn't make sense. I'm so glad you've been there, though. I'd have been out of my mind by now but just knowing you were keeping an eye on him . . .' Her voice trembled with the dread images of all that could have been.

A mug of strong tea and a fried egg sandwich, followed by a tin of rice pudding with cranberry jelly allayed my hunger. I browsed through the evening paper as I slurped. There was a heart-rending lead story about the little girl who needed a kidney for Christmas and a plea for more people to join the donor scheme. I flicked through and studied the page with ideas for last-minute presents but none of it would do for Ray. He wanted a CD. I wouldn't even have to go into town; there was a shop the other side of the park, on Fog Lane, that sold recent releases and did a roaring trade in second-hand music too. But what CD would he like? I should ask Laura maybe, he might have dropped her a hint. I turned the pages back to a report on the ill health of the city. We were already top for coronary illness and lung cancer, infant death rates and dental decay. The latest study showed a similarly gloomy picture for mental health. Suicide rates and depression levels rising. One forthright GP said the biggest challenge and the only effective one to improve health was to tackle poverty. A voice in the wilderness. Poverty wasn't sexy. The poor don't vote. Another health worker blamed the breakdown of traditional communities and of marriage, the isolation of families. A third of those interviewed were depressed. It was a shocking figure.

I thought of Adam, bullied at school and now deeply unhappy. Why? Who or what was he looking for in York? Had he ever been happy and settled? His mother clearly loved him, and she was warm, likeable. What was going wrong for Adam?

And Roland. The loss of his mother was bound to disturb him. He'd be dealing with it for the rest of his life. Would he heal? Would he reach the point where life felt worthwhile? Where he could trust and love again?

They both had people who cared and neither of them were living in the harsh material conditions that crushed so many childhoods. Would that be enough?

Prompted by thoughts of Roland I stirred myself to use the phone and check my messages.

Connie Johnstone had rung and left a message.

'I've talked it over with Martina and Patrick. We'd still like you to carry on, and Roland knows that but I've told him there's no pressure on him to be involved at all. When we meet again we'll come to you or we'll sort out a time when Roland isn't around. That's it for now. If there's any problem you can ring me. Thank you. Goodbye.'

On the whole I was pleased. Glad that I could pursue the leads I had; show the photos to Sharon and maybe make some progress on that front, and I was relieved that the decision to carry on had been discussed among them and that Roland's opposition was acknowledged and out in the open. But I was a little worried about his removal from the process. Wasn't it a bit too pat to think his absence equalled acceptance – 'what you don't know can't hurt you' sort of thing? And there was still the niggling feeling that Roland's attitude might conceal more than his grief. A notion that I couldn't shake.

Laura was visiting Ray. He'd got Moby on in his room; he only ever puts music on when she's visiting. As I went upstairs to look in on the children, I could smell her perfume. I found it overpowering but said nothing. I couldn't think of a way to mention it that wouldn't be hurtful.

The children were both asleep as I'd expected. Tom was hidden beneath the duvet. I pulled it back a little so his head was uncovered. Sweat had dampened the curls around his temples and they were flattened like feathers against his head. I kissed him.

I went over to Maddie and bent to kiss her. She brushed at me with her hand and turned onto her other side. There was a thick green felt pen on the bed, a pool of dark green ink on the sheet. Washable, supposedly. I'd heard that one before. I moved it onto the bedside table. Had Ray paid Vicky Dobson? I'd have to remember to check with him in the morning.

I wasn't ready to go to bed yet. I needed a bit of quality time. I wanted to see Stuart but he'd be busy at the cafe-bar. Twenty-four hours. I sorted out clothes for the following night, checked that the things I liked didn't need washing. I should talk to him about how we arrange our dates. It would be so much easier if we set a date each time we parted. Then I wouldn't get in a state wondering whether to call or get fed up with him for not calling me. But would that seem too rigid? Were we ready for that? Was he? All I could do was talk to him about it. And about Christmas too. My idea of a night away on our own. See what he thought.

Time to relax. I'd got a *Sopranos* episode on tape still to see. That and a couple of glasses of Shiraz would do very nicely.

CHAPTER THIRTY-ONE

It was warm in bed. It was cold out there. I didn't want to move. Just give me five, ten, fifty more minutes, a couple of hours, the morning.

I didn't want to have to chivvy the kids to get dressed, unearth their book bags, brush teeth. I didn't want to make packed lunches and sort out PE kits, make toast, find Tom's missing glove, pump up the back wheel on my bicycle, set off for school, return to find Maddie's forgotten recorder, set off for school take two, deposit children, coats, scarves and bags in the correct classrooms.

But I did.

I'd brought my bike because it was neither snowing, raining nor sleeting and the distances between my various places of work were in the couple of miles league. Doing my bit for the environment.

First call was Susan Reeve. I asked to put my bike round the back and she went to open the back gate. The garden was a tip. Obviously no one had kept it tidy for ages; dead weeds stood waist-high and an old mattress lay rotting alongside the skeleton of last year's Christmas tree. What a shame, I thought, not just the gardener in me but also the parent. Four kids and a garden going to waste.

I accepted a cup of coffee and then recounted the trek Adam had made.

She listened attentively and shook her head in bewilderment as I finished.

'Why knock at first but not later?'

'I don't know. You've not been able to think of any connection?'

'No.'

'Any estranged relatives?' I said. 'People Adam might have looked up?'

'No.'

'Mrs Reeve, this might sound like a silly question, but is Adam adopted?'

'What?' she said incredulously. 'Adopted? No. Whatever gave you that idea?'

Oh, well. Worth a try. 'It could have been a possible explanation, for his behaviour, if he was tracing family . . .'

'No,' she said. 'Besides, I'd have told you.'

'Like I said – silly question. But I had to check. Some people keep it a secret, even from the children. So, what did your husband say about York?'

'I . . .' She looked uncomfortable, mouth half open but no suitable words. 'He wouldn't know anyone.'

'You didn't ask him?'

She played with her mug, her fingers dancing lightly round the rim. She sighed. 'No.'

'Why not?'

'He doesn't know?'

I frowned. 'What doesn't he know?'

'About you,' she went pink.

'Oh. I just assumed . . .' Too much obviously. 'Why?'

She tucked her chin in, looked down at the mug in her hands. 'The money. Things are very . . . difficult. The building society are talking about repossession. We've only been able to pay the interest for the last six months. Ken's work, most of it's commission, sales have been right down. He's worried sick. I couldn't . . . he'd never have agreed.'

I felt sick. She was up to her ears in debt, they were about to lose their home yet she'd hired me. What was I supposed

126

to do now? I couldn't afford to reduce my fees and I felt cross at being put in this awkward position.

'But Ken won't know about anyone in York, really. I'm the one who keeps in touch with people, does all the Christmas cards, that sort of thing. He's so busy with work. I can't remember the last time he socialized with anyone.'

'In the contract . . .' I began, still weighing up money and time.

'Have you done the two days?' she said with dismay.

'Almost; there's a couple of hours or so left.'

'Only I was thinking last night, if you could find out who lives in that house, it must mean something. If we knew who the people were then I could perhaps get in touch myself. See if they knew Adam. Like you said, some people have to do it themselves. I'd try asking him first. Probably tell him I knew he'd been to York but it would be easier if we had their names.'

'I can do that,' I said. 'And as for the money you can pay me in instalments. I think finding out who lives in the house is the next logical step. Yesterday, just before he left to come home, Adam was very upset. He was crying.'

'Crying?' Her face creased with emotion.

'Yes. We still don't know why Adam is so unhappy. You said before he wouldn't go to the doctor?'

'Our GP isn't the most approachable man I can think of.'

Maybe she should change her GP then.

'Is he eating all right, at home?'

'He's a bit fussy . . . why?'

'He didn't have anything all day yesterday, maybe he didn't have enough money with him, or it could be another problem.'

'Oh, dear. I just wish he'd talk to me,' she said with feeling. 'All I want to do is help.'

'You said Adam had friends before he moved into sixth form?'

'Well, it was Colin really. Colin Fairbrother. Adam's never

127

been one for a big gang or anything but he and Colin spent time at each other's houses, saw each other out of school.'

'And did Colin leave?'

'Oh no. He's in the college too but we've not seen him this term. They seem to have drifted apart.'

'Perhaps you could suggest to Adam that he invites him round. A friend might help.'

She smiled a little sadly. 'Anything I suggest will be ignored. I will try and I'll mention the doctor again but . . .'

'What did he say last night?'

'Said he'd been out and it wasn't that late and to stop treating him like a kid. Then he stormed upstairs. Least he didn't spin me a load of lies.'

'Why, though?' I was puzzled. 'If he's not prepared to tell you what he's up to, where he goes, why he's started acting like this, then he's obviously hiding something. If he really was intent on keeping it from you wouldn't he have rung last night, said he'd be late for tea, made some excuse so you wouldn't grill him when he got in?'

She considered this. 'Go on.'

'Well, it looks to me as though Adam is drawing attention to himself, not diverting it.'

'You think that's it, attention-seeking? A cry for help?'

'Feels like that. You've sensed all along that he needs help – in some shape or form.' I thought of the lad waiting on the hill, shivering in the easterly wind, his face rotten with misery.

'And soon,' she said. 'Before he gets any worse.'

CHAPTER THIRTY-TWO

I cycled from Burnage down Kingsway and up Anson Road towards Rusholme. My eyes watered with the cold air and I had to stop twice to wipe my nose. I arrived at the Whitworth centre unscathed. No car driver had cut me up or forced me off my bike. No near misses, no emergency stops. Impressive.

Sharon was at her desk and greeted me warmly. 'Do you want to see Eddie?'

'No, it was you I was after.'

'What've I done?' she joked.

'The man you saw, the one who was asking after Miriam.'

'Yeah.'

'I've brought a couple of photos. Would you have a look at them, see if either of them is the man you remember?'

'Yeah, all right.'

I handed her the photos of Albert Fanu and Nicholas Bell. She looked at them quickly then shook her head. 'No.'

Any excitement I had felt drained away. 'You sure?'

'Yeah. This one, he's too short, too fat. And this guy looks a lot older. He wasn't bad-looking, for his age, younger than these. When he first came in I thought maybe he was from the council, arrived a bit early. They were due at half twelve and they had to be away for two. We'd got sandwiches in so they could work over lunch. I started telling this chap about the lunch and then he says he's looking for Miriam Johnstone. I should have realized – he wasn't in a suit or anything.'

I took the photos back and put them in the envelope. 'And

he never said why he wanted to see Miriam, where he was from, anything like that?'

'No.'

I must have looked brassed off because Sharon asked, 'Things not working out?'

'You could say that.'

I had anticipated a resounding yes from Sharon and planned to act on that as the next step for the Johnstones. Now the rug had been pulled from under me. There were still friends and contacts of Miriam that I hadn't spoken to but I thought I needed to consider where to start. After all people like her dentist, optician and so on weren't likely to shed much light on the events of that Thursday but it was just about possible she'd rung someone else as well as Hattie.

I cycled back to my office, turned the fire on full, nipped home to fetch some milk and set to work.

I tackled Susan Reeve's request first. Even in this age of the information superhighway, the law states that electoral rolls are only available for the public to see in written form. The rolls for York would be held by the local authority and probably by main libraries. I couldn't ring them and ask for information about who lived at 21, Blandford Avenue. They weren't allowed to tell me. I could go up there and see but the prospect of making that journey was a turn-off. If I only knew someone in York. I racked my brains. Came up empty. Did I know anyone else who might have connections there?

I made a coffee while I mentally crossed off various candidates. As I took the first sip I found inspiration. It's amazing what a hit of caffeine can do.

I punched the numbers on the phone.

'Platt, Henderson and Cockfoot. Can I help?'

'Please can you put me through to Rebecca Henderson?'

'Who's calling?'

'Sal Kilkenny.'

A pause and some soothing strings came on the line. I

guess most people contacting solicitors need soothing not geeing up.

'Sal?'

'Rebecca, hello. How are you?'

'Fine. Fine. Doing lots of work compliments of The Human Rights Act. You?'

'Fine, yes. Busy.'

'And what can I do for you?'

'Am I right you've got another office in York?'

'Wetherby but we do a lot in York and Leeds.'

'Do you have any freelancer investigators up there?'

'Like you, you mean? Is this a tender for work?'

'No, the opposite. I need to check the electoral register up there, I'd like to pay someone else to do it.'

'Got you. Hang on.'

I listened to strings some more.

'I'm going to have to speak to Jeremy in Wetherby, he's got the info. Save you ringing back you could give me the query and I'll forward it. Unless you want to negotiate a different rate?'

'No, standard rate. That sounds good.'

'He won't need any background?'

'No, it's pretty straightforward.'

I gave her the York address and told her I wanted latest registered occupants. I left my mobile but also my email address.

'Excellent,' Rebecca said. 'Probably be a day or two.'

'Great. Thanks a lot.'

It took me an hour to type up a draft report for Susan Reeve detailing with dates and times my trips to Parrs Wood Sixth Form College, The Arndale Centre and York. I saved the file. Once I had the details of the York inhabitants I could complete it and give it to her. I totalled my receipts for expenses and drafted an itemized invoice. My bill would be a knock-back to the household, especially at Christmas. I'd already told Susan Reeve she could pay in instalments; perhaps if I suggested deferring any payments until January it would soften the blow. Would she be able to hide the fact that she was paying me from her husband. How? Using the child benefit money? Getting a loan?

I turned my attention to Miriam Johnstone. Sometimes it helps me to draw out the cases I'm working on like diagrams. Placing the people and the pieces of information here and there, drawing in lines of connection and coincidence, highlighting uncertainty and confusion with large question marks.

I put Miriam in the centre, placed around her the people I had talked to. I began to consider the gist of what I'd learnt, where the queries were.

I ended up with a rash of question marks. I got a fresh sheet of paper and listed these alongside my thoughts and comments. In some cases I was playing devil's advocate. When I'd finished I read it over.

1. Police failure to examine car park pedestrian entrance videos (at pay station). Laziness or something nastier? Minimal enquiries made – no attempt to establish how Miriam got to the scene. No appeal for witnesses etc. Police never knew about phone call or grey-haired visitor.
2. Why a multi-storey car park?
   Miriam couldn't drive. Afraid of heights – vertigo. Would this fear increase or not under stress? Surely former is most likely.
3. How did she get there?
   Bus ticket? No record of . . .
4. Grey-haired man – who?
   Could be irrelevant?
   Why was Nicholas Bell so rude? (get over it Sal!)
5. Where was M. Between 12 & 4?
   This is what I'm being paid for!
   (rang Hattie J. at 2.00)

6. Roland's music/Mrs Boscoe.
   Who is right?
7. If R is lying sheds new light on refusal to talk/attitude to
   Connie's quest
   Why would he lie?

I studied my list. The discrepancy between Mrs Boscoe and
Roland rankled but Martina had backed up, without any
apparent pressure, her brother's story of coming in after
she did. The school would keep attendance records but they
would probably only divulge the information to a parent or
carer. Connie could check but that would mean alerting her
to the vague and unfounded suspicions I had about Roland.

Where to go next?

I decided to ring round the remaining friends to see if
anyone had heard from Miriam on the afternoon of 6 October.

The calls took a long time. Miriam had died a sudden, violent
death. People needed space to react to my opening comments
and some of her friends wanted to share their regrets with me
and even to reminisce about her. Only when we'd been through
that could I focus on the direct questions I had.

There were a couple of people I couldn't reach but of the
others there were no reported phone calls.

'No, she didn't ring. But I saw her.' I gripped the receiver
tightly and leant forward. 'When was this?'

'About one o'clock,' Mrs Green said. 'I was going into
church as she was coming out. I could tell she was troubled,
then. Usually we'd have a bit of a chat but she just passed me
by. She looked like she'd got the whole weight of the world
on her shoulders. It was plain for all to see. Deeply troubled.'

'She was on her own?'

'Yes.'

'Was there anyone else in church?'

'Only Reverend Day. People don't call in as often these
days.'

I felt a rush of indignation. Reverend Day, who had been

so unhelpful when I'd called him, had actually seen Miriam himself. Now why hadn't he told me?

As soon as I'd finished talking to Mrs Green I rang Reverend Day.

'Miriam Johnstone came to your church the afternoon that she died.'

'Mmm,' he grunted assent.

'You saw her?'

'Yes.' Coldly.

'Why didn't you tell me? You knew I was working for the Johnstones when I rang before. Why didn't you say anything?'

'You were asking about a grey-haired caller, I believe,' he said pedantically.

'And I told you we were trying to retrace Miriam's movements that afternoon.'

'I don't recall that. You certainly didn't make yourself very clear.'

Bloody liar.

'What colour is your hair Reverend?'

'What!' That had him riled.

He will punish me. God or his representative? I felt a flush of apprehension in my guts.

'Were you intentionally keeping it from me? Would you ever have mentioned it? As their minister I would have thought you'd do everything you could to support Miriam's children.'

'My ministry is a matter for me, my God and my congregation. If you failed to make yourself clear when you first approached me I can hardly be held to blame. You call yourself a private investigator, am I right?'

'I am a private investigator.'

'But you have no authority as such.'

'Pardon?'

'Anyone can set themselves up in your business. There's no regulation or anything.'

134

If he was trying to throw me off the scent he had another thing coming. 'That's right,' I said, 'like churches, anyone can set themselves up as a minister. But if you wish someone to vouch for me before you answer any more questions I can ask Connie Johnstone to contact you.'

He sighed. 'I am rather busy,' he said evasively.

'I'll be brief then. How long was Miriam there?' I said icily.

'Half an hour, a little more.'

'And she left about one o'clock?'

'About then.'

'How did she seem?'

'She was praying. I left her in peace.'

'She didn't seem upset?'

A pause. Was it a tricky question?

'I don't remember.'

But Mrs Green did. It was plain for all to see, she said.

'You didn't speak to her?'

Comfort the sick.

'I left her to her prayers.'

A friend in need, eh? Father to the flock. Couldn't he have found a kind word for her? Or sat beside her and lent his presence? Why had he done nothing? 'If you remember anything else Reverend, I'd very much appreciate a call. It's Sal Kilkenny and I'm in the book, under Kilkenny and under Private Investigators. I know Connie Johnstone and the family would be very grateful too.'

I put the phone down and did a little jig of annoyance round the office.

What was his game? I'd met people like that before, too many of them. They have some power, a bit of influence, some authority or status in the community and they adopt an arrogant, supercilious stance as though normal co-operative ways of interacting are somehow beneath them. They are so insecure in their position that any approach is filtered first as a threat. Was that why he led me such a merry dance?

Was there any more to it? Miriam had been fine at midday when she'd left the Craft Centre. An hour later Mrs Green saw her leaving church in a terrible state. Reverend Day was the only person I knew had seen her in that crucial hour. Was he hiding something? Had he threatened to punish her? What on earth for? Or was it simply his own inadequacy that led to his churlish behaviour? Had he been discomfited by her distress? Fearful even? I wondered if he had conducted the service for Miriam. And what Connie thought of him. And what colour was his hair?

I'd run out of time but at last I had found something concrete out about Miriam's whereabouts that day. She had gone straight from the Whitworth Centre to the church and remained there till one o'clock. And then?

CHAPTER THIRTY-THREE

'Mummeeee!'

Pandemonium from the kitchen. I ran in and found Tom bawling his head off and Maddie looking worried.

'What on earth's the matter?'

Tom doesn't cry much so we always know it's something big when he does.

He was incoherent.

I ran my eyes over him searching for signs of injury and saw nothing. I scooped him onto my knee.

'What's the matter?'

He was red faced and tears were squirting out of him like mini fountains. 'Tell me, Tom.'

He fought for a breath. 'My tooth,' he wailed. 'I ate my tooth.'

I peered. His loose tooth had gone.

'He was eating his sandwich,' Maddie said.

'It's gone,' he sobbed.

'Don't worry,' I reassured him. 'You'll still get the money.'

'The tooth fairy won't come.'

'You'll still get some money, Tom,' I was not going to get into philosophical debate about the rules and regulations of an imaginary fairy. 'It's all right.'

I gave him a tissue. 'Wipe your nose.'

He did.

Maddie moved closer and put her hand on his shoulders. 'Think of something nice,' she said gently.

'Will it bite me?' he said in panic and his face creased up again.

'No, no. It'll probably melt away because your tummy's got really strong stuff in to melt all the food.'

'Or it'll come out in your poo,' Maddie added.

Tom beamed at such a naughty idea and looked at me for confirmation. I nodded. 'It could do. But it definitely can't hurt you whether it stays in your tummy or comes out the other end.'

He sighed.

'Let's think of something nice,' Maddie said again. 'Like presents.'

'Stockings,' I said. 'Where do you want to hang your stockings?'

'By my bed,' said Tom.

'Have we still got them?'

'Yes. You know when I was little we used real stockings like women wear, not ones with nice pictures on.' And how strange they had looked hanging in the dawn light, distorted, detached legs with angular shapes straining against the nylon.

'Mine's a snowman,' Tom reminded me.

'And what do you think there'll be in it?'

'Chocolate money,' they chorused.

'Yes.'

'And an orange,' said Tom.

'Satsuma,' Maddie corrected him.

I nodded.

'And toys.'

'I got a Slinky last year,' Tom said brightly. He had been virtually inseparable from the coiled metal toy, wearing it as a bracelet when he wasn't watching it flip over and over down the stairs.

'I got a mouth organ. How many things will we get, Mummy?'

'You'll have to wait and see.'

138

'And we can open them straight away, Tom, and eat all the money, can't we?'

Crisis over, we chatted for a while longer about their stockings and by the time Ray came in Tom was proudly showing off the gap where his tooth had been.

CHAPTER THIRTY-FOUR

Stuart found the sight of me in cagoule and cycling helmet somewhat amusing. 'Very fetching,' he said.

I had hoped to remove my helmet before he answered the door but I didn't get my gloves off in time.

'Rather I risked head injuries?' I muttered.

'No! But a blue cagoule might go better with . . .' He teased.

'Shut up.' I wheeled my bike in and divested myself. Beneath I was quite presentable; soft grey fleece, cream top, grey trousers. Underneath I wore something impractical in peach.

It had looked the part in the mirror but the lace didn't half tickle when I rode my bike.

At least I hope it looked okay. My underwear had been a strictly private matter for a long time, letting someone else see it, and hopefully remove it was a novelty. When I'd started going out with Stuart I'd had to go shopping, to replace my comfy cotton briefs with something a tad more sensual.

'Wine?'

'Yes.'

Stuart had a wonderful log-burning stove in his lounge. It belted out heat. I took off my fleece and got comfortable on the sofa while Stuart brought wine and a plate of titbits from the kitchen. I nibbled a pastry and olive concoction and took a big, satisfying swig of wine. Then sighed with pleasure.

'How's things?' he asked.

'Good,' I nodded. 'Work's a bit frustrating.'

'Oh,' he groaned and stretched. 'Let's not talk about work.'

I was a bit taken aback. I hadn't been going to say much more, I save my confidences for Diane. But then Stuart proceeded to launch into an account of the shenanigans at the cafe-bar.

'Three people did a runner without paying on Sunday, had the most expensive meals of course. Went after them but they were long gone. Then we'd no bread yesterday, had to send out to the local bakers. Can you imagine it?'

'No ciabatta?'

'Sold out; we had to make do with barm cakes and Manchester cobs.'

'Very exotic – it might catch on.'

'And Jonny's off.'

'Yes, what happened with the baby?'

'A girl. Angie had to have a caesarean so he wants more time off to help out. Temps are a nightmare this time of year. Christmas rush.'

I was beginning to glaze over.

Then my mobile rang. Maddie? My mind raced round freeze-frame disasters; fire, electrocution, poisoning, kidnap, car crash, as I got my phone out.

'Sal, it's Jackie Dobson here. There's a young lad at our house wanting to see you. I tried to explain that you weren't here, that downstairs is just your office but he's quite upset. I said I'd try and contact you.'

Adam Reeve. Had Susan told him, then? And he'd found out where I worked. Tracked me down in the Yellow Pages?

'He's called Roland,' Jackie said. 'Roland Johnstone.'

Oh, shit.

'Keep him there,' I said. 'I'll be straight round.'

I turned to Stuart. 'Oh, Stuart, I'm really sorry, crisis at work. One of my clients has turned up at the Dobsons'. I'm going to have to go and sort it out.' I gathered my things together.

'How long will you be?'

141

'I don't know. I'll ring.'

'Okay.'

We kissed goodbye. A long, slow kiss. It made me a little dizzy. A promise of what lay ahead once I got back.

'I'm sorry,' I mouthed as Jackie Dobson met me in the hallway.

'Don't worry,' she said. 'He's in the kitchen. I've given him a coke.'

'I'll take him downstairs.'

'Unless you want to use the kitchen?'

'No, no. We'll go down.' I opened the kitchen door. 'Hello, Roland.'

He looked tightly wound up, his shoulders and neck held rigid, mouth tight with tension. He nodded sharply and muttered hello.

'We'll go to my office downstairs,' I told him.

He stood, looked at the coke can and made half a move to put it down.

'Bring it with you,' I said.

I went ahead to unlock the door and switch the light on. The room was bitterly cold. I plugged in the heater, set it to full power. I pulled out a chair for Roland and sat down opposite him.

'You want to talk to me?'

' 'S about Ma. There's something . . . if I tell you, you've got to swear you won't tell them I told you.'

I felt a shiver across my shoulders.

'Who?'

'My sisters.'

'I can't do that.'

'Why not?' He shouted making me jump.

'First of all I don't know what you're going to tell me and secondly Connie is my client. I'm working for her. I'm hired to find out about what happened to your mother and I report anything I find back to Connie.'

'Why?' His face was contorted with frustration.

'It's my job Roland,'

'If you tell them,' he shook his head, his eyes glittered. 'I can't tell you if you're going to do that.'

'It might not be as bad as you think.'

'Oh, yeah, right,' he said derisively. 'It's only my fault, innit?'

'What is?'

'That she . . . what she did.'

I swallowed. Waited a moment. 'Why do you think it's your fault?'

He shook his head. 'You'll tell them.' He pushed himself away from the desk and stood up. I thought he was going to bolt but then I realized that the intensity of his emotions made it impossible for him to sit still. He rocked on his heels, one hand plucking at the cuff of his coat.

'You may feel responsible in some way, Roland, but your mother committed suicide.'

He flinched at the words.

'You know that.'

'And I know why,' he insisted. 'That's what I'm trying to . . . but if you tell the others . . .'

'Hang on a minute,' I said. 'I think they will be glad to know. That is all Connie wants, to understand, to try and make sense of it. Okay it might be something difficult,' I was deliberately vague as I'd no idea what he'd been hiding, 'or very upsetting but in the long run if it helps to explain things then it's better than not knowing.'

'Is it?'

'I think so.'

He stood there for a long time. I didn't push or pressure him. Occasionally he shifted his position, his hands fidgeting, his mouth worked, his breathing irregular and audible in the quiet basement. I couldn't think of anything else to say that might help him. It was up to him. And the fact that he had come this far and waited to see me meant I was fairly sure he would eventually talk.

143

He finally sat down. Put his head in his hands. I couldn't see his face.

'It's hard,' I said. 'You feel you're to blame. That's an awful burden to carry around.'

'I never should have done it,' he said softly.

'What?'

'My dad. It was him that put her in the hospital the first time when he walked out. Oh God,' his voice wavered.

'What did you do, Roland?'

'He'd never seen me, you know. Not when I was born or nothing. Never tried. They all gone on so much about what a bad man he is, a waster and all this and we never talk about him. His name is dirt, you know? And I think, I start to think I'd like to meet him, make up my own mind.' I heard longing in his voice. 'You know, there's no photograph or nothing. I didn't even know what he looked like.' He raised his head, stared at me. I nodded for him to continue.

'And,' his voice slid higher, his eyes filled, 'he wasn't a monster. He was just a man. A bit down on his luck. Not living the high life or nothing. And he was really pleased to see me. Sorry too about how things had gone. So,' he breathed shakily and sniffed hard, 'I wanted to tell Ma and my sisters but I knew they'd be in a rage and so we worked it out, Dad and me. He'd come to the house and I'd be there and it would be like a new start. Talk to Ma first, mending . . .' His mouth stretched with pain. 'I got stopped leaving school,' he began to cry, the tears sliding down his face and his account coming in spasms. 'And I was late . . . no one there . . . he'd turned up and she's, she's lost her mind and the . . . and the next thing Ma's dead.'

The grey-haired man. Miriam's ex-husband. Roland's father. I got the box of tissues out of my desk drawer and slid them across to Roland. I wanted to hug the child, to hold him as he sobbed, wracked by guilt and grief but it didn't feel right. Instead I went and stood beside him, placed one hand on his shoulder, and left it there until his crying stopped.

He used half the box of tissues, wadding them into small balls afterwards. A pile on the desk.

'You have to tell them?' His voice was hoarse from crying.

I sat down. 'Yes. But not straight away. I want to talk to your father first. Have you seen him since?'

'No. He rang us once, just after. I couldn't. I don't want to see him.'

'You can give me his address?'

'Yes.'

'What did you do when you realized no one was home?'

'I waited a bit. I didn't know what else to do.'

Mrs Boscoe had been right.

'After a while I knew it weren't going to happen. I went out then, just to the park. Waited till home time then went back, like I'd been at school. Ma wasn't there. Martina started getting worried . . .'

'Roland, don't blame yourself. No one could have predicted that seeing your father would have such a devastating effect on Miriam. No one.'

'I wish I'd never done it.'

'I know. But you were trying to make things better, sort out a reconciliation, so you didn't have to be secretive about seeing your father. There was nothing wrong with that.'

'How can you say that?' he demanded. His eyes were very dark.

'Because it's the truth. You had good intentions. You hoped to heal a rift. Like I said before no one could have dreamt either that you'd be delayed or that Miriam would self-destruct.'

'You're trying to make it come right,' he said. 'It won't. It's my fault,' he thumped his chest. 'It's my fault and they'll blame me too.'

'At first you might get recriminations, that you said nothing, for one thing. But once it's sunk in they'll understand. You can't be held responsible.'

'I am though.' He looked at me, his eyes stark.

'In your view. And you've got a choice about that, Roland.'

He frowned, put a hand on the coke can and twisted it to and fro.

'You can spend the rest of your life stewing in guilt and condemning yourself or you can forgive yourself. It won't be easy, in fact the easy way is probably to martyr yourself. It's up to you. What would your mother want you to do? Think about it.'

I insisted Roland accept a taxi home. It was cold, late, dark and he'd be a prime target for any muggers or troublemakers out on the streets that night.

I wrote down his father's address and promised that I wouldn't be talking to Connie and the others until after I'd seen Horace Johnstone. 'It'll probably be Thursday or Friday. Have you got a mobile?'

He nodded.

'Give me the number and I'll give you mine too. Now, I'll let you know when I'm coming round and you can decide whether to make yourself scarce. And let me know if you decide to talk to the family before then.'

He agreed. 'It will be better, honestly. Once it's all out in the open and the shock's passed. It'll be easier for you and I think it'll make it easier for Connie to accept, knowing it was your father's visit that set it all off.'

He looked at me with bloodshot eyes, he was exhausted.

'Will they be worried about you, now?'

He shook his head. 'I said I was going down the Aquatics Centre. Be fine.'

I saw him into the taxi and returned to close up my office. I still wore my coat, the place hadn't warmed up. I felt drained and saddened by Roland's story and distressed at the awful pressure he'd been under.

It wasn't that late, Stuart would be waiting to hear from me. But I wanted some time on my own. Would he understand? I hoped so. I didn't want to go round there and be preoccupied by what I'd just heard and I didn't feel like pretending.

I wasn't in any mood for romance or talking about our relationship. I needed solitude. I rang and explained.

'It's been pretty heavy, I'm afraid I'm not really fit for anything at the moment. I'm really sorry. Can we rearrange?'

'Okay,' he said shortly, or was I imagining it? 'I'll give you a ring.'

That was it. He'd hung up before I could suggest a date. And that made me feel insecure again. It wasn't my fault the evening had been spoilt and a touch of sympathy from him would have been very welcome. I realized how little I still knew about Stuart. I didn't know how he would react when he was brassed off about something, whether he'd sulk like Ray or pick a fight or come right out with it? Had he been tight-lipped with me? I tried to recapture the exact tone he'd used but I still couldn't tell if he was being curt or practical. The uncertainty added to my worries but I pushed it away. Enough for one day.

Jackie Dobson was in the kitchen making mince pies and, she complained, hunting for the snowman they always had on their cake. I thanked her and apologized for Roland barging into their lives, if momentarily, and told her everything was under control. Then I unlocked my bike, strapped on my helmet and rode home, snatches of Roland's story circling my mind.

He didn't deserve such pain. No one did. I'd promised him that Connie would understand eventually, would find relief in an explanation for her mother's death and not blame Roland.

I prayed that I was right.

I woke in the night from a frightening dream. Miriam was falling, Roland crying. There was an audience. Just before Miriam hit the ground I looked and saw that it was me, me falling. I shouted to them to stop but I couldn't speak. I couldn't move. I reared awake, my heart thudding frantically.

Thankful then that it was just a dream, that's all, just a stupid dream. Not real. Nothing to worry about. Everything's all right. Just a stupid dream.

And it kept me from sleep for the rest of the night.

CHAPTER THIRTY-FIVE

I couldn't visit Horace Johnstone until the next afternoon. I had a dental appointment mid-morning; yes, even private eyes have to get their teeth done. This time, two fillings had to be drilled and refilled.

It wasn't a pleasant experience. With my mouth prised open I fought the impulse to clench my teeth in fear and I performed peculiar glottal swallows to avoid drowning in the saliva that pooled in my throat. The suction device whooshed and roared like an espresso machine but couldn't keep pace with the volume of liquid flooding my mouth. I listened to the pop music, the trivial natter about what would be the Christmas number one on the radio, gazed at the corrugated light and wished for an out of body experience.

I came away with a card for six months' time; a numb face, peculiar new textures for my tongue to explore and an unshakeable sense of defilement. There's something deeply disturbing about having a stranger mess about in your mouth. It strengthened my resolve to keep to the hard line with Maddie and to insist that anything sugary was saved for meal times, even birthday treats from school and lollies that well-meaning shopkeepers handed out. Sometimes it felt as though the whole world was intent on bathing her little pegs in sugar from dawn to dusk.

I made a cup of tea at home and sipped carefully. It was hard to tell how hot it was and difficult to drink without dribbling. Chewing was out of the question so lunch was soup and noodles. I put dirty clothes on to wash, wet clothes in the dryer and dry clothes in the right piles for Ray, the kids and myself. A handful of Christmas cards had arrived, I opened them and put them on the hall table. We ought to start hanging them up, keep the kids happy till the tree materialized.

Feeling began to return to my face bringing increased control along with deep aching where the needle had gone in and along my jawbone. I tried talking to the mirror. Everything looked as it should.

Time to tackle Horace Johnstone. He was only living a few miles away from his estranged family. In a maisonette in Collyhurst, north of the city. It was a poor area. Money had been poured into it recently to smarten it up in time for the Commonwealth Games and some of the more obvious signs of vandalism and neglect had been cleared away. Nevertheless, the squat rows of maisonettes and the tiny houses, with narrow windows like horizontal versions of the slits on Norman castles, looked grim in the dim, grey weather. A carrier bag fought for freedom in the branches of a solitary tree. At the roadside a car had been abandoned, probably stolen, its interior charred, tyres gone. The bus shelter had been worked on too, fragments of glass glittered on the pavements, and lay in frosted heaps.

Mr Johnstone had an upstairs flat, reached by exterior stairs. I rang the bell and was greeted by gruff barking but no one came to the door. I tried again. From the landing I could see the three tower blocks down on Rochdale Road towards the valley bottom and beyond them the sweep of Cheetham Hill, the outline of Strangeways prison and beside it Boddingtons brewery. All those men locked up and smelling the yeast of the beer-making each day. Reminding them of what they were missing. A train made its way along the track towards Victoria station, in between the old warehouses and mills. Some of these were rotting, roofs gone, walls bowing, wood crumbling in the broken window frames. Others clung on, housing workshops and storage.

East Manchester was the wrong side of town. It was home to a large population but no one else ever had cause to go there. There was nothing to go there for. Unless you were a cycling fan and went to the Velodrome. People would travel through here to the stadium for the Games, the arterial roads would be kept spruced up but the estates behind wouldn't change much. And when it was all over, when the medals had been handed out and the last trumpet blown, I imagined the area settling back into its timeworn role as the dead end of town.

I wrote a note asking Mr Johnstone to ring me and pushed it through the letter box. Down the stairs a pasty-faced woman, wearing a thick brown woollen coat and what looked like a tea-cosy on her head, was waiting.

She eyed me up. 'He's not in.'

I nodded. 'Thanks. I've left a note.'

'You've taken your time, haven't you. They said last Wednesday, then it was Monday and yesterday they said they couldn't promise anything. And what's a note going to do? He's had warnings before. I'm fed up with it. The television's that loud I can follow what they're saying. I've a heart condition, you know. I shouldn't be having this stress. And the dog's barking all bleedin' night while he's at the pub. That's where he is now. You should go down and sort him out not just leave a note and then bugger off for the next six months. He's there more than he is here. Bleedin' alki. 'Cos he's black int'it? All this Equal Opportunities malarkey means you can't get nothing done if they're black, in case they say it's racist.'

Did she believe this crap?

'I don't sleep. Friday night . . .' she began.

I interrupted her.

'Which pub?'

'The Cat and Ferret, Jersey Street.'

'I'll try and catch him.'

'He'll be there all afternoon.'

I escaped without even trying to correct the misunderstanding.

The Cat and Ferret was warm and smoky and busy. Huge plastic cartoon cut-outs of Santa and Rudolf, sleighs and bells had been taped to the walls, garish against the flock wallpaper. Dingy streamers were strung about. Brewery posters advertised Christmas Fayre and family fun. I was marked as a stranger as soon as I walked in. Conversations were suspended as people waited to see why I was here. I scanned the room. Horace Johnstone sat with a group of men. He was the only black person. I was the only woman.

The resemblance to his son Roland was striking. I braced myself and crossed to the table. They were playing cards. One of the men shuffling the set.

'Mr Johnstone?'

He turned, peered at me. His grey hair was wiry, just covering the top of his ears. 'Yes?'

I moved closer, lowered my voice. 'I need to talk to you.'

He frowned. 'Who are you?'

'Sal Kilkenny. I'm working for your daughter Constance.' His eyes widened in surprise. 'Roland told me where to come.'

A burst of laughter came from the bar where more men were watching a television suspended up in one corner.

'If we could talk in private?'

He looked at me cautiously, nodded once and picked up his glass. He swallowed it down, his Adam's apple rippling as he did. He pulled the coat from the back of his chair. 'Deal me out, Dave.'

The men were clearly tight with curiosity but Horace didn't furnish any explanation and they were unsure of me enough to forego any banter. I was an official, they knew that much: the social, the council, the filth. Someone to be given a wide berth.

Horace Johnstone pulled on an olive-green flat cap and buttoned his coat. He took his time. I sensed the ferocious

151

concentration of the habitual drunk in the slow way he moved.

We walked in awkward silence, into the wind, and back to the maisonettes. There was no sign of his downstairs neighbour.

The dog barked loudly as Mr Johnstone unlocked the door.

'Don't mind him,' he said. 'He's in the kitchen.' He stooped to pick the folded paper from the floor.

'I left a note,' I said, 'before I came to the pub.'

The door led into a narrow hallway. Mr Johnstone hung up his coat and took me through the door ahead into a small, rectangular, low-ceilinged room. No one had cleared up for a long time. The navy carpet was covered with dog hairs, bits of lint, crumbs. Yellowing newspapers were piled up on the sideboard and the room smelt stale, like the morning after a party, old beer and cigarettes and the meaty scent of dog. There was no sign of Yuletide, not even a card.

Mr Johnstone gestured for me to sit in one of the shabby armchairs and he sat in the other.

'I'm a private detective. My name is Sal Kilkenny. Constance hired me because she was unhappy about the inquest into her mother's death. She wanted to know more about the day itself, where Miriam had been, who she'd seen; that sort of thing.'

He regarded me suspiciously. 'And Roland?'

'He told me that he'd found you, that he'd been seeing you in secret. He said you'd arranged to meet at Heald Place. He hoped you and Miriam would let bygones be bygones.'

He gave a sigh, he sounded exasperated.

'One moment.' He went out and returned with two cans of cheap lager. He popped one and drank from it.

'I'm the first person Roland's told. He's convinced that seeing you drove Miriam into a panic. He blames himself for what happened.'

He frowned, took another swig. 'That don't make no sense,' he said.

152

'I know but he does.'

'No,' he held the can out towards me to emphasize his point, 'I don't mean that. It makes no sense,' he said carefully, 'because Miriam never saw me. She wasn't home when I called at the house.' He nodded solemnly and took a drink.

'What did you do?'

'I thought maybe Roland had cold feet. I waited a little bit and I asked at the shop. They told me about this centre she goes to. I wondered if she'd be there or if Roland had gone there maybe, to give her some warning about me. I thought he said twelve fifteen then I got to thinking if I had it mixed up and then . . .' He shrugged. His speech was slurred. 'I went to the centre and she gone.' He shifted and pulled a tin of tobacco from his pocket and some Rizla papers. He began to roll a cigarette with slow, practised movements.

'Miriam had left. I missed her.' He struck a match and lit his roll-up. He took a drag and blew smoke into the air, drank some more.

'What would you have done if she'd been there?'

He shrugged. 'Don't know. Was all Roland's plan and he was nowhere in sight.'

'Have you seen him since then?'

'I rang him and he said to keep in touch.'

Really? Roland's version was that he had hung up the phone, refused to talk to his father. Why this little lie? Was it all lies?

'You never went to the funeral?'

'I wasn't welcome. Miriam and me we parted with very, very bad feelings. She turned them all against me. She never let me see my son.'

'Did you try?'

'She wouldn't let me, no way,' he said evasively.

'She became ill just after you walked out,' I said. 'It must have been difficult for them.'

'She had a weakness,' he said. 'Some people, that's the way they are.'

'Were you surprised when she killed herself?'

'No, ' he took a long drag. 'It's like a bomb waiting to go off, you know? Sooner or later . . .' He made a gesture with his hands tracing the shape of an explosion.

He was the only person I'd talked to who had known Miriam and hadn't expressed surprise or disbelief at her suicide. He hadn't seen his wife for fourteen years – maybe that had something to do with it. Perhaps emphasizing her mental vulnerability and the inevitability of her fate was a means of absolving himself of any responsibility for the way her life had gone. If Miriam was weak and destined for suicide his walking out would be neither here nor there. Was that it?

'You had no contact over the years?'

'No.'

'Did you contribute financially?'

'No,' he said defensively. 'I can't do that. I never had lots of money and why should I pay? I never see my own children. I don't have food cooked or my washing done or nothing.'

But we were wandering, now.

'After you'd called at the centre, what did you do?'

'I thought about trying the house again. Maybe she walked a different way. But I decide to give her a bit of time. I went for a little drink.'

'Where.'

'The Albert.'

I knew it. I nodded.

'I stayed there awhile and I thought, you know, maybe Roland he set me up. Some sort of silly matchmaking and that's why he wasn't there. Though he must realize that it's going to be a big, big shock for her if I turn up out of the blue and no Roland to have his say.'

'He was delayed,' I said. 'He got stopped leaving school.'

He peered at me, trying to take in this new scenario. 'Delayed?'

'Yes.'

154

The ash fell from his cigarette onto his trousers, he rubbed it in. Had a drink.

'He's a fine boy,' he said. 'He came to find me. His sisters, they never bothered. Father,' he pointed to himself, 'and son.' He pointed away. He had a last suck on the roll up and dropped it in the beer can. There was a tiny hiss.

'Then I was thinking, in the Albert, I was thinking if Roland had come back and his mother they were maybe waiting for me. I got some Dutch courage and I went back to the house.'

I imagined him a little worse for wear, walking along to Heald Place.

'What time was this?'

'They were still serving.'

Before three thirty then.

He stifled a belch. Popped his second can. 'But Miriam had her own business to attend to,' he said sarcastically.

'What do you mean?'

'She was busy, going out with her fancy man.'

I stared at him.

'You saw her?'

He nodded. Belched. 'Both of them. Come out of the house and get in the car.' Nicholas Bell? Albert Fanu? 'Bloody cowboy.'

For a moment I thought he was referring to the style of the vehicle or the attitude of the man driving. Cowboy builders, cowboy mechanics. A con man, a wide boy, flash and trashy. But it was simpler than that.

'Like Wild Bill Hickock. Big mess of a beard and them cowboy boots.' He made a sucking noise with his teeth.

Eddie Cliff.

My stomach lurched and my scalp prickled with unease.

Eddie Cliff.

What the hell was *he* doing there?

155

CHAPTER THIRTY-SIX

'I was gobsmacked,' I told Diane. 'He'd already claimed that Roland wanted to keep in touch which I knew was a lie and then he sprang this. But I couldn't see that he'd be making it up. As far as I know he'd never clapped eyes on Eddie before.'

'Bit weird.' She agreed. 'What's this Eddie like?'

'All right. Well, I thought he was. Good with people, passionate about his work. Helpful.'

'So, ask him about it.'

'Oh, I intend to. As soon as possible. It's a bit awkward though because it means he wasn't being straight with me. And I can't see why. Of course the other side of all this is Roland, who thought his father turning up on the doorstep had led to his mother cracking up and that wasn't it at all. He must have been to hell and back, poor kid. Now I can tell him how wrong he was, once I've talked to Eddie Cliff and got things a bit clearer.'

'Another?' Diane held up her beer glass.

'Please – and crisps.'

While she was at the bar I worried some more about Horace Johnstone's version of events. There was a possibility that he was writing himself out of the picture because he felt guilty, though I'd not seen much sign of that. Maybe he had met Miriam and she'd freaked out. He'd panicked and left her. Later he hears she is dead. But the description of Eddie Cliff was too close to be coincidental. He must have seen him. Could he have seen him at the centre and then invented the bit about the car. Possibly, but why? To point me in a different direction? That only made sense if Horace Johnstone had done something he wanted to keep hidden. The more I chewed it over the more muddled I became. I thought about the timing – it wasn't exact but presumably it was after Roland had gone off to wait in the park at two-ish and before Martina got in around four o'clock.

Diane returned with our drinks and two packets of cheese and onion crisps. I took a swig of beer, opened my crisps and ate a handful.

'What about the other lad, the one that was running off?'

'Curiouser and curiouser,' I said. I trailed him twice. He spent one day mooching around the Arndale and the next on an odyssey to York.'

'York?'

'York. Stood outside a house, watched the occupants, went home in tears.'

'Aw!'

'And I've no idea what's going on there. I thought perhaps a girlfriend, unrequited love. But there was no girl the right age. I even asked his mother if he was adopted, thought he might be tracing his roots. She thought I was bonkers.'

'Is he stalking them?'

'I thought about that but it's the first time he's been up there so that doesn't fit. He even stopped to ask me directions.' I pulled a face.

'What did you do?' Diane exclaimed.

'Bluffed my way through it. Seemed to work. All I can do now is find out who lives in the house, hope it means something to his mother.' I took a drink. 'Mmm.' The beer was just cool, tasted full and bitter and had a creamy head that meant you had to lick your lips after each drink. Perfect. 'So, tell me about Iceland.'

'Thunderbirds are GO. All on schedule. Bit of a panic when the airline couldn't find a note of my booking.'

'You're joking.'

'They'd just lost me somewhere.'

'Over the North Sea.'

'Saves on the catering. It's sorted now.'

'You go Friday?'

'Yes. Thermals are packed and Christmas cards posted.'

'Mine aren't.'

'So how's Christmas shaping up in the Kilkenny/Costello household?'

'Nana 'Tello is on the brink of accepting Ray's offer. She'll spend all day needling Laura if recent form is anything to go by.'

'How does Laura cope?'

I grinned. 'She smiles sweetly and replies politely. She's got far more control than I ever had. You can see it drives Nana 'Tello mad; she wants a scrap.'

'Why's she like that?'

'Jealousy? I don't know. Yours truly can do no wrong these days.'

'You're joking.'

'Flavour of the month. I think I preferred being the devil within.'

'Does Ray say anything?'

'Oh, yeah. He blows up after so much and then she goes all quiet and cold or tearful. But I think I'll stick my oar in if she starts this time. It's horrible for the kids let alone Laura. Goodwill to all men.'

'You're really looking forward to it then.'

I gave sickly smile. 'I'd rather come with you.'

'The course is fun. Oh, and they've got a television crew coming over from Germany, arts documentary, so that's another spin-off.

'Brilliant. And after Iceland?'

'The world,' she said in a phoney American accent. 'Warrington actually,' she went into broad Mancunian. 'Children's library.'

158

I raised my eyebrows.

'I like libraries.'

'It was the children's bit.'

'Nah. Won't have to do much with them, a design work-shop. Well-behaved group of schoolchildren, teacher present.'

I smiled.

'And New Year, of course.' We'd both been invited to the party at our old friends'. 'Are you going to Harry and Bev's?'

'You bet. Means I can bring Maddie; babysitters are pretty scarce at New Year. Are you?'

She screwed up her nose. 'You know I hate New Year. I might just rent a video and curl up with some smoked salmon and single malt.'

'Chris and Jo will be there. Be a chance to catch up with people.'

'You bringing Stuart?'

I grimaced. 'Don't know. Probably not. We haven't talked about it really. He might be doing something with his family. And if not that would mean me explaining who he was to Maddie.'

'Still a secret?'

'Yeah,' I said slowly. And I didn't like it, I realized. One of the things I was becoming more uncomfortable with was the secrecy we'd imposed upon ourselves. It had seemed sensible at the time, for the sake of the children, to give us chance to work out whether we were suited before involving anyone else, but I wasn't so sure any more.

It's the secrecy I can't stand, Susan Reeve had said, *the lies and the secrecy.*

From a completely different perspective I agreed.

I tried phoning Stuart at his place when I got in. A woman answered the phone.

'Is Stuart there?'

'Who is this?'

I was thinking the same thing.

'Sal Kilkenny, I'm a friend.'

She put the phone down.

I felt like I'd been slapped.

How dare she? Who was she? Some other new conquest that Stuart had forgotten to mention? My cheeks burned with outrage and I found myself talking aloud, spluttering with indignation. It really wasn't worth it. Crikey, seeing someone after years in single-parent purdah was tough enough without rude behaviour from anonymous third parties to contend with.

I got ready for bed and lay there rehearsing my speech to Stuart, adapting it to suit his reactions. But whichever version I chose, penitent Stuart, blasé Stuart, misunderstood Stuart, bastard Stuart, I always ended up reaching the same final line.

Goodbye.

CHAPTER THIRTY-SEVEN

I felt sullen the next morning. Too little sleep and too much unresolved ill temper. I still felt resentful of Stuart though I realized I was being unfair in leaping to conclusions and passing judgements before I had the facts. I packed my swimming things. If I could fit a few lengths in it would help with the slow burn in my stomach.

Ray was walking the children to school so I took half an hour to warm up and practise some holds and jumps from self-defence. I went through my kicks; forward, side, back and stamp. Concentrated on getting the force and weight into my leg, nowhere else. Forward, back, side, stamp. I imagined jaws, knees, balls. Then I moved onto a pull and roll technique that always made me feel good when I practised it at the class with Brian. The idea was to wrong-foot an attacker by moving with them rather than against. Brian would lunge at me and I'd grab his arms and roll back and down pulling him over as I went. Once he'd landed behind me I would recover forward and run. It wasn't the same without a partner but I could still rehearse the roll. I had a troublesome shoulder and it was important to fall without incapacitating myself.

'You won't get a chance to warm up,' Ursula had always told us, 'maintaining general levels of fitness is important, keeping supple too. That's the groundwork for all the rest. You need to minimize the risk of pulling a muscle or spraining something in a tricky situation.'

I followed my exercises with a hot shower and felt a great deal better. From the office I rang Eddie Cliff at the Whitworth Centre and asked if I could call in to talk to him.

'I've the Craft Club till twelve,' he told me, 'and at one I've a meeting with funders about monitoring and evaluation. You know I spend more and more time raising the money and justifying the work with targets and weights and measures and performance indicators and less and less actually working with people. Sorry,' he said. 'Soapbox. Right . . . erm . . . best come at twelve. Squeeze you in then.'

'Thanks.'

I checked my emails and sent one to Harry and Bev to tell them we'd be coming to the New Year's party. Then I spent more time transferring files from floppy discs I'd brought from home and trying to design a more efficient way of organizing my folders.

As I worked my mind circled around my forthcoming appointment with Eddie Cliff, tentatively, never quite reaching out and shaking the thing out to have a good look at it. I prowled round it with eyes shut and face averted hoping that the whole thing was a mistake, an illusion. Not real. Not a lie. A flat, hard, ugly, awkward lie.

'What?' Eddie looked genuinely puzzled. His blue eyes narrowed and shadowed with confusion.

'Someone saw you there,' I repeated. 'At Miriam's, getting in the car with her.'

'They can't have,' he said. 'I wasn't there.' He looked at me and shook his head in disbelief. 'Who said this?' He sounded hurt.

'You don't know them but they knew Miriam.'

'It's a mistake,' he said firmly. 'Either it was someone else or it was another day and this person's got them mixed up. That's the only explanation I can think of. Could that be it?'

'Possibly,' I said guarded.

'You know I was here, at the Centre,' he pointed out, 'I told you, we had the visit from Central Grants. I was up to here with it,' he measured the air above his head.

'That finished at two.' Sharon had told me.

He gave a short laugh. 'They may have left the building at two but the work didn't stop there: papers to clear, displays to remove, supporters to thank.' He frowned. 'I feel I'm having to defend myself,' he put his hand on his chest. 'And I don't even know who's told you this. But they're wrong. I didn't see Miriam after she left here. I wish I had. Maybe I could have done something . . .' He shrugged.

Reverend Day had seen her. Was that why the clergyman had been so awkward? Because he'd seen how distressed she was and he'd failed to help her? Did her agitation frighten him? Was it guilt that had sealed his lips, not wanting it to get out that he done nothing, said nothing and left her to her fate? Crossed on the other side of the road?

'You say it could have been another occasion?' I asked Eddie.

'We went to GRUMPY,' he saw me look quizzical. 'It's a resource centre, for community groups, they collect waste materials and recycle them, lots of arts and craft stuff. It's very cheap. We're members. We went to stock up on materials. I took Miriam.'

'When?'

'The day before, the Wednesday. That must be it,' he said. I could sense him waiting for my agreement. And I realized I would have to be as persuasive as he was being. I knew Horace Johnstone was a drinker, but I believed his story. He hadn't been to Heald Place before Roland invited him. Unless he was manipulative beyond belief he had seen Eddie with Miriam and it had been the day of her suicide. Eddie Cliff was lying but I didn't want him to know that I didn't believe him.

'On the Wednesday,' I shook my head, tutted. 'God, I am sorry. That fits,' I nodded. 'Makes a lot more sense. It wasn't the most reliable of people but I had to check it out.' I smiled, it made my mouth ache. 'Hope you don't mind.'

'You had me worried there,' Eddie said.

'Don't. Really. This sort of thing comes up all the time. It's amazing how muddled people can be . . . and asking people to recall things from months ago. Well. Anyway I'm glad that's cleared up. It really didn't make sense.' I smiled again. 'And now, I'd better be on my way. You look busy?'

I nodded at the piles of Christmas parcels, the table decorations, the crib with its carved figures.

'Christmas Fair. You must come.'

'Yes, I will. Sharon mentioned it.' When she told me about Melody. I could have asked Eddie if he'd heard about Melody but I held back. I wanted to get out of there. Away from him. Eddie Cliff. Liar. I felt sick inside.

I got to the baths at twenty to one. The last twenty minutes of adult hour. I ploughed up and down, feeling my heartbeat speed up, my breathing quicken, the blood flow faster round my arms and legs. All the time I chewed over the interchange I'd had with Eddie Cliff. He'd been plausible, concerned, friendly. And he'd maintained his false story. Why?

The question echoed to the rhythm of my strokes. Why, why, why?

He had something to hide. Whatever business he had with Miriam Johnstone that Thursday afternoon he wanted to keep it hidden. He had a secret. A secret I needed to unearth. He was the last person to see Miriam alive. Not at 12.00 when she had left the Whitworth Centre but over two hours later when she was already distraught according to both Mrs Green and Hattie Jacobs.

I don't remember getting dressed. I was too busy concentrating on my next step, and the best way to unpick the truth.

CHAPTER THIRTY-EIGHT

The Health Food Shop in Withington were selling pricey organic Christmas pudding, vegan mince-pies and carob tree decorations. I could just imagine Maddie's horror if she opened one of them and found it wasn't authentic Cadbury's chocolate. I steered clear of all that and bought a spring roll and a flapjack for my lunch and some mixed nuts, black mustard and sesame seeds, oatmeal and herbal tea for home. I imagined Nana 'Tello's reaction: birdfood. I dropped my purchases twice and queried the change before I clocked that I wasn't functioning properly.

I was shocked that Eddie Cliff was lying to me. And apprehensive about what the lie might conceal. He was so convincing though. There'd been nothing obvious in his body language or the tone of his voice to betray him. He was a good liar. Skilled. If he'd lied about Miriam, what else had he lied about?

In among my distaste and anxiety I was completely keyed up, adrenalin buzzing along my spine, mind racing about. The weather was changing, a storm was forecast and I could feel the pressure in the air. The sky had darkened to a moody blue and the first tugs of wind were starting. I hurried back and devoured my lunch, chose strong coffee over herbal tea and had a most uncharacteristic (after so many years) craving for a cigarette. Then I got on the phone.

Eddie had worked in Hull, Sharon had said, at a similar project called Horizons. I started with the local authority.

Like all councils it seemed to have only one phone line which was either engaged or unattended. On my sixth try I got through and was transferred to social services. I told the man at the other end I wanted the number for Horizons, a drop-in centre I'd heard of where they did arts activities.

'Not a day-centre?' he asked.

'Don't think so, open to anyone.'

'Just a minute.' I could hear him relaying my query to his colleagues. One of whom knew exactly where I meant.

He came back on the line. 'Horizons,' he said. He gave me the address and phone number.

Bingo.

I flexed my shoulders and stretched my arms.

When I got through to Horizons I asked for the manager.

'Who shall I say is calling?'

I told her.

A pause, then, 'Bryony Walker speaking.'

'Hello, my name's Sal Kilkenny. I'm ringing in connection with a Mr Eddie Cliff who used to work there.'

'Sorry?'

'Eddie Cliff.'

'No. No one of that name.'

'It would be about three years ago, more or less.'

'No,' she said directly. 'I've been here since we started and there's never been a Eddie Cliff.'

Another lie. He'd made up the job?

'He had a reference from you,' I said.

'There's obviously been a mistake. We're a small place; if there had been anyone called that I'd remember the name.'

So he'd written his own reference. I'd heard it was common for applicants to embellish their CVs but a non-existent position and false references was pushing it. And could get him the sack.

'Sorry to bother you, then, thanks.' I was about to ring off when I heard myself talking again. 'This man, he's got a beard, long hair, dresses like a cowboy.'

Silence.

'Hello?'

'Oh, God,' she said. 'Who are you again?'

'Sal Kilkenny. I'm a private investigator.'

'Oh, God.'

'You recognize the description?'

'Yes.'

Another pause. 'We had someone like that here. Clive Edmonds he was called.' She sounded breathless.

Yes!

She cleared her throat. 'Listen, I just need a few minutes. Erm . . . can I ring you back?'

'Yes.' I gave her my number and paced the room waiting for the phone. When it rang I pounced.

'Sal Kilkenny speaking.'

'Bryony Walker. Listen do you have any proof of your identity? Something you could fax me?' It was a reasonable request. I could have been anybody. I was dying to know what lay behind her stunned reaction.

'Driving licence?'

'Fine, yes.'

'And is there anyone who can vouch for you?' she asked. 'Someone who knows you professionally?'

I thought. 'There are a firm of solicitors I work for.'

'Good.'

I gave her Rebecca Henderson's number. She was certainly being very cautious.

'I'll give these people a call. Meanwhile if you can send me the copy of your driving licence.'

'Yep.'

'If that's all okay I need to make absolutely sure that we're talking about the same man before I say anything else. I'll fax you a photograph and can you confirm it is the right person?'

'Yes, of course.'

We exchanged fax numbers and I set my machine to receive a fax. I was practically dancing with anticipation.

Eddie Cliff had changed his name. Got a job under false pretences and more important to me he'd lied about Miriam Johnstone. The woman at Horizons knew the man and what she knew was certainly not good.

I was wired with curiosity. What had he done? What could she tell me? And as I waited for the fax to arrive the fingers of dread stroked at my neck.

CHAPTER THIRTY-NINE

It was him. I looked at the grainy copy, a shot with a group of people beside a statue. Even with the poor quality there was no doubt in my mind.

I gave it two minutes, then I rang Bryony Walker.

'That's him.'

'You said you were a private investigator. Do you mind telling me are you working for the local authority? Is this an official enquiry?'

'No. I'm working for someone privately,' I said. 'Their mother attended a club run by Mr Edmonds, Mr Cliff as I know him.'

She groaned. 'So he's working again.'

What did she mean?

'And he claims to have a reference from here?'

'Yes.'

She exhaled sharply. 'Look I'd really like to help but I can't talk about this over the phone. There's a lot at stake and much of it is sensitive or confidential.'

'Could I come to you?'

'Where are you?'

'Manchester.'

There was a pause. 'I'm travelling down to Birmingham first thing tomorrow, for the Christmas break. Maybe we can meet up somewhere?'

'Yes. I take it you never gave him a reference?'

'No.'

'And he left under a cloud of some sort?'

'Yes.'

She wasn't giving much away. I would die of suspense if I had to spend all night speculating. Had he run off with the funds or been drinking on the job or had he forged his last references?

'Could you give me any idea of what happened?'

'I'd rather wait till tomorrow, talk about it face to face. The club you mentioned, it's similar to our set-up here?' She checked. 'Caters for vulnerable people, mental health survivors, people with learning disabilities?'

'Yes.'

She sighed. 'Where can we meet?'

'Are you driving?'

'Yes.'

We established her route and arranged to rendezvous at a services on the M62. I told her I'd be wearing a grey coat with a red beret and I'd wait in the cafe.

'I take it he doesn't know you've contacted me?' she asked.

'No.'

'Good. Keep it that way. He mustn't know.'

I felt shaken by her tone. Whatever he had done was heavy enough for her to insist on secrecy and to refuse to tell me about it over the phone. I was buzzing with curiosity, and tension settled in the pit of my stomach.

Where had he worked before Horizons? Digging around in his past had brought me Bryony Walker; might there be more to uncover out there? I wondered if I could find out. It wouldn't do any harm to try and might ease my sense of suspended animation while I waited to hear what his former employer had to say.

My old friend Harry was the best person for the job. I rang and gave him the details: aliases Eddie might use, locations, timescale. I asked him to find any press coverage or maybe references from Local Authority or Social Services public information. He said he'd do his best though it might be a day or two before he got back to me. I knew my enquiry was in competent hands.

Once it got to four o'clock I rang Roland Johnstone on his mobile, assuming that they'd be banned during school hours. I wanted to reassure him.

'Roland, it's Sal Kilkenny. I got to see your father, I wanted to tell you what he said.'

' 'Kay.'

'He never met Miriam. When he got to the house she was out. He tried the Whitworth Centre but she'd gone. She never saw him that day.'

'Oh.' That was all he said.

'It had nothing to do with your father.'

An intake of breath. 'You going to tell my sisters?'

'Eventually,' I said. 'But things are completely hectic at the moment, it's going to be a couple of days at least before I get round there.' And I wanted to go back with a fuller picture. I was making progress but I needed to tread carefully. What I could tell them at the moment begged more questions than it answered. 'I'll let you know separately when I'm coming,' I said, 'then you can decide if you want to be there.'

'Right, yeah.'

'Are you all right?'

He sounded a bit stunned. He'd spent two months blaming himself for his mother's suicide and now his reasoning had been stripped away. Would he go easier on himself now the facts had absolved him? Guilt's a hard burden to relinquish.

Then Stuart rang. I'd been so preoccupied with work that I'd not had time to dwell on my irritation but as soon as I heard his voice my pulse quickened and I became short of breath as unpleasant things happened to my diaphragm.

'I rang last night,' I said.

'Oh, I was out.'

'Were you?'

'Sal?' Least he had the grace to notice the sharp tone.

171

'A woman answered. She hung up on me.'

'Oh, God,' he groaned. 'Sal, I'm so sorry . . .'

'Someone new?' After all we'd never sworn to be monogamous or anything – he had a right.

'Christ, no,' he exclaimed. 'You didn't think . . .'

Obviously I did.

'It was Natalie. The kids were staying at mine because Nat had an early start this morning.' Natalie, his ex, did something in wardrobe for Granada TV. 'I was working all evening so she had to babysit.'

'I thought things were sorted out between the two of you.' He'd always claimed they had a very civilized relationship. I wouldn't have gone out with him if there'd been a messy marriage break-up festering away.

'They are. Sal, I'm sorry. I think, well, Nat – she finds it hard. It's the first time . . .' He dried up, suddenly inarticulate. 'I'd like to see you,' he added.

'We need to talk,' I replied noncommittally.

Once I'd put a question mark over the future of our relationship I realized I couldn't delete it. Self-fulfilling prophesy. Was I using Natalie's hostility as an excuse? Was I just being stubborn? Cutting off my nose to spite my face?

'Tomorrow?'

'Haven't you got the kids?'

'Grandma's all weekend.'

But I had self-defence.

'Saturday would be better.'

'Fine.'

Where should I suggest? Not here. If I ended the relationship, which was a possibility, I wanted to be able to walk away. Stuart's? Or somewhere neutral? Thing is neutral would mean public which could make it all the more awkward.

'I'll come to you,' I said, 'about eight?'

'See you then and erm . . . if you'd like to stay?'

Ah! I winced. Lousy timing. 'Right. Erm . . . don't know.'

The invitation seemed poignant. There he was thinking

about the possibility of waking up in the same bed and there I was thinking of dumping him just in time for Christmas. Shouldn't I give him, give us, a second chance?

Ray was supposed to be making tea but there was no sign of him by five o'clock and the children were starting to whine. I didn't even know what he was planning. There wasn't much potential in the kitchen cupboards or the fridge, even the freezer was low. I discarded some out-of-date Thomas the Tank Engine yoghurts and several little foil-wrapped bundles which I vaguely remembered saving from meals gone by but which didn't warrant further inspection. Dinner was decided by default. Spaghetti hoops on toast.

We'd just cleared our plates when Ray and Laura breezed in complete with a bag of Indian takeaway.

'We just had tea,' Tom yelled, delighted at this example of adult folly.

'Oh, great,' Ray retorted giving me a moody glare.

'They were starving,' I protested. 'I'd no idea when you'd be back.'

'You can have two teas,' Laura told Tom, trying to improve the atmosphere.

'It's only twenty past,' Ray continued.

'Sorry,' I said without sounding it. 'If you'd let me know you were getting takeaway I wouldn't have done anything.'

'It was going to be a surprise,' he muttered.

'I love takeaways.'

Thanks, Maddie.

Ray stomped about a bit getting fresh plates and cutlery and then we all sat down again. The kids didn't manage much, and Ray had bought more than necessary. I ate a samosa, a small portion of aloo saag which was so hot I couldn't taste either the potato or the spinach, and half an onion bhaji.

Seeing as things were already strained I took the opportunity to push it a bit further; preferable to having to wait for him to stop sulking which could take ages. 'We need a big shop,' I said. 'And lots of frozen stuff.'

'Yep,' he said curtly.

'We could get the Christmas stuff at the same time.'

'I'm getting the turkey tomorrow.'

'But we need other stuff too.'

'Right,' short and crisp.

I saw Laura's mouth twitch ever so slightly, just the smallest suggestion that she found his attitude risible. I was getting to like Laura more. At first I thought she was a bit too accommodating but I'd come to see that she decided when and where she'd get drawn into things. I also used to worry she'd be the downfall of our house, whisking Ray off to nuclear bliss in a Hartley semi. It was still possible but they seemed quite content for now and she kept her flat on. I'd even reached the point where I could see her joining our household and it working. Though whether she'd ever countenance that I didn't know. The kids were both very comfortable with her. A few days before she had suggested a trip out once school was finished, somewhere they could climb trees and play hide and seek. Ray had protested that he'd no time until he'd finished his furniture so Laura and I had agreed we'd take them anyway. It would be the first time we'd done something without Ray; a chance to get to know each other better.

I left Ray and Laura clearing up. Spent some time helping Maddie with her reading and then a delightful hour delousing her head. Bed time followed and I made up the latest instalment of our home-made saga about Smokey, the baby dragon and Silver Moon, the orphaned Indian girl. Maddie or Tom, depending on whose turn it was, detailed the elements they wanted in the story and I joined the dots. Some surreal adventures ensued. But they all ended happily ever after in a world where people showered in waterfalls, rode on dragons and where sweets grew on trees.

I really had to write some Christmas cards. I found my address book, the stack of cards, a pen and began a list of people to send them to. Progress was slow, I found it hard to concentrate as my mind kept sliding off to speculate about the morning, what my meeting with Bryony Walker would bring. Eddie Cliff had taken me in, just like he had everyone else. I still found it hard to credit.

My mobile began to chirrup. It was Susan Reeve.

'I'm sorry to ring you this late,' she said breathlessly, 'but it's Adam. He's had a row with Ken and he's just stormed off. He hasn't even got a coat on and it's horrendous out there. Ken's out looking for him now but I thought if you could, if you wouldn't mind . . .'

Oh, great. Just the ticket. There are times when my job loses its appeal.

'Okay,' I put her out of her misery. 'You've no idea where he's gone?'

'No, but he hasn't any money so he won't have been able to get the bus or anything.'

'What was the row about?'

She gave a sigh. 'His attitude; he never said a word at tea time, wouldn't eat his food. It was driving Ken up the wall. I thought it'd all calmed down after that but Ken went up to try and talk some sense into him and he just blew up. Yelling and shouting. The girls got that upset. It was bedlam. Then he ran off. Ken's gone out in the car.'

'What if I find him?'

'Please, bring him home, if he'll come.'

'He still doesn't know about me?'

'No.'

'And your husband?'

'No. But I'll tell him if it comes to that.'

I knew my time was pretty much used up but I wasn't going to be picky about it. I didn't like to think of the poor lad out on such an awful night. I told her that I'd drive around for a bit, and to ring me again if she heard anything.

Ray and Laura had gone to his room. I could hear a Marvin Gaye tape playing. My Marvin Gaye tape. Maybe I should get Ray a CD of it for Christmas. I knocked on the door.

'Yes?' Ray's voice.

'It's Sal,' I spoke through the door. 'I've got to go out for work.'

'What's happened?'

'Someone's done a bunk, a teenager. I said to his mum I'd see if I could spot him. See you later.'

I was halfway down the stairs when Ray's door opened and he came across the landing. He was wearing his dressing gown. 'Sal, it's nothing heavy is it?'

'Oh, no. Nothing like that.'

He raised his eyebrows a fraction, giving me the chance to amend my story if I was underplaying it. 'Really. Go back to bed.'

'Be careful.'

'Thanks.'

We'd had awful arguments in the past about the risks my job involved. Hence my self-defence classes. But he still worried.

CHAPTER FORTY

The storm had hit, gusting wind, heavy rain falling as I unlocked the car. I put the heater on and the windscreen warmer. I put a tape on too. If I was going to cruise the streets of South Manchester on this foul night at least I'd have some decent sounds to accompany me. The Buena Vista Social Club swung into life and I pulled out of the drive and headed for Burnage.

If Adam had no money then he'd be limited to travelling on foot, unless he tried hitching. I decided to work methodically starting with the streets near to his home and gradually working my way further out. The rain spattered across the windscreen with each surge of wind. It was very hard to see much of anything. I meandered along the roads off Burnside Drive then I drove down Kingsway towards town and circled the roundabout at the bottom and drove in the opposite direction. I scoured the pavements, bus shelters, shop doorways. Nothing. At one point I came across a group of lads outside a boarded-up shop and slowed right down but I couldn't see Adam among them. I wove my way through the council estates that straddled Kingsway. There were lots of cul-de-sacs and small avenues. Plenty of privet hedges to crouch behind and every house had a garden; he could be in a shed somewhere or under someone's pergola.

The tape finished. I substituted it for Macy Gray but that made me think about finishing with Stuart so I swapped that for Fat Boy Slim. My mobile went off and I pulled in to the side of the road and answered it.

'Ken's back,' she said, 'I can hear the car.'

'Has he got Adam?'

'I don't know, I can't see . . . wait a minute. No,' she sounded defeated. 'No, he's on his own. He'll have had enough. If it was me . . . Please will you . . .'

'I'll keep looking a while longer but if he's found somewhere out of sight to shelter then it'll be impossible to find him. He has run off before.' I reminded her. And he came back.

'But the row. I've never heard him like that. I'm really worried. If he did something stupid . . .'

'You could call the police,' I suggested. Though I wasn't sure how much help they would give her. After all Adam had run away several times even if the circumstances hadn't been exactly the same. But if she thought he was at risk? Wind buffeted the car and the connection began to break up.

'I'll try a while longer,' I said.

'Thank you so much.'

Where would he shelter? Would he pass in a pub? Soaking wet and on his own? He'd draw too much attention. Besides, I reminded myself, he's no money. I thought of his previous outings. Sitting on the bench at the Arndale Centre, on the bench at the bus stop. The vigil that had left him in tears. Where would he sit down round here. Forget about garden, no way could I start looking in them. I'd passed the main bus stops. I got out my bumper size A–Z and my Maglite and studied Burnage. Kingsway and the railway line divided the area in half. It was heavily built up. The only open spaces were at Cringle Fields which was quite a way away and Ladybarn Park. I couldn't recall any shelter at Cringle Fields. I'd only ever been there to the travelling funfair. It was a wide, flat, open space ideal for the large fairs. Ladybarn was smaller and nearer. I drove there and parked on Mauldeth Road. The park was fairly open, a large row of poplars marked the southern boundary. It was pitch black, impossible to see if anyone was hiding beneath them. I played my torch over them, the beam rippling over the trunks and saw nothing. A squall of rain hit again and I tightened my hood. There were two deserted picnic areas, tables with fixed chairs, I think they'd been put there as a place for the youngsters to hang out. But not on a night like this. I walked along and round the corner so I could see into the bowling green and the basketball courts. Empty. Thunder cracked and rumbled in the distance and there was a single flash of sheet lightning that lit the sky momentarily.

But no Adam. I made my way back to the car. A train rattled past on the bridge above. The station? There was a modicum of shelter there. Only two platforms but express trains ran through all night; this was the airport line. I did a three-point turn and drove up the slope which led to both the railway station and B&Q. I parked by the steps which led up to the platform.

He was there. Hunched on one of the fixed metal seats in the shelter, his back curved, shivering. The wind was barracking the plastic glass, making the overhead wires sing and the trees roar. A torn poster advertising the Snow White pantomime at the Palace Theatre whipped against the shelter. He didn't hear me approach.

'Adam,' I called.

He started and stood, emotions flashing across his face; confusion, fear, defiance. 'Go away. Leave us alone.'

He didn't even know who I was but he didn't want company. He took clumsy steps to the platform's edge, his shoulders shaking with cold, his lips blue. It was only a few feet down to the rails and the gravel around them but there was a recklessness in the movement that scared the shit out of me.

'Your mum sent me,' I told him. 'She wants you to come home.' It was impossible to talk intimately, the racket of the wind meant that I had to shout to be heard. 'She's worried about you.'

Behind Adam at the farthest point of the tracks I saw the unmistakable yellow pinprick light of a train appear. My heart stammered. I swallowed. 'I'm a private detective,' I told him.

'She knows?' he said incredulously, shock startling in his eyes.

'What?'

He looked as puzzled then as I was.

'Come and get in the car,' I yelled.

He shook his head.

The train light had grown a little larger. I willed him not to look back, not to get any daft, dramatic ideas. He shivered, a violent jerk that made his teeth rattle.

The wind flung more rain at us, bucketfuls. It sounded like stones hitting the shelter. It ran off my cagoule and soaked my knees, I could feel tiny cold rivulets running down my neck and soaking into my clothing. 'Adam, she's really worried. She asked me to find you.' He shook his head, his brow creasing.

'Adam.'

'Is he there?' he said with loathing.

'Your father? He went out to look for you. He's back home now.'

'Did she tell you about him?'

'She told me that you had a row.'

He waited as if there was more. He looked down at the track.

I thought I could hear the beat of the train galloping along the wires. A different rhythm from the wind. The light was bigger. I wiped rain off the tip of my nose and my forehead.

'Adam.'

'What's the point?' He turned away from me. He could see the train.

My pulse drummed quicker.

I stepped closer, trying to judge the distance so I could possibly reach him if needed but not get so close as to crowd his space and maybe force his move. His sweatshirt was plastered to his back. He was painfully thin, his neck looked

180

white and scrawny, his elbows sharp points, the hand at the end of his arm too big for the rest of him.

'She cares about you,' I answered him. I inched a bit closer. 'She loves you.' The train was much nearer now, I could make out the shape of the cab. It was travelling at great speed, clattering towards us. The Airport Express, it wouldn't stop here.

He was standing on the very edge of the platform beyond the white line which marked the safety zone. One of his trainers was gaping open at the side where the stitching had gone.

I glanced at the train again and its hooter blared like a foghorn, loud and urgent and unending. Adam flinched at the sound. I shifted one foot forward, stared at his neck. I'd use my right arm to grab him and pull back. Safer than trying to clutch his sweatshirt which could tip him over the edge.

'She needs you, Adam,' I yelled. 'She needs you.' Remembering how Susan had talked of his protective attitude towards her.

Was he going to jump?

I got ready to spring, then he turned my way, just as the train entered the station. It hurtled past us and we both ducked and moved back as the force of the air pushed at us and the scream of the hooter sounded again.

It clacked away leaving us with only the moan of the wind. I tried to read his face but I couldn't. He looked glazed. Would he have jumped? Had he been bluffing? Had it been a show for me or had my arrival thwarted his plan?

If things were so bad what on earth was going on in his head? He needed help. But first he needed to go home, get warm and dry.

'Adam, come on.'

He followed me silently, bowing into the wind.

We got in the car and I found an old j-cloth in the glove compartment and used it to dry my hands.

Adam stared at his knees. He'd shut down on me. He shook spasmodically. I drove him home. I was wet through to the skin. I concentrated on the physical, not wanting to dwell on the emotional trauma of the last half hour.

I drew into Burnside Drive and stopped opposite the house. The lights were on. I wondered if the heating was. If there was hot water. The car was in the drive. Ken Reeves' car. I stared at it.

Shock rippled through my cheekbones, made me swallow fast. Silver Mondeo, and in the barley-sugar glow of the streetlight, a crumpled bumper.

Adam moved to release his seat belt.

'Don't.' I started the engine and drove on round the crescent, stopped again.

'York,' I said to him. 'Blandford Drive. It was your father.'

And he began to cry.

CHAPTER FORTY-ONE

I kept the heater running in the car and soon the windows were opaque with condensation and the air redolent of wet hair and male body odour. Adam cried for a while, gulping and sniffing. Wiping his face on his sleeve. 'She knows?' he had said at the station when I'd told him I was a private eye. Meaning about his father. When he quietened he said in a husky voice.

'She doesn't know, does she? You didn't either?'

'Not till now.'

'Don't tell her.'

I sighed. 'I have to, Adam.'

'Why?'

'It's my job. Your mum wanted me to find out what was happening with you. Now I have.'

'Please don't tell her,' he begged me.

'It has to come out. Your mum knows you went to York and I've promised to find out who lives in the house. 21 Blandford Drive.'

'You followed me?' he said dully.

'Yes. And we couldn't work out why you were there.'

He didn't say anything for a moment then he cursed. 'Bastard, fucking bastard.'

I knew who he meant.

'How did you find out?' I asked him.

'Colin, this friend. It was his birthday, in the summer holidays. We went to York. The Viking place. I got him a voucher, you know, for Comet and Superdrug, and there was a Comet in York. Colin was getting a mini-disc player, he'd saved up and he'd enough with the voucher.' He took a long breath in and out, pressed his palms between his knees. 'He was there. I saw him kissing this woman at the counter. He goes off and she's still waiting. I thought I'd gone mad. Maybe it was a double. You get that sometimes, doubles. She was ordering a dishwasher. I wanted to be wrong, so I listened for the name and the address.'

'Blandford Drive,' I said.

'Mrs Reeve,' he choked on the words.

I exhaled. Listened to the rain slapping against the car. Heard an alarm start, a high-pitched keening.

'I had to make sure. I so wanted to be wrong. You can't tell her. You can't,' he was impassioned. 'She'll . . . what will she do?'

'I don't know. But don't you think she's entitled to the truth? Can you imagine carrying on like this? Keeping it from her? Missing college, not looking after yourself, messing up.'

'I'll go to college.'

'It's not just that.'

'It'll wreck everything.'

'Adam, bigamy's a serious offence. A crime. I need to talk to your mum. Not tonight but tomorrow when your Dad's at work. I don't know what'll happen but she'll need your help, you can be sure of that. You go home in a minute, don't say anything. Go to college tomorrow and come straight home after. Will you do that?'

He nodded. Stared desolately at the windscreen.

'I am sorry,' I said to him.

'Will he go to prison?' he said tightly.

'I don't know. I'll try and find out what the law is before I see your mum.'

'I hate him,' he said. 'I bloody hate him.'

'Yes.'

'If you talked to him, told him we knew, that he had to stop it . . .' He knew he was talking a fantasy. As though one family could be dropped into a hole and buried out of sight and the truth concreted over.

'No, Adam. When your mum hired me she'd no idea what you were involved in. Could have been drugs, crime, anything. She still wanted to know. She was beside herself worrying about you and she almost didn't care what it was, once she knew then there was a chance she could help.'

A little sob escaped.

'What she hated most was the secrecy, not knowing. I have to tell her.'

I cleared the windows, turned the car round and took him back. I watched him get to the door and someone open it. He disappeared inside.

Sleep was fitful. Gale force winds roared round the house and blew about anything they could shift. A car alarm was ringing on and on, unattended.

My thoughts wove endlessly round the daunting events that awaited me the following day. Meeting Bryony Walker, breaking the news of her husband's bigamy to Susan Reeve. I got a swing of anxiety too. Would Adam Reeve do anything foolish in an attempt to spare his mother? I nearly rang her but what could I say? She was anxious for him already, she hardly needed someone else to tell her to keep an eye on him. And perhaps now the secret was no longer his to bear he'd be able to settle once the shock waves had passed. However his mother took it their lives would change completely once I broke the news.

At four thirty the wind abated but the alarm shrilled on, a dog did an occasional duet with it. Impossible to ignore. I went down to the kitchen and made a cup of tea. Digger lay beside the armchair and made no protest when I used him for a footstool. I could feel his warmth through my slippers.

I sipped the tea and tried to think of things domestic. We could get the tree on Saturday. I'd promised them, after all.

Ray could get it when he was doing the big shop. Would he prefer new music to Marvin Gaye? Would he think I was making a point if I got him Marvin Gaye? I looked through the pile of cards that needed stringing up. Another job. Laura wore hats a lot. There were some nice fleecy ones about. What did I really fancy for Christmas dinner?

It was too cold to stay up and there was nothing productive I could do in the middle of the night so I returned to bed and covered my head with the duvet to muffle the alarm. Slowly I slipped into sleep.

'Mummeee!' Maddie's yell pierced like tin. I sat bolt upright, then went quickly to her room before she screamed again.

'Mummy, it was a dream. There was a giant ant and it was trying to eat me.'

I gave her a hug. 'It's just a dream. It's gone now. You lie down and go back to sleep.'

'What's that noise?'

'An alarm.'

'Why doesn't someone stop it?'

'I don't know.'

'Is it robbers?'

'No, the wind set it off.'

'What if I have another bad dream?'

'I don't think you will.'

'I might.'

'Maddie, I'm really tired.'

'Can I come in your bed?'

'No, you're too wriggly.'

'I won't wriggle.'

'Lie down.'

'Can you get giant ants?'

'No. Even the very biggest ones are so small they couldn't eat a person.'

'But if there were bizillions of them and they all had a small bite . . .'

'Maddie, I don't want to talk about ants, I want to go to sleep. There's no giant ants and that dream won't come back. Think about something nice.'

'What?' Sulky tone.

'Christmas. We're getting the tree on Saturday.'

'Really?'

'Yes. Think about that and the presents.'

She lay down and I covered her with the duvet. 'Night-night,'

Sleep take three.

I must have got some. It was dawn when I awoke. I certainly hadn't had enough though, not for the day that lay ahead.

187

CHAPTER FORTY-TWO

I had two cups of strong coffee which might have kept me awake but also made me feel slightly nauseous. I joined the other poor sods whose work lies via the motorway network and set out for Birch Services on the M62.

I concentrated hard; the lanes were busy and plenty of drivers made manoeuvres that had me cursing and stabbing the brakes while adrenalin squirted into my stomach. I tried various tapes but nothing suited my mood. In the end I found a radio station with audible reception but the laddish drivel got to me and I snapped it off.

I was more or less on time, got myself a banana milkshake and egg on toast. I was already ravenous. Pale food. I seemed to be having a lot of it. Comfort food or invalid food. Okay, maybe I needed some comfort but, although tired, I had survived my night in the rain without a sore throat or anything. I was not an invalid. I usually try and eat colourfully – a rainbow diet is a healthy diet, well as long as the colours aren't artificial. Blackpool rock wouldn't count.

I scanned the cafe. The staff wore sprigs of holly or tinsel on their hats and the tannoy let out a trebly rendition of Christmas songs: Bing Crosby, John Lennon, Slade wishing it could be Christmas every day. Want their head examining, I thought. You could sense the seasonal tension in the air, most of the conversations you heard, especially between women started with 'Are you ready for Christmas then?' A frenzy of planning and buying and then wrapping and cooking, and when it was all over there was the huge gap in the bank account to worry about.

I was sucking on my milkshake and contemplating whether stuffed aubergine and ensalata verde would be nicer for Christmas than chestnut, mushroom and asparagus pie when Bryony Walker introduced herself.

'I'll get a drink,' she said. 'Do you want anything?'

'No thanks, I'm fine.'

She was older than I'd expected. Her hair was sprinkled with grey, cut into a practical bob. She wore rectangular gold-framed glasses and golden earrings, a striped cotton sweater, long, dark skirt and Doc Marten boots. The boots were a nice touch.

She returned with her tea and a pastry. 'Where shall we start?'

'Can you tell me what happened at Horizons?'

She nodded, took a bite of pastry and a drink of tea. She had the style of someone constantly in a rush. She swallowed a second mouthful of tea.

'Clive Edmonds joined us in '94. He was an excellent worker, enthusiastic, prepared to take the initiative, good rapport with staff and users. He built up a very successful arts project, regular workshops leading to fixed practical outcomes.'

I was trying to translate the last bit when she tutted at herself. 'Sorry, jargon. Means they actually made things, there was a goal. Some workshops are open-ended, so the outcome there might be self-esteem rather than a painting. Anyway, he was even good at raising funds which is a godsend in a set-up like ours. Year after year we have to raise the money to pay ourselves before we even think about funding projects. It's precarious and it's bloody awful as far as planning ahead goes. So, everything seemed fine. Then in '96, out of nowhere, one of the long-term centre users, girl called Katy, who'd been through the mental health system and back, told her mother that Clive

Edmonds had been abusing her.' She sighed briskly. Took a drink.

I stared at her, my mouth half open, a falling sensation in my stomach.

'Unfortunately the girls' mother, who should have known better, confronted Clive directly. He denied everything, said Katy was making false allegations. It didn't help that the girl had a fairly unreliable record. She'd been involved in petty crime, shoplifting, credit-card fraud at quite a young age and there was a background of abuse in the family.

'Anyway the management committee were all informed and they were running around trying to establish how the disciplinary procedures worked when Katy withdrew the allegations. She refused to put it in writing and didn't want to talk about it to anyone.' She shrugged her eyebrows. 'Social services had been informed but basically there was no case against Clive. The trouble was by this point I believed he was guilty.'

'Why?'

'Gut feeling. No more than that. He acted exactly as you'd expect an innocent person to act. He was patently hurt by what was being said. But deep down I believed Katy . . .' She tutted. 'Of course, any suspicions like that were taboo, completely out of order. If I'd breathed a word of it to anyone else and Clive got to hear of it then he could sue for constructive dismissal or defamation or whatever. As far as everyone else was concerned it was over, finished. Things carried on. Then Katy died. Took a bottle of Paracetamol. It was awful.' She shook her head slowly.

'One of her uncles came down to Horizons, barged in and laid into Clive. Clive fought back, more than was necessary. He hospitalized the guy. Another bloody awful mess. Clive left. Said the trust had gone and he couldn't work with the shadow of suspicion hanging over him. Never mind that we could hardly let him carry on when he'd used gross violence like that. He didn't work his notice or anything. Just went.'

'When was that?'

''97. It was almost another year before we found out anything else.'

I was all ears.

She drained her cup, set it down. 'I'm a counsellor. Part of my role is to be available for people who want to talk. What I'm saying now is strictly confidential,' she looked at me. Her eyes were the muddy green of river water. 'I have no proper proof for any of it and it won't stand up as evidence.'

I nodded my understanding.

'It was about a year later, I was doing a counselling session with a young woman. She became very agitated and she disclosed to me that Clive Edmonds had sexually abused her on several occasions.' She drew breath. 'Two months later, completely unsolicited, I had the same story from another user. Even though he had been gone so long they were both still extremely fearful of talking about it. It seems he'd threatened them constantly about what would happen if they ever told anyone. He would make sure they were sent to secure mental hospitals, they'd be detained indefinitely. No one would ever believe them. Only him.'

Miriam's call to Hattie. *They'll put me back in hospital . . . he'll punish me.*

'At the same time he was telling each of them how special she was, how gentle, beautiful, bright. How they had to be careful because no one would understand how they felt about each other.'

Oh, God. I pictured Miriam, getting into his car. Fancy man, Horace Johnstone had said.

'What could I do? The women flatly refused to make any complaint or have their accounts passed on to anyone. He was God knows where. I couldn't break confidentiality so,' she gave another short sigh, 'I tried carefully worded memos to social services in other counties because I knew he'd have started somewhere else doing the same thing.'

Was that what had triggered Miriam's collapse?

'But of course he'd changed his name. And to be frank, as far as Social Services are concerned he is way, way down the wanted list. They've loads of people they are already trying to nail with a lot more evidence; documented abuse stretching back years, survivors willing to testify, and even then it's not easy.' She leant forward. 'The only hope of stopping him is to do every step by the book. Get enough evidence to drown him and bring in the police. And that is only a hope. Half the time the police don't want to know, or they cock it up. See it as a woman's job, not macho enough, hunting abusers. This woman, the one whose family you're working for, she's made a complaint – will she testify?'

'She can't. I should have explained. She's dead. She committed suicide back in October.'

'Oh, God, I am sorry.'

'And I've no idea whether he was abusing her.'

'If not her then he's found someone else.'

I shook my head. 'What you've told me just now . . . there's never been so much as a whisper of anything like that from anybody. Nothing.'

'But I'm confused now,' she peered at me. 'What made you ring me in the first place? Why were you interested in Clive Edmonds?'

'The family wanted to know more about the hours before she died. That's why they hired me. Eddie Cliff, Clive Edmonds was the last person that we know of to see her alive. But he lied to me about that afternoon. I don't know why but he lied about when he'd seen her and where and I thought I'd try and find out more about him.'

'I got completely the wrong end of the stick. So no one where he works has made any complaints? Or made any allegations?'

'No.'

'So he just carries on.' She bit her lower lip.

'It's so hard to believe,' I said. 'He's so . . .'

'Nice? Great guy, solid.' She said bitterly. 'Only last year I had the same sort of conversation with someone who had heard of him, in Bristol, back in the eighties. Rumours, but it was him.'

'I was completely taken in.'

'So was I. I went out with the bastard.'

My jaw dropped.

'Oh, yes. Hook, line and sinker. So this is personal too.'

'What now?'

'Be vigilant.' She shook her head. 'I don't know.' She lifted her glasses, rubbed at the bridge of her nose. 'Until there's any complaint, your hands are tied. Do you know anyone on the Management Committee?'

I thought of Sharon but she was a worker now. And she thought Eddie was the bee's knees.

'Not really.'

'In some authorities the police and social services have mechanisms in place to work together on this sort of thing. You could alert them. A sympathetic police officer with the clout to act can make all the difference. You must prepare so that if and when allegations are made, everything is in place to protect the victims and prosecute him.'

It's not going to be up to me, I felt like saying; I'm a PI, this is just one of my cases, I don't work at the centre.

'But, basically, we have to wait for it to happen?'

She looked bleak. 'Unless someone comes forward from the past and is prepared to go to court.'

'It's like a trap.'

'Stinks. But that's how they get away with it. No report, no crime. No evidence, no testimony, no crime. It's all hidden. And no one wants to look.'

And Miriam? The picture I had of her was not some lonely girl desperate for attention. She had raised a family single-handed, worked for much of her life. She had friends, a place in the community. She was happy. Even that morning she'd been happy. No hint of depression. I found it hard to believe Eddie Cliff had been regularly abusing her. So maybe it had only happened the once. With such a severe reaction.

'There was no forensic evidence,' I said.

'Maybe you're right and she wasn't one of his victims. His pattern was the same according to the two I heard from. No full intercourse. He'd,' she cleared her throat, 'he'd feel them up, touch them and then they had to perform oral sex on him. That plus the threats and the promises.'

I didn't know lots about forensics but presumably sperm would disappear from the mouth more quickly than from the vagina. How long would traces remain? And if he used a hanky?

The sense of purpose with which our meeting had begun had dwindled into a shared sense of despair.

'There doesn't seem to be much you can do,' she said.

'There's the false references.'

'That could cost him the job but he'd move on, up to his old tricks.'

'Could the deception be publicised to prevent him applying for other posts?'

'The networks aren't there. You could notify social services but there are all the voluntary sector outfits, charities as well. It wouldn't be any hindrance to him. And until he's convicted he can't be put on the sex-offenders register. Square one.' She looked at her watch. 'I really ought to make tracks.'

'Thank you for coming.'

'You said he'd lied to you about this woman?'

'Yes.'

'Keep that to yourself,' she said. 'Don't challenge him.'

My stomach twisted.

'He's not stupid and if he senses he's going to get rumbled he'll be planning his way out.'

'I already have.'

'Oh, God.'

'But I accepted his explanation; we agreed it had been a misunderstanding.'

She looked doubtful. 'Are you a good liar?'

'Not brilliant.'

'Be careful' she said. 'He feeds off people. He's no qualms. If you corner him he'll do anything to escape.'

I imagined a rat going for my throat.

'You need a watertight case before you challenge him, you or whoever.'

A trap. But traps need bait. Who was the bait in the trap now? Jane with her endless chatter? Or sulky Pauline, or Sandy with her weight problem?

Who was the special one, seduced by his promises, silenced by his threats. Waiting for his summons, for a kiss, his touch, the breadth of his hand around her head as she knelt before him. Who was it this time?

CHAPTER FORTY-THREE

On the drive back I was reeling from the revelations, my head filled with questions clamouring for answers. Had he abused Miriam? Had it happened before or was that day the first time? It seemed to fit so well with her sudden breakdown but I forced myself not to accept it as fact. It was only supposition.

I was incredulous too. He was such a nice man, with his friendly nature and his apparent care for those he worked with. It was like Jekyll and Hyde, making beautiful things at the same time as he destroyed lives.

I tried to examine the evidence. There had been nothing in the postmortem report about sexual violence or even recent sexual activity. Or had the postmortem been shoddy too? They were supposed to check for those signs as a matter of routine along with looking at the major organs and documenting the appearance of the body, but would they? If the police were telling them it was suicide cut and dried? Would they bother? Would they do it cursorily? Or not at all?

It might never have happened. Just because he had done it at Horizons it didn't necessarily mean he was doing it to women at The Whitworth Centre. But if (and it was a big if) he had assaulted Miriam then it gave him a very good reason to lie to me about seeing her that afternoon.

Bryony Walker, who was more of an expert than me, was convinced he would be abusing wherever he worked. There were people like that – serial offenders: rapists, paedophiles.

If Harry came up with any more information on Eddie Cliff's previous places of work, there may well be victims there. Perhaps even someone willing to point the finger, a little less in fear of him with the passage of time?

My inbox held a solitary email. From Platt, Henderson and Cockfoot – the solicitors' firm whose freelancer was checking the electoral rolls for me. It confirmed what I now knew; Address: 21 Blandford Drive, York. Registered occupants: Mr Kenneth Reeve and Mrs Denise Reeve.

The man who had done the job for me added that the couple had been registered at the same address for the last ten years.

I found it hard to imagine the mindset of someone who could sustain a double life for so long. This wasn't just a short-lived affair but the man had two fully fledged families. Children being born, starting school, mouths to feed, relatives to visit. What drove someone to do that? And was he the same person in each household? Did he have identical clothes in both places? How did he manage holidays? Christmas? What on earth did he do at Christmas?

I printed a copy of the message out and put it in my file. I planned to see Susan Reeve early afternoon, before her children were due back from school. Enough time to break the news and stay with her as she tried to take it in. I rang to check it was convenient. She sounded subdued but thanked me for bringing Adam back. She had seen my car from the house. I was dreading having to tell her what was really going on.

I needed to find out what the score was for the offence of bigamy. Rebecca Henderson was in court but a colleague gave me a resumé. Basically, it was a case for prosecution and the police would go ahead even if none of the wronged individuals chose to press charges. Sentences varied widely; prison was an option but not a matter of course. It would all depend on the circumstances. I put the file in my bag.

I thought about Bryony Walker's advice. Find allies in social services, and a decent police officer. Who did I know in social services? No one. But I did have a social worker friend, Rachel, who might know who to try. I dug out her number and left her a message to call me.

As for the police, my dealings with them had often been messy and a little tense due to the nature of my work. I had no tame contact. A very nice PC had attended our last attempted break-in but he would be way down the pecking order. I needed someone with a bit of seniority. I wasn't even sure whether there was a sexual crimes unit in the city. I mulled it over for a few minutes but rather than go off half-cocked trying to identify someone, I thought it would be better to discuss it with social services first who would be up to speed on who did what and how.

I didn't know anything about the Management Committee at the Whitworth Centre apart from the fact that Sharon had been on it before she'd gone for the job. If I asked her for a list of members, without explaining why, could I trust her to keep it to herself? Would she be allowed to give out that sort of information? Was it in the public domain somewhere? It should be, if the centre was a charitable body. I was a bit hazy on the details but I was pretty sure the names of the committee would be published with reports and accounts. I could only try. Maybe ask her to fax me an annual report? If she wanted to know more I'd just have to bang on about discretion and confidentiality and apologize a lot.

I dialled the number.

But Eddie Cliff answered my call.

'Is Sharon there, please?'

'No. Is that Sal?'

Shit. 'Yes, erm . . .' I thought rapidly. 'She talked to me about the fair . . .'

'Volunteers. Can you help?'

I was taken aback. Why would he want me around, unless it was to keep an eye on me. Work out whether I still suspected him.

'Yes,' I said before thinking it through. Anxious only that I made the right noises. 'Just for an hour or so.'

'Excellent. We've a couple gone down with the flu so we are really pushed. If you could come midday? Help set up and with the initial rush? And then I think we'll manage. We usually do one way or another.'

'Fine,' I managed.

'See you then. I'll let Sharon know.'

'Thanks.'

My mouth was dry and my hand shaking as I replaced the receiver. He doesn't know you've met Bryony Walker, I told myself. He can't possibly know that. He probably just wants to suss out the lie of the land. A devious bastard, she'd called him.

I sat back, a blizzard of images and questions in my mind.

Had he assaulted Miriam? She arrived at the centre well and happy. No one saw her leave, but by the time she reached her church she was in a state. The whole weight of the world on her shoulders. The Craft Club members had noticed nothing but it had been a chaotic morning. Jane burning her arm with the batik wax, Melody upset. Why? A row at home; Eddie had said that. Another lie? Hiding something worse? Melody and Miriam had to clear up. Had Miriam told Melody? Had Melody seen something? She no longer went to the club. She was suicidal. Melody upset. *If not her then he's found someone else . . .* Bryony Walker's words.

I searched through my notes. Found the jottings I'd made at the sewing circle. Melody Gervase. Unusual name. I looked it up in the phone book. Just one. It had to be it. And the address in Barlow Moor. A few minutes away.

Mrs Gervase didn't want me to talk to Melody. At first she thought I was a journalist wanting to do a follow-up on the dramatic suicide rescue story that all the local papers had covered.

I showed her my card and explained who I was working for and what the Johnstones had asked me to do.

'I saw Melody at the sewing circle,' I said, 'and I realized later she'd spent Thursday morning with Miriam at the Whit-worth Centre.'

'She's not up to talking about all of this.'

'Five minutes,' I asked her. 'Please. It could be a real help. I promise I'll be as careful as I can be.'

I was aware that I was being less than honest with her but I sensed that any mention of my suspicions would earn me a swift exit from the house.

She hesitated.

'Please. The family are desperate to learn anything they can. They lost their mother. You understand. Even the small-est things become important.'

She hesitated.

'Please, Mrs Gervase.'

'She may not talk.'

I gestured 'so be it'.

We went into the back room where Melody was watching television. A lunchtime confessional show. Pain and betrayal writ large. Just the job. I could never work out the appeal in shows like that; did people like the there-but-for-the-grace-of-God aspect or was it sheer voyeurism, a load of sad losers to gawp at?

Melody had bandages round her wrists, just visible beneath her baggy sweatshirt. She looked younger than I remembered. She wore sports pants and sheepskin slippers. There was a crossword puzzle book on her lap.

Mrs Gervase used the remote control to turn off the televi-sion and asked me to sit down.

'Melody, this lady would like to have a word with you about Miriam; Miriam Johnstone.'

Melody gave me a guarded look, bent to pick at her nails.

'Melody, I met you at the sewing circle. Do you remember?'

Brief nod.

'I'm trying to find out everything I can about that Thurs-day, back in October when you were all doing batik at the Craft Club. I think someone or something upset Miriam, something that happened at the centre. If you can tell me what you remember it would be a real help.'

Melody continued to pick at her nails.

Her mother shook her head at me.

'Did you like Miriam?'

A nod. 'She died.' She spoke quietly and began to rock backwards and forwards.

'Melody,' her mother said anxiously.

'Yes,' I said. 'Was Miriam upset?'

'You better go,' Mrs Gervase said.

'It's a sign,' Melody said, her breathing speeded up, she looked at me, her dark eyes wide with panic.

'A sign?'

'That's enough.' Her mother stood. 'I can't let her get upset like this.'

'Melody?' I made a last attempt.

'She promised to help. She died. Don't say anything.' She implored but whether she was talking to me or to Miriam I couldn't say. 'Don't say anything, please. Please don't. You mustn't tell.' She was becoming frantic. Her mother moved to hold her, shushing at her till the 'please' quietened and the rocking slowed. I slipped into the hall and waited there.

Her mother came out, lips tight and marched to the door.

'Mrs Gervase, there have been rumours about one of the workers at the Whitworth centre. About abuse. I think that's what Melody was saying in there . . .'

'She's ill.'

'This man,' I began, 'I've found out . . .'

'You better go. I need to see to my daughter.'

'Do you understand what I'm saying?'

She stared at me, unspeaking. Silence is consent.

'Has Melody told you?'

'No, nothing,' she said quickly.

'And you don't want to find out what really went on?'

She shook her head impatiently, her face creased with distaste.

201

'Why? Because he threatened her?'

'She has to recover. She has a life ahead. This . . .' she had no word for it, 'dwelling on it can only damage her more. I will not have that,' she said fiercely.

'So you pretend it never happened?'

'I will not sacrifice her.'

She opened the door. The message was clear. Her look implacable.

I walked slowly to the car, breathing in the cold, misty air, fiddling with my gloves, feeling angry and sad about the whole bloody mess.

I unlocked the car and got in. Closed my eyes and thought. The new version: Eddie Cliff had been abusing Melody, Miriam had found out. I didn't know whether Melody had said something or she'd found out some other way. She'd been upset. Gone to church then home. Rung Hattie, panicking and talking about punishment and whether to say anything. A moral dilemma, fearful of her own safety. At what point had Eddie Cliff realized that Miriam knew? He comes to the house and she gets in his car. Why? If she knew what he was up to why on earth go anywhere near him? I didn't understand. And then what? Where did he take her? What did he do to her? Miriam at the car park. Had she been alone. I shuddered. Told myself not to be ridiculous. Was it that ridiculous?

I had information but none of it was any practical use in prosecuting Eddie Cliff. Melody wouldn't testify. Even if her health improved, her mother would never give her the support to stand up and bear witness. Would she heal? If there was no acknowledgement of the violence that had been done to her?

What would I do, if it was Maddie? Force her to give evidence? Make her speak out and so prevent others suffering? Or would I protect her? Spare her the pain of reliving the ordeal, the trauma of going over the abuse? Allow her the refuge of silence knowing that it gave space for others' cries to go unheard?

CHAPTER FORTY-FOUR

The day had turned out overcast, the light bleak. No wind or rain, a thin mist suspended still and grey. A briny smell hung in the air. The world was littered with broken twigs and branches, torn fences, stray rubbish; the legacy of the previous night's storm.

At home I ate a bowl of soup and began a shopping list for Ray. If I left it to him he always forgot essentials like sunflower oil or soap. I sometimes forgot to take the list but still remembered most of the stuff. Something to do with women's brain architecture. We also needed things like crackers for Christmas and it was nice to have traditional snacks about, like dates and nuts. I finally ran out of steam.

'I don't want to go, Digger.' The dog pricked up his ears at the mention of his name and slid his eyes my way. I procrastinated for another ten minutes, shoved a load in the washing machine and left.

'I'm afraid I've got bad news,' I told Susan Reeve.

'Oh, no,' she put her mug down, clasped her hands together. 'What's wrong? What's he done? What's happened?'

'It's not about Adam.'

'But . . .' She stopped, her face slack with incomprehension.

'It's about your husband.'

'Ken?'

There was no easy way to tell her. No helpful euphemism. I plunged on.

'The address in York, your husband lives there.'

'What?' she said crossly, as though I'd got it all wrong. Trying to slow down the impending blow.

'He's married to someone else, Susan, he's a bigamist.'

'No,' she said sharply. 'No.' She half rose from her seat.

'No,' she flung her arms wide, shoving the cup beside her which smashed against the cabinet and broke, splashing coffee on the floor and the cabinet door.

'I'm sorry,' I said.

I waited for some sign that she was ready for me to continue but she spoke next, her hands grabbing the table's edge, her face mottled with emotion.

'You said there were children?'

'Two.'

'No . . . no . . . no,' her yells rose in pitch and volume and she pulled at the table. I moved back quickly, my drink spilt on my legs. She heaved it onto its side, the papers and tray of bits and bobs scattered across the floor. She flung her chair aside too. Then she began to cry, her hands over her large glasses. I left her for a minute then went and righted the chair, put it behind her. Placed my hands on her shoulders. 'Sit down.'

I set the table upright. I looked around for a kitchen towel roll but couldn't see anything. She was crying almost soundlessly, her face wet with tears and mucus.

'Have you any tissues?'

'Toilet roll – upstairs.'

I brought it for her. I found a small dustpan and brush under the sink and cleared the shards of pottery. Wiped the cabinet and floor down and made fresh drinks. She wept all the while.

'Thank you,' she blew her nose. 'I'm sorry. I feel like I've been in an accident or something. I was in a car crash once and it felt just like this.'

'The shock.'

'There's no chance . . . it couldn't be a mistake?'

'No. I've checked the electoral roll. It's him.'

'You're sure, absolutely certain?'

'Yes.'

'How on earth did Adam know?'

'It was a complete fluke. He went to York with his friend Colin in the summer.'

'Colin's birthday!'

'Adam saw Ken and his . . . wife. They were giving delivery details in a shop. He overheard the address.'

'Oh, Adam.'

'He asked me not to tell you. Last night when I brought him home. I realized then, you see. The car, it was the same car I'd seen in York. I told Adam then that I'd worked out why he was in York. He begged me not to say anything. I told him it had to come out in the open. That I'd see you today. He was in quite a state last night,' shivering at the edge of the platform, 'he was worried about you.'

'Oh,' she stifled her cry with one hand, rubbed at her face. 'You never imagine . . . How could he do that to us? Working away, staying in B&Bs and all the time he's there. All this time poor Adam . . . And the house? We're going to lose this house . . . I can't take this in. The bastard, the rotten, bloody bastard.' She wiped her face again. 'Do you think she knows, the other one?'

'I doubt it.'

'How long?' Her face was hard, prepared for another slap.

'The couple have been living there for ten years.'

Her face fell apart. 'Oh, God,' she covered her nose and mouth with her hand; her eyes were wounded. 'Since Penny was born, before the twins. I won't have him back in this house. How could he? And the children . . .'

Daddy one day, Judas the next. Would they share her sense of betrayal?

'I just feel so angry,' she said. 'I want to get all his things and tear them up and throw them in the street and smash the car up and humiliate him . . . but the children . . . I can't

205

do those things because I care so much about . . .' she broke down. 'That's the difference, isn't it?' she said eventually. 'That's how he can do this and live with himself, because he doesn't really care?'

I didn't answer. I didn't know.

'I feel such a fool,' she said. 'It all makes sense now. Times when he had special sales exhibitions on, nights when the traffic was bad. Things he missed, Penny in the concert at the Royal Northern College,' her eyes shone with a harsh conviction, 'and the time Rachel was knocked down. I was in MRI with her and he was working, or so he said. He'd probably got his feet up . . . I blamed the job. I never once thought . . . not even an affair.'

She thought for a moment. 'We've been struggling; the bills, I can't keep Adam in shoes and trousers, everything has to be the cheapest, discounts, second hand. We haven't had a holiday in years. No bloody wonder is it? He'd be paying out for two families . . .' She choked on the thought.

'How can you be so wrong about someone? When I met Ken he'd just been promoted. I thought he was Mr Wonderful. He had a great sense of humour . . .'

She talked on recalling their courtship and marriage, the ups and downs, what had attracted her to him, how he was with the children when they were babies. The sort of reminiscence people do when someone has died, trying to capture a sense of the person as they were. Or in this case as they were before they were unmasked. Her account was coloured by a bitter irony that bled into everything. As she talked, the past was being rewritten in the light of his betrayal. Memories tainted; the picture skewing like water bleaching old photographs. Every so often she'd interrupt herself, taken aback anew by the magnitude of his wrongdoing and its implications. 'What do I tell the children?' she'd say, and 'all those lies,' but most of all, 'how could he?' and 'the bastard.'

'You need some legal advice,' I told her. 'Do you know anyone?'

She shook her head.

'I'll give you a number. It's likely he'll be prosecuted. Bigamy is a criminal offence. Sentences vary but he could go to prison.'

'Good,' she said bitterly. 'I hope he rots there. How could he? I just can't understand it. I can't. It doesn't make any sense.'

She talked on, an endless litany of moments of betrayal and expressions of shock.

At half past two I heard the sound of someone coming in the front door. I turned in my chair.

'Adam,' she said. 'He finishes early on Fridays.'

He came into the kitchen, his face strained with apprehension. 'Mum?'

'It's all right Adam,' she kept her voice steady. 'I know. I know everything. Big shock, eh? Your dad'll be leaving.'

'Have you talked to him?'

'Not yet. I've got the name of a solicitor.' Relying on the practical to make her way through this. 'I'm going to ring them in a few minutes, find out what we have to do. I might need your help, okay? We got to stick together now.' I could see tears standing in her eyes but she held them there, determined to be strong for him.

'Mum,' he wobbled a bit.

'Be for the best in the long run,' she said. 'Come here.'

She hugged him briefly, fiercely. 'It's going to be okay, yeah?' She let him go.

'Yeah,' he said hoarsely.

'Put the kettle on then, will you? And get me a couple of Paracetamol. And put the heating on as well, eh? Warm this place up a bit.'

Self-defence was gruelling. It was the last thing on earth I wanted to do, but I dragged myself down there and knuckled under.

'Had a hold-up on Tuesday at the shop,' Brian, the security guard, told me. 'Kids with bloody great guns.'

'Oh, Brian.'

'Shitting myself, I was. Did all the right stuff, no one got hurt. Still makes you think. Not much of a job is it? Only so long you put up with that sort of thing. Fourth time this year.' He shook his head.

'What else would you do?'

He shrugged. 'Dunno. You like your work, don't you?'

'Depends when you ask me.'

'Not had a good week?'

Bigamy, sexual abuse, deceit and betrayal, lives falling apart.

'There've been better.'

'Oi, you two,' Ursula yelled, 'stop nattering and get on with it.'

CHAPTER FORTY-FIVE

I couldn't settle that evening. I wrote half a dozen Christmas cards which would arrive too late no matter when I posted them and I drank too much wine. Easy drinking it said on the label and it was. Absolutely no problem at all.

The phone rang late. Rachel, my social worker friend. I explained to her that I'd got embroiled in a case of suspected sexual abuse but there was no clear-cut evidence at this stage.

'Children?'

'No, vulnerable women. Well, woman singular at this stage. It's all at a place for people with mental health problems or low self-esteem; some have learning difficulties. It's all very circumstantial, no proof like I say. I need someone to talk to who's had experience of this, knows the ropes.'

'Probably Geraldine Crane . . . it is Manchester?'

'Yes.'

'Let me check. If not, there's a new guy, Toby Smith. I'll find out. There is an emergency service if someone needs getting to a place of safety immediately.'

'No, it's not like that.'

'I'll get back to you first thing after Christmas and you can talk to Geraldine or Toby then.'

I thanked her and we exchanged some brief news about ourselves before ending the call.

What would I tell them? Everything I suppose; the facts like Eddie Cliff forging references for his job, the rumours, the unsubstantiated claims from the clients at Horizons, my meeting with Melody. They would know what, if any, action could be taken. Maybe they could start a covert enquiry; it happened in cases like this didn't it? Get the help of other agencies and invite people to talk to them about incidents from the past. If Bryony Walker was right there would be a trail of victims from Eddie Cliff's life. Whether any of them would have the courage to testify was another matter. When I got the information from Harry it could be a starting point for further enquiries; a route map of his career. And if one person spoke out, that chink could be like a break in a dam. Others might come forward and there would then be no way to hide it all again.

Meanwhile Saturday awaited and my appearance at the Whitworth Centre Christmas Fair loomed. I had to go and behave as naturally as possible. Anything to reassure him that I was no threat, that I had accepted his explanation of being seen collecting Miriam on another day. But it would be hard to stomach, now I knew what had happened with Melody. Now I knew how he operated. When my every instinct was to have him seized and see him stand trial. However the detective in me was also aware that there could be opportunities for picking up some more information now I had a different perspective on events.

'We've put you on table decorations,' Eddie grinned. Nice as pie. What was really going on behind those crinkly eyes? 'That's your table. Sharon's got some red paper for cloths, once that's on you can put out this box. And if you sell out there's spares in there.' He pointed. 'Someone will be bringing round a float. Everything's a pound so no worry with change. Leave you to it?' Brisk and breezy.

I nodded, smiled, hoped it didn't look as false as it felt.

'Charles,' he called. 'Give us a hand with the Grotto.'

Sharon arrived with a roll of red paper edged with holly motif. Together we unrolled it and cut it to fit.

She moved onto the next table and I lifted up the box and

brought out the contents; candle holders, table and tree decorations, concoctions of fir cones, berries, glitter and tinsel, silver and gold spray. A woman gave me a saucer and £20 in coins and notes.

'Okay everybody, we're opening the doors.' He had changed. Cowboy to Santa Claus. Ho ho ho. I felt sick.

A steady stream of people came in and the next hour passed in a blur of chatter and sales. I finally got relieved by another volunteer.

I ran into Jane in the toilets. She had a ring of tinsel on her head, her hair was just right for the Christmas fairy but her face looked red and angry from the eczema.

'Hello,' she remembered me. 'I've nearly spent up.' She held aloft a bulging carrier bag.

'I bet you made half of them, didn't you?'

This tickled her. 'Yes, I made half of them and now I've bought them. And I made half of them.' She laughed.

'Jane, you know the day you got burnt?'

She pursed her lips and frowned. 'It hurt, that, really hurt.'

'How did it happen?'

'It was hot, the wax in the little pan. I was stirring it and it tipped onto me. I was screaming and they said "oh, get Eddie, get Eddie." '

'Eddie wasn't there?'

'He was in his office, he had to get a letter for Melody to fill in. Miriam ran to get him and you know what he said? Only a little burn. I was on fire, it felt like. Really hurt. I said take me to the hospital.'

'Where was Melody when you got burnt?'

'In the office,' she laughed as if I was stupid, 'getting the form.'

I nodded.

'You said she was upset?'

'She was crying in here. After they put the dressing on me I saw her. Miriam was looking after her. She had a row at home.'

Two women came into the washroom. I changed the subject. 'Are you going to buy anything else?' I asked Jane.

'I'm going to see Father Christmas.' She shrieked with laughter. 'Have you seen him? It's Eddie dressed up. Last year I got nail varnish and some stickers.'

I went out with her into the melee and had a look round some of the stalls. I bought two trinkets for our tree. Sharon, sporting a holly head-dress, was at the entrance in conversation with a tall, smartly dressed Afro-Caribbean woman.

'This is Mrs Wood,' Sharon said. 'Chair of our Management Committee. Sal's been helping us out.'

'Thank you,' Mrs Wood said.

'Sal's a private eye,' Sharon said.

'Really?' Her eyebrows rose and fell. 'That sounds intriguing.'

'Can be. This is very successful,' I nodded to the hall.

'Yes. The whole project has done extremely well. Immense amount of work though, not just today but week in week out. Sharon,' she turned to her. 'I'll stay here for a while, you go see to Chantelle.'

'Great.' Sharon left us.

'You employ people here, that's part of your job?'

'The committee as a whole, yes. Plus policy, planning, training, health and safety, you name it.'

'So if anyone had a complaint who would they talk to?'

Her brow creased, she looked at me sharply, alarm in her eyes.

'To me in the first instance.'

I felt in my bag and fished out a card and pen, ready to take her number.

'Touting for business?' Eddie Cliff walked towards us, still in his red and white robes.

My stomach tightened. 'Every bit helps,' I joked. I passed Mrs Wood my card. 'So yes,' I said. 'Tell your friend to give me a ring, it's completely confidential.' I prayed she'd cotton on and not say anything to Eddie. She looked slightly unsure but took my card. I struggled to maintain some semblance of calm.

Eddie Cliff looked at me brightly, inquisitive ultramarine eyes, then at Mrs Wood.

'It suits you,' she said drily.

'I'd better go,' I said and fled with my skin crawling.

I knew Ray was expecting me back so he could go shopping but I needed to straighten my thoughts. I drove the car round to nearby Plattfields and parked on the roadside. I concentrated.

Eddie Cliff and Melody Gervase had been alone in the office when Jane burnt herself. He was probably well out of order leaving the group unattended but I bet no mention of that was made in any accident report. So, Jane got burnt and Miriam hurried to get Eddie. She walks in on them. A big shock all round. Eddie has to see to Jane, apply first aid and calm her down and meanwhile Miriam and Melody go to the toilets, the only place he's not allowed. Melody is distressed (at being caught out? At something Eddie has said?) and Miriam promises to help. Melody maybe asks her not to say anything. She's very frightened. *Don't tell, don't tell.* She never goes back to the Craft Club after that. She heard about Miriam's death. *A sign*, she said. *She promised to help.* She died. Look what happens. Never dared go back. Waited, not knowing if her withdrawal would be enough to spare her. She must have been terrified when I showed up at the sewing circle asking questions.

So, the group leave. Melody and Miriam are supposed to clear up. Then what? Does Eddie make more threats? Underplay it? Pretend it never happened? He could probably rely on his threats keeping Melody quiet. But Miriam, who had stumbled upon the abuse? There were no sweet promises or soft kisses to bind her to him. When Miriam rang Hattie Jacobs, she had talked of being put in hospital if she told them, that it was awful and he would punish her. Eddie's threats?

Why then had she let him in, gone in his car? She was scared, she knew what he was doing. Why hadn't she just locked her door and refused to come out? He hadn't physically forced her into the car or Horace Johnstone would have said so.

And then what?

One way or another, Eddie Cliff had driven Miriam Johnstone to her death.

I couldn't carry it on my own another day.

I went to the police.

CHAPTER FORTY-SIX

Elizabeth Slinger police station is a large purpose-built facility in Withington, near the hospital. I spoke to the desk sergeant who checked and told me the inspector who had been in charge of the police enquiry into Miriam's death was on leave for Christmas. I then explained to two different people, at intervals of ten minutes, why I was there and that I had new information relating to that death, that I suspected foul play. After hemming and hawing and raised eyebrows and throat clearing and several suggestions that after the holiday would be better, they finally took me through to a small interview room where I could wait to see someone in the serious crimes section.

I rang Ray and told him I would be a while longer.

Detective Sergeant Elland made careful notes while I went through my story. I told him what I knew, what I'd heard and what I suspected. He checked some details and then asked me if I had spoken to anyone in Social Services regarding the alleged abuse.

'Not yet; I hope to as soon as possible.'

'We do try to work together on cases like this. Now, the suspicion of foul play, that wasn't raised at the inquest?'

'No, although her family have said all along that her fear of heights would have made her incapable of jumping off that building. Plus she was sane and healthy that morning.'

'It's not hard evidence, though.'

'I know,' I tried not to show my frustration. 'But this man

lied to the police about when he last saw the victim. He said he'd seen her at midday but he picked her up after two o'clock.'

'According to the ex-husband?'

'Yes. And Miriam rang her friend and said he would punish her and send her to hospital.'

'She didn't identify him by name.'

'No but together with the fact that he lied and the history he has . . .'

'Alleged history. He has no criminal record that you are aware of?'

'No. But the police never spoke to this friend that she called, or to the ex-husband; it's new evidence. They never even checked all the CCTV tapes, they could have seen him driving in with her. They didn't even ask for it, only the one for the top floor and that wasn't working.'

'Well, if it appeared to be suicide . . .'

'And if it had been a white man, would any more effort have been put in? A rich white man, no hint of illness, well connected – what then?'

'We don't work like that,' he said coldly.

'She was black.' I said. 'She had a history of mental illness, she got second class treatment.'

'Look, I didn't work the case and I haven't got the papers here, but the facts at the time led to a suicide verdict. The coroner was satisfied.'

'The family weren't. There weren't enough facts.' I stressed the words. 'No one contacted her friends, no efforts were made to establish how she got to town, she didn't drive, she didn't have a car. But no one bothered. Mad, black woman, jumped. End of story.'

Even I had been sure that they'd reached the right verdict when Connie had first hinted at other possibilities. But I hadn't known then how token the official investigation had been.

'I can't agree with you,' he said. 'And I don't think wild

216

allegations about the conduct of the enquiry will help you get a fair hearing. As for this new information, I'll discuss it with my colleagues in the unit and a decision will be made as to whether any further enquiries need to be made.' His eyes were glazing over; he'd heard all he wanted to and now he wanted rid of me.

'And they might not be?'

'Hard to say. What you've got is pretty shaky. To be frank there is always a question of priorities and resources.'

'Murder must be a pretty high priority.'

'Oh, yes. But what you've got is barely grounds for re-opening a case. If it was in my hands I'd want a word with this Mr Cliff again, particularly if he's been giving false information. But it doesn't follow that there'd be a fresh investigation launched. It may be that there's more of a case to make on the sexual abuse allegations. I suggest you discuss it with social services as you planned and meanwhile I'll have a word at this end.'

'When?'

His jaw tightened a fraction. 'As soon as someone from the initial investigation is back from leave.'

'When will that be?'

'I'll have to check.'

'Will you ring me, let me know what they say?' I was determined to hound them until I had a response.

He considered this.

'I'll need to know if I'm talking to social services, won't I?'

'You can ring here,' he said. 'But I suggest you leave it till near the end of the week.'

'And who should I ask for?'

'You can ask for me,' he said crisply.

And that was it.

The clock would creep round slowly, the world would keep turning, Eddie Cliff would go about his business and at some point the police would consider their response. I'd wanted action, swift and decisive, vindication, recognition. But it doesn't work like that. Not in those circumstances. And I was haunted by the notion that he might just get away with it all. That he could go on because he was too clever and those he hurt too afraid to stop him.

From the car I called Connie Johnstone.

'I was going to ring you,' she said. 'I'd not heard anything.'

'Yes. I need to see you. Can you do it tomorrow, can you come to the office?'

'When?'

Laura and I were taking the kids out at some point. We'd promised. I'd been neglecting them at weekends. If we were to go anywhere the morning would be better for that. It would be dark early.

'About two?'

'Yes, Martina has a dance class so it would be just me and Patrick.'

'That would be better actually.'

'Have you managed to find out any more?' I heard the anticipation in her voice.

'Yes,' I said. 'I'll see you tomorrow.' It was impossible to say anything else without launching into a full blown account.

I rang Roland on his mobile and told him I'd be seeing Connie and Patrick the following afternoon.

'And you're gonna tell them about my dad?'

'Yes.'

He was quiet.

'It'll be okay,' I said, 'There's a lot of other stuff going on, Roland. The thing with your dad, it's not going to be that important really.'

I finished the call and sat for a few moments, my heart leaden in my chest. I thought of Miriam getting into Eddie's car, the drive to Cannon Street. Why there? Driving up the ramps to the top floor. Miriam beside him, quiet or crying or talking, perhaps trying to make sense of it all. Eddie opening

the car door, her door, pulling her, lifting her, Miriam clutching her handbag, rendered senseless by her crippling fear of
heights, twisting to get away but not enough strength, like a
dream, running in sand . . .

I rubbed at my face, shook my head in an effort to clear
the images. I took a couple of slow breaths and then started
the car and drove to my office. Harry had sent me an email
and a pile of attachments. I opened these in turn and speed-
read them. They were cuttings from newspapers, most of
them. References to a Cliff Edwards, manager of a residen-
tial home in Exeter, and a Clive Edmonds, project worker
at a new arts centre for people with learning difficulties in
Shrewsbury, a picture showed 'Clive' and three clients holding pottery they had made. There were also several items on
Eddie Cliff, who was a minor golfing celebrity in the eighties and bore no resemblance to the man I knew and lastly a
feature on Clifford Eddy receiving a civic award for work in
the community from Bristol City Council. The same man,
variations on a name, a list of jobs each giving him access
to vulnerable girls and women, putting him in a position of
trust and of power.

If the police did nothing and social services were willing
to begin an inquiry I could give them this lot to start with.

While Ray went shopping I got the Christmas decorations
and the cast iron tree stand out from the cellar. The children
helped me sort through what we had, we threw away some
broken ornaments. The fairy lights still worked. I cleared a
space for the tree in the corner of the lounge.

My mobile began to tweet.

'Sal Kilkenny.'

'This is Mrs Wood. You wished to talk to me.'

My pulse quickened. 'Yes. In confidence.'

'Of course. You mentioned a complaint?' She didn't sound
happy about it.

'Yes.'

219

'*Jingle bells, Batman smells, Robin's run away . . .*'

'Shush,' I hissed at the children and pointed to the play-room.

'Sorry,' I went on, 'I'm afraid it's very serious and I don't want to speak out of turn but it involves Eddie Cliff. I've actually been to the police about it this afternoon though it might also be an issue for social services. I wanted to get your details, as chair of the management, so that I can pass them on to the authorities. It's out of my hands now.'

'Good grief,' she said. 'What's going on?'

I took a deep breath. 'There may have been some incidents of sexual abuse.'

'Surely not,' she said sharply. 'Eddie! Have you any proof?'

'It's hearsay at the moment,' I admitted. 'I'm convinced there's substance behind it and I realize how important it is that it's dealt with properly. There have been allegations in the past.'

'In the past?'

'There were similar incidents at Horizons in Hull where he worked.'

'But they gave us references.'

'He forged them.'

'You know this for a fact?'

'I've spoken to his former employer. Yes.'

'This is awful,' she said.

'I know. And there's more . . . other . . . suspicions that I've asked the police to look into.'

'What?'

'Eddie Cliff lied to the police when they were investigating Miriam Johnstone's death.'

'The lady who committed suicide?'

'That's right. The police may want to speak to him again. They haven't decided yet.'

'Why would he lie? Exactly what are you suggesting?' she demanded.

'*Rudolph, the red-nosed reindeer,*' the kids began, their

220

voices carrying and becoming louder; they were out of sight so I couldn't gesture to them to shut up. I bent down, trying to shield the phone with my body.

'He may have had some involvement. It's possible.'

'What sort of involvement?'

I didn't want to spell it out. Until there was solid evidence against him I sensed she would be protective of him. 'I think he may know more about what happened than he is saying. He was the last person to see Miriam alive.'

'You think he was a witness?'

Worse. 'Yes,' I said.

'I can't believe it,' she said, 'any of it. Of all the people I've worked with in my time . . . there's never been any concerns expressed. Quite the reverse and then this.'

'. . . had a very shiny nose, like a lamp post . . .'

She exhaled then became businesslike. 'Well, we obviously need to get to the bottom of it. If you're making some terrible mistake I would want to quash any rumours before they take hold. Who else knows about all this? You say you've spoken to the police already?'

'Yes. I hope to talk to social services after the holiday. And the police have said they will be considering whether they intend to take any further action. I'll give them your details so they can liaise with you as his employer. Social services will know the proper procedures and everything.'

'False allegations are not unheard of,' she said. 'As his employers, the committee will have to make sure that he gets treated fairly at the same time as we ensure that there's no risk to any of the people who use the centre. But if there is gross misconduct going on I can tell you now we will act swiftly and decisively. If this is just hearsay, though . . .'

'. . . called him names, like tomato face . . .'

'Yes,' I interrupted her. 'As yet, no one has been prepared to speak openly about what he's done, either here or in his previous place of work. If social services or the police can't get anyone to testify, I don't know what will happen. And,

221

like I said, the police will have to decide whether he has further questions to answer about Miriam Johnstone.'

'Good grief,' she said again, the realization of crisis rocking her formal efficiency. 'I hope you're wrong.'

I said nothing.

'. . . *in any reindeer games, like Monopoly . . .*'

'If I could have your number?'

She gave me her work and home phone numbers. Exchanged terse goodbyes.

I put my phone down and went into the playroom. 'I was on the phone,' I said. 'I couldn't hear.'

They looked at me as though I was speaking Mandarin then went on with their game.

As I went through to the kitchen I heard strange sounds coming from the cellar; rustling noises. The door was ajar and I switched the light on at the top of the stairs and went down. The sounds were coming from the little room underneath the front of the house. We use it for storing stuff. I felt a stir of unease. Something was in there. Rats attack if they're cornered. Oh, God. I went into Ray's workshop and selected a long piece of doweling. I went slowly back and used it to pull aside the curtain we had tacked up there in place of a door.

Digger was crouched over, gnawing away at part of a body. I felt a wave of nausea rise in my throat and shock charge through me. 'No, Digger!' I yelled.

He peered up at me and stole out of the room and past me. I heard the kids coming, alerted by my shout.

It was the turkey, just the sodding turkey. Relief made my legs shake. I let the curtain fall back.

'What is it,' Maddie said. Tom behind her, eyes alight with interest.

'Nothing, it's all right. Digger was after the turkey.'

'Where is it?'

'In there,' I pointed.

'Let's see,' said Tom.

222

I obliged.

Digger had chewed away most of one thigh but the rest looked intact.

'Gross!' Maddie said.

'It's all spotty,' said Tom.

'Like goose bumps,' I agreed, 'but those are turkey bumps.'

'I'm not eating any of that,' Maggie announced.

Neither was I.

'It'll be fine; we'll give it a wipe and once it's cooked you can decide.'

'But Digger's licked it and everything.'

Tom chortled. 'And he licks his bum.'

'Well, you can always have a veggie Christmas dinner with me.'

'That's worse,' she said.

Reluctantly I picked the thing up and took it to wash off the grime from the kitchen floor. I put it back on a shelf in the same room but way out of Digger's reach.

Ray arrived back not long after with several boxes of provisions and a big, bushy spruce. The children related with glee the story of Digger and the turkey. I reassured Ray that not much damage had been done. The four of us dressed the tree together, sharing out the baubles and tinsel equally between the children who kept squabbling.

I thought of the Reeves family. What sort of Christmas awaited them? And the family in York – when would the bombshell hit them? Would Ken be spending Christmas in either household? Or in a B&B somewhere getting drunk in his room and missing his children? How long would it take the police to move and begin proceedings against him? What a hopeless mess. It had been a peculiar case. From a professional point of view I'd done a good job. I'd been successful in getting to the root of what was behind Adam's troubled behaviour but the outcome had been devastating rather than satisfying. The best that could come of it was that Adam would settle again, rediscover his direction in life and that Susan would be able to hold the family together, help them adjust to a new life.

And the Johnstones. The first Christmas without their mother. Still grieving and tomorrow I had to tell them that I thought Miriam had been killed. That she had not chosen to leave them, that she'd not been so distressed that death seemed the safest place but that she had been taken from them, forcibly, that it was murder. And almost worse than this I had no real, solid proof. So the chance of being able to pursue justice was by no means guaranteed. The police may or may not review the case. It would be in their hands and they had hardly given their all the first time round. I had to tell them the truth as I saw it. But it wasn't some gleaming, bright clear thing but a weight; sordid and slippery and hard to bear.

I climbed on the chair to put the star on top and the tree was done. We turned off the light and plugged in the fairy lights. It was lovely, the tiny lights glowing and twinkling, the scent of pine filling the room.

'I can't wait till Christmas,' Maddie said, 'I just can't wait. Are you excited, Mummy?'

'Mmm,' I said.

But all I felt, burdened by the dirty truth, was apprehension, drumming its fingers on my heart, clutching at my belly; a tense tattoo of dread to accompany me onward to what lurked ahead.

CHAPTER FORTY-SEVEN

Stuart took one look at my face and his expression shifted. The warmth replaced by uncertainty. Oh, Stuart. Did I really have to go through with this? But I couldn't switch back to how I felt before, my emotions wouldn't rewind. I didn't feel excitement now just embarrassment and I realized I felt sorry for him. Not a healthy basis for anything.

'Come in,' he said. 'I've opened some wine.'

'Thanks.' I took my coat off and sat on the sofa, took the glass he offered me. There was the evocative aroma of wood smoke from the stove. I wondered if he was burning something special – apple or cherry – in my honour. Fluttering in my stomach.

'About Natalie,' he said. 'I'm sorry. I had no idea she'd do something like that.'

'Stuart, I've been thinking. This – us – it isn't what I want at the moment.'

'But you can't hold me responsible for how she behaves. I'll talk to her.'

'No. It's not that, well not just that.' I sighed. I could feel my cheeks burning and it wasn't the fire. 'Maybe it's the timing, I don't know. Maybe I'm not ready for a relationship, too long on my own. I don't know.' I cupped the glass in my hands, studied the ruby surface, the reflections from the stove and the candles.

A pause.

'You never said anything. I thought we were getting on really well.'

I thought back. We had been and then we hadn't. Or I hadn't. When had it changed? When did I start to notice those little flaws, like how he was better at talking than listening, how he took his time to return my calls? And, once noticed, they seemed to grow until they were all I could see. If there had been more of a pull, more than a general sexual attraction, it might have been worth talking to him about all that, investing in trying to make it work but there wasn't.

I drank some wine.

'It was good,' I told him. 'But it's changed for me. I'm sorry. I can't really explain it very well but I don't want to carry on. I'm sorry.'

'Can we talk about it?' He stared at the fire.

'I've made up my mind.'

He exhaled. Filled his glass and drank some.

I felt awkward and desperate to leave.

'If you need some time . . .'

Oh, don't!

'No. Thanks but . . . I think I'll go.'

I'd been there all of five minutes.

'That's it?' He asked. 'No chance to talk about it, nothing?' Emotion edged his voice. 'You've decided so that's it? It was good, you said so yourself, maybe it could be like that again? If we don't talk about it . . .'

'Stuart . . .'

'Please, Sal, listen.'

It was the last thing I wanted to do. Was I being unfair? I gave a small nod.

'I like you, I like you a lot. You're the first person I've met since Nat and I broke up that comes anywhere near the sort of relationship I'm looking for.'

I gazed into the stove, watching the tongues of fire lick about the wood.

'I'm not saying it would last forever, it's too soon to tell but I don't want to lose you, not just end it,' he sighed. 'There must be things that would help, we could give it another few weeks, talk about what might work for us at the moment . . .'

'Stuart,' I couldn't let him go on; it hurt to realize how much he wanted me. His honesty was salt in the wounds. 'I'm really sorry, but I can't change how I feel now.'

'You like me.'

'It's not enough. I don't want to pretend.'

'God,' he sighed, put his head in his hands.

'Anything else would just be messing you about. That wouldn't be fair.'

'And this is?'

'I'm sorry. I'm going to go now.'

We stood up, both leaning forward for my coat. A ripple of embarrassment. I took it from him, slipped it on. He saw me to the door. I imagined us shaking hands. It made me want to laugh. Nerves. I didn't want him to kiss me. He didn't try. We hugged. I could smell his cologne, a light, grassy scent. He had thought I might stay. He would have made up the bed, perhaps bought treats for breakfast. Don't do this, Sal. The sex had always been good. But sex wasn't enough, there was everything else.

I pulled away. We said goodbye.

Was I mad? He was a nice man and there weren't many available. Would that be it for the next few years? The sum total of my relationships? Would I always be so picky? Yes, Stuart had flaws but the good things far outweighed them. And he really liked me. He'd been gutted. Was a single life really preferable to compromising? I was turning my back on sex and affection and someone to stroke my head and laugh with. Why wouldn't I settle for anything less than perfect?

I wanted to ring Diane and go out to a club and get rat-arsed with her and dance myself stupid but Diane was in Iceland. Everyone else I knew well enough to tell about it was snugly settled in happy coupledom and well out of the clubbing habit. Not that I'd even know which clubs were playing what these days. And I shouldn't get drunk anyway. Laura and I were taking the kids for their promised walk in the morning while Ray cracked on with his furniture and I was seeing the Johnstones at two. A hangover wouldn't help. I shouldn't get drunk. But shouldn't and wouldn't are two different things. So I did.

I sat by the tree with a lamp on and a bottle of Merlot by my side and wrote more hopelessly late Christmas cards. I stayed up to watch the film until the wine ran out and my eyes began to dehydrate.

I drank two pints of water, knowing it wouldn't come close, and got to bed. I don't remember getting into bed but that's where I woke up on Sunday morning. With my head lanced with pain, a churning stomach and a large pebble where my tongue should have been.

'Where are we going?'

'To the caves.'

The children bounced around like ping-pong balls in the hall while Laura and I gathered outdoor clothes together.

'Why isn't Daddy coming?' Tom asked.

'He's got to finish his chairs,' Laura told him.

Digger yelped as Tom trod on his paw which made Maddie scream. A thin needle of agony stitched through my temple. I was hoping the Nurofen would kick in soon. It had been half an hour.

'Don't scream,' I said carefully. No one heard.

My phone rang and I shooed them out to the car with Laura while I took the call.

'It's Bryony Walker. I'm sorry to ring you over the weekend but I thought you'd like to know, I've got some good news.'

My pulse increased and my head throbbed more.

'What is it?'

'I was with an old friend in Brum last night. She's been working on an inquiry down in Devon and Cornwall with the police. Guess whose name came up.'

'Eddie Cliff.'

'Bingo. Except he was going by the name of Cliff Edwards, working there way back in the mid-seventies. Anyway, to cut a long story short, there are two women who have come forward and are prepared to talk about what happened.'

Oh, yes! 'Brilliant. And they'll be able to prosecute?'

'Fingers crossed. I'll give you the name of the officer in charge of the inquiry and you can pass it on to the authorities at your end.'

'Thanks,' I took down the details. Digger was outside barking with frustration and Maddie began calling my name.

'Sounds like you're wanted,' she said.

'Yes, thanks for that. It's a real breakthrough. Great.'

'I nearly rang you in the early hours. Managed to restrain myself. Anyway, have a good Christmas.'

'You too, and a happy new year.'

It was good news but I felt a shiver of anxiety as I left the house. I blamed it on the drink. Not content with messing me up physically, it was having a go at my emotions. Fresh air, I told myself. Fresh air and fun and a huge lunch later.

'Come on,' Maddie bawled.

I got in the car.

Alderley Edge is twenty-five minutes' drive on a good day. It used to take longer but the new bypass removes the need to crawl through the traffic jam in Wilmslow town centre.

The village at Alderley Edge nestles at the foot of the big hill and is renowned as the champagne capital of the north. It's celebrity territory; Posh and Becks country. A desirable Cheshire location within reach of Manchester and the airport, occupied by footballers, soap stars, those at the higher reaches of the media and entertainment business. And up the hill, past the mansions with their landscaped gardens and double garages, their turrets and follies, monkey-puzzle trees and orchid houses, their horses and dogs, stands the Edge. A sandstone escarpment, stuck on the Cheshire plain,

229

covered with woods and riddled by old copper mineworkings, quarries, caves and gullies. Local legends tell of the wizard who sleeps beneath the Edge, a story immortalized in the children's book by Alan Garner.

We stopped at the main car park and meandered through the woods towards the Edge, stopping en route at the small Druids' stone circle where the children played stepping stones. The stones were small and low but some were too far apart for either of them to make the jump. Digger ran off exploring and made his way back to us when called.

Further on, we climbed up to the site where they lit the beacon to warn of the Armada. I read the plaque out to the children; a ritual of our visits.

Most of the trees were bare, their branches and twigs laced against the pearly grey sky, bird's nests, tangled balls of twigs clearly visible. Underfoot lay a soft carpet of conifer needles, orange beech leaves and beech nut cases and mud. Here and there a Scot's pine or a holly tree remained evergreen. A brisk wind shook the trees and blew our hair about, wafted the sharp aroma of leaf mould and crushed vegetation our way.

A couple with a string of dogs passed us. The dogs rooting for scents around the base of trees. We walked on. Maddie and Tom ran ahead to hide.

'Is Stuart coming for Christmas?' Laura asked me.

Ho hum.

'No,' I cleared my throat. 'It's all over.'

'Oh, God, I'm sorry.'

'Don't worry. My decision really.'

She sighed. 'When was this?'

'Last night.'

'Hence the hangover?'

'Yes.'

'How do you feel?'

'Headache's gone. Crap really,' I blinked hard.

I felt queasy and tired. As though my blood was too thin

and my muscles too weak. And I still felt uneasy about work, anxiety slopping around inside and cloaking my shoulders. Why couldn't I just shake it off?

'Careful,' I called to Tom who scrambled down the sandstone edge. As we reached it we could see the fields which lay far below; in one, cows the size of paper clips. The further vista beyond the first farm was shrouded in mist. We all followed Tom down onto the cliff-side and along to one of the caves that peppered the hill. The soft walls, striped russet red and golden with the layers of rock, were smothered with carved initials and drawings. This was supposed to be a magical place, wizards and all, and pagans held it sacred. The remnants of a fire and some lager cans lay near the entrance. Maddie refused to go any further in – there be monsters – but Tom had no qualms. Giggling with excitement he made growling noises and chattered about bears and dragons. Laura and I followed him. The wall and ceiling narrowed suddenly so we had to go on our hands and knees. The place reeked of damp rock. It was impossible to see further into the small tunnel. We could hear the wind deep in the stones.

'Next time we'll bring a torch,' I told him. 'Then we can go further in.'

We turned and crept back out, Laura and I squatting until it was safe to stand up. Maddie was waiting, silhouetted at the mouth of the cave. As I got near to her I could see a woman with a Dalmatian dog descending the path towards us and at the side of the path a man: grey and brown hair, leather jacket, denims, cowboy boots.

'Laura,' I turned to her and spoke urgently, keeping my voice low. Tom was next to Maddie, jumping up and down. 'Take the kids, get them an ice-cream. Ring the police.'

'Sal,' she peered at me. Was I serious?

I returned her look, showing that I'd never been more so. I put my hand on her shoulder and squeezed. 'Tell them I'm being . . . someone's following me. Hurry . . .'

'But . . .'

'Laura, please.'

She speeded up. Called Tom and Maddie and challenged them to a race up the hill. Off they went; Digger appeared from nowhere loping after them.

I stood in the entrance to the cave. Waited. My mouth dry, my heart flopping around in my chest like a landed fish.

I had acted instinctively. He shouldn't be here. Things could get unpleasant and my first thought was to get the children clear. Looking back with the benefit of hindsight, I'd probably have been safer sticking with them. But it's easy to think that now. And I never imagined he would take such breathtaking risks.

'Sal,' he stepped down the ridges made by the tree roots, stood level with me.

'You followed me,' I said. It couldn't be chance. From home, then. How had he got my address? Oh, God. I remembered; we'd chatted about Withington, I'd signed their petition, home address. Stupid.

'Things to talk about,' he said.

Another family headed for the cave.

'Here?' I tried to convey my incredulity.

'Shall we?' He gestured to a rocky outcrop beside one of the small brooks where we could sit. We walked over there. I could feel tension singing along my limbs, spiralling inside. Give them chance to get back to the car and then I could run for it if I had to. What could he possibly have to say?

He climbed up and sat on one of the boulders, I perched on the one next door.

'I don't like being set up,' he said. His eyes were flinty, the blue flat and artificial even though the lines still wrinkled the edges.

I looked away. 'What do you mean?'

'Oh, you know. Snooping around, then you accuse me of lying, next thing you're in a huddle with the chair of my management committee.'

I tried to laugh. 'She has a friend, needs a private eye, a domestic thing.'

'Yeah, yeah,' he was dismissive. 'I really don't understand this vendetta. I bent over backwards to help you and then you start twisting everything. I won't have you spreading lies about me.' He was icy.

I stood up. I didn't need to hear this. I could feel his anger simmering, he was fuming. Gone the sharing, caring cowboy.

He moved round quickly and blocked my path.

'Excuse me.'

'You're making a big mistake,' he said, 'I can't let you do that.'

I wheeled away in the opposite direction off the path and into the trees. I'd circle through the lower woods, climb up to the car park further round. But he came crashing after me. I ran. The ground beneath the tangled undergrowth was soft with mud. I stumbled twice, rolling as I fell to keep my speed up. I pulled off my gloves and threw them away. I couldn't get a proper hold of anything; the wool was too slippery. I kept moving. There were no paths down here, little chance of meeting dog-walkers or families out for a stroll. I glanced back, the distance between us was increasing. I ran up and over one of the small ridges. He wouldn't be able to see me now. There were bushes to the left, rhododendrons growing in a gully. I ran round. Further along was an overhang, thick with brambles. I wriggled beneath them, gasping as the thorns tore at my face, curled into a ball. I smelt earth and rotting plants. My breath roared in my ears, I tried to quieten myself. He wouldn't hear above the rustle of the wind surely. Still I buried my face in my hands, trying to sip only a fragment of air, not make the noisy gulps. My heart was burning. I could hear him now. Getting closer. He stopped walking. I could hear him panting. Then another sound, someone moving, light and rapid through the woods. Snuffling, closer. Digger worming his way into my hiding place.

'Go,' I mouthed and shoved at his head. 'Get away.' Stupid bloody dog.

It was too late, footsteps my way. I pulled myself out and struggled upright just as Eddie Cliff reached me. He launched himself at me. I ducked and managed to side step him. I ran, he was close on my heels. He caught up again. Knocked me down. I brought my hands up to protect my head. He had his weight on me. He was heavy, solid. I could feel mud beneath one hand, brambles with the other. My face was buried in the leaf mulch, cold and gritty with sand. The miasma filled my nostrils, robbing me of breath.

He was panting, harsh and fast. 'You had to interfere, didn't you? Just like . . .'

Like Miriam. Who had seen Melody with him. Who knew him for what he was.

He rolled me over and knelt astride me, his hands went round my throat. He began to squeeze, he was incredibly strong. He was choking me. My eyeballs hurt, my vision went. Help. Get off. I lifted my hands up, clawing at the air, his head, his face. He bit my finger, the deep pain made me whimper. Bastard. I was angry. As soon as he released my hand I lunged, found his nose and jabbed my nails into the orbs above. Hard as I could. He howled and released his stranglehold. Pungent air rushed into my windpipe making me splutter and saliva washed into my mouth. It was only a moment but enough for me to roll him partly off me, and begin to wriggle backwards. As soon as I could I kicked at his face and hit his nose. He yelled again. His eye was all bloody and his nose began to bleed too. But he came at me again. I rolled over, kept going, half crawling, half falling down the steep slope. I could taste blood in my mouth. Was it my throat?

He scrabbled after me. 'They know I'm here,' I called, but my voice was cracked and weak. 'The police are coming.' If he heard me he took no notice.

At the bottom of the hill there was a stony path and a barbed wire fence separating the woods from the private farmland.

I got to my feet, my knees soft and heavy as sand. I tried to run but it was hard to achieve any speed. He was catching up. My skin was burning with the exertion, my heart thumping. Cramp stabbed through my left calf. Up ahead were more fences, we were nearing the far end of the estate. I began to climb the bank, the sheer gradient made it horribly slow. Up at the top there'd be people. The police would be on the way by now, wouldn't they? Faster. He was at my heels, his breath ragged. He grabbed my ankle. Please, no. I used the other one to kick down hard, connected with something and his hold slipped. On the skyline among the trees I made out a horse and rider cantering, surreal against the steely light.

I reached a plateau and stumbled across it. In the centre was a large pit, an old quarry. Trees crowded the slope behind it, I'd have to skirt it then keep climbing. I spat blood from my mouth, wiped the string of saliva as I moved. He was on me. His hands grabbing my neck again. No. I collapsed, deliberately, dead weight pulling him over, making him let go of my neck. I scrambled to my feet and took a step away. The quarry behind me. I didn't have enough air to run any further, not uphill. Both legs were cramped. He stood swaying, blood slicked his face and one eye was swollen shut.

'The police,' I tried to shout but the words were hoarse. 'You can't . . .'

'Bitch,' he ran at me again, roaring, arms coming up to push me. For a moment he was slow motion, I watched his arms, getting ready. As he got to me I reached out to grab him, and went into a backward roll using his momentum to guide him over me and on over the rim of the pit. It was clumsy and he banged my head with his knee but it was effective. I heard a thump and the brush of foliage as he landed.

I lay there knowing I had to get up, go, escape. Trying to move, feeling weak and uncoordinated as a newborn. Move. Move. I rolled over and got on my hands and knees. I shuffled forward and looked down, panting. He was looking back at me, with his one eye. A bright blue marble. He kept twitching his arms and legs but he couldn't get up. I noticed then that one leg was bent strangely, the knee didn't look right. His face had gone the colour of lard.

I hesitated, wanting to make sure he couldn't come after me any more. Trying to slow down the breaths that hurt so much. Then I heard a shout, a child. I looked up and saw a man and a small boy slithering down the hillside.

'Help,' I shouted, 'help.' My voice croaky.

The man swung his head, caught sight of me. I knelt up. 'There's been an accident. Get an ambulance. And the police.' Shouting made me feel sick. I clamped my mouth shut and tasted the tang of blood.

'Come on, Rory,' he turned and took the boy's hand, led him up the bank.

Eddie Cliff had stopped twitching. Both eyes closed. He was moaning, a little like the sound a dog makes in pain. I put my legs over the edge of the quarry and went down on my bottom. My hands were freezing and bright red like lobsters, swelling too. I'd torn a thumbnail deep and it hurt as much as my throat. When I got to the quarry floor I walked over to him, my legs trembling. I fell twice; the place was a jungle of fallen trees and brambles hiding uneven rocks. He had fallen onto a rock. He lay across it like a sacrificial victim. He heard me approach and opened his good eye, the other eyelid flickered, looked like cranberry jelly inside.

'I know about Miriam.'

'Suicide.'

'She was scared of heights. Did you know? Did that make it easier? She'd have been frozen, incapable, drowning in fear.' It hurt to talk. I coughed and spat blood. I wiped my face with the palm of my hand.

Beads of sweat stood on his forehead and nose and ran into the lines on his face. All those laughter lines. Ha ha ha.

'Why did she get in the car?'

He didn't reply.

'She knew what you'd done to Melody, she'd promised to

236

help but Melody begged her not to tell. She was frightened, they both were. Threats. Someone like you, it wouldn't take much to have someone sectioned, sent to a secure unit. They knew you had the power, people would never doubt anything you said. But Miriam knew she should speak out. She wanted to do the right thing. And you couldn't rely on her keeping quiet, could you; she wasn't one of your victims, she was a witness. Was that the first time, eh? Oh, I know it wasn't the first case of abuse – you've been doing that for years, haven't you? But was it the first time someone actually caught you at it?'

He'd gone paler, his lips tinged with blue. Shock. He moaned. He was going into shock. It can kill. Hypothermia. I could go. Spit on him and walk away. Leave them to find him. I looked at him. It was hard to get my coat off, my hands were stiff and puffy. I draped it over his chest. White foam flecked the corners of his mouth.

He shook and his face spasmed in pain. 'Help me,' he said hoarsely.

I bent and whispered in his ear. 'Why did Miriam go with you? Why?'

No answer.

I could smell the salt of his skin and the acetate note in his breath.

'Why did she get in the car?' I demanded.

'Help,' he moaned.

'Tell me first.'

He groaned again, his face was waxy, covered with a sheen of sweat.

'Tell me. Why did Miriam go with you?'

He smiled. It looked like a death rictus. 'See Melody. Told her . . . misunderstanding, sort it out . . . told her Melody wanted Miriam there . . . support.'

'She believed that?'

'Social worker wants to see us all,' he struggled to speak, I bent close to hear. 'Take statements, Melody asking for you, Miriam.'

237

The bloody liar. Able with his clever words and ready assurances to persuade her to go with him, in spite of everything. Ladling on how much Melody needed her. Miriam confused, appalled at what had happened, frightened but wanting to do the right thing for the young woman. Promises of a civilized meeting, social workers and all.

Bemused and disoriented she had gone, for the best of reasons, sitting tight, loathing the man beside her and with no idea how brutal and ruthless he was. She had gone. In the car. How long till she realized he wasn't taking her to see Melody and a social worker? Perhaps he said they'd meet at the Town Hall. But he drives another way, towards the Arndale Centre, into the car park. Her panic mounting, her terror of high places freezing in her veins. Perhaps still hoping that it would all come right, that nothing could happen here, in a busy city centre car park. That Eddie would never . . . Then what? He forced her from the car? Pulled her to the edge. Petrified she had finally seen his plan. Struggled then, for her life, for her children but he was stronger. Had she begged? Screamed for help? Had fear eaten her words? Those last frantic moments, calling on her God, praying for Connie and Martina and Roland.

He shook, the smile faded and his eyes slipped back inside his head, revealing one white orb like a hard-boiled egg, one crimson pulp. Blood dripped on my jumper, I felt the trees stagger and suddenly my knees buckled. I landed on bracken, wet grass, branches. Above me a Scot's pine was silhouetted, spiky black stretched out against the smeared grey sky. They wouldn't be long now, would they?

A little later something warm and wet wriggled across my face, making the cuts sting. Digger licking me. He grinned and sat. Stinky breath curling from his lolling tongue. No barking, no fetching help, nothing. I closed my eyes. You, I thought, must be the most bloody useless dog in the whole known universe.

CHAPTER FORTY-EIGHT

I don't often abuse alcohol for sustained periods of time but I spent that Christmas in a protective haze of gin and tonics, wine and whisky, depending on the time of day.

I wept a lot, which is very easy to do with all the schmaltz on the box. Ray was annoyed with me again which I thought was a bit rich. After all, I had done the self-defence course and I had used what I'd learnt to great effect. Ursula would be proud of me. It was hardly my fault that Eddie Cliff chose to attack me when the kids and Laura were around. If I was a vicious, manipulative, psychopath I'd have chosen a better moment, but honestly . . .

Connie Johnstone had rung my mobile when I failed to appear at the office. There was no answer. She tried my home number and Ray, not knowing who she was of course, told her that I'd been in an accident and was in Wythenshawe Hospital.

As there was a beds crisis, flu sweeping the nation and affecting staff as well as patients, they didn't even keep me in overnight. I didn't need a bed anyway, I would only have used it to sleep in. My wounds were cleaned and stitched, needles stuck in me, painkillers prescribed. I was told to rest my voice.

The police wanted an initial statement which I supplied with the sort of numb indifference that comes after a trauma. Well, indifference alternating with hilarity which is a disturbing combination. They wrote it down and told me I'd be seen again.

Would I press charges?

Too bloody right, I would.

I told them I'd already seen a detective at Elizabeth Slinger. That I'd tried to report a man for suspected murder. The same man who had just tried to kill me. They nodded. I gave them the policeman's name. They wrote that down. I told them about the abuse inquiry too, in Devon. They nodded, made another note. And went away.

I had to talk to Connie Johnstone. Once I got home I rang her and asked if she would come and see me.

'You sound awful,' she said. 'Are you sure? Your husband said there'd been an accident.'

Wrong on both counts.

'I'm sure.' I had to get it over with. I had to tell her before the police called round or there was anything in the papers.

'Don't bring Martina or Roland.'

'All right.' She sounded worried.

It felt strange, clients in my living room.

'Good God,' Patrick exclaimed. 'What's the other fella like?'

'Patrick!' Connie was shocked.

So was I; bit inappropriate cracking jokes before he knew what the 'accident' had been.

'Sorry,' I realized he was tense. He knew something heavy was coming. His Adam's apple bobbed and he apologized again.

'It's all right,' I said. 'He's worse than me; dislocated hip, fractured knee, lacerated eye, plus he's looking at a long stretch inside.'

'Blimey.'

'Please, sit down.'

They settled on our sofa, side by side. 'Roland told us,' Connie said, 'about meeting Horace.'

'He thought that was what had set Miriam off,' Patrick added. 'Poor lad had been tearing himself apart with it. But apparently the meeting Roland had set up never happened. You spoke to Horace?'

'That's right.'

'If only he'd said something. But I know why he didn't.' Connie gave a rueful smile.

'I'm glad he's told you himself. He was so worried. Has he said anything about keeping in touch with his father?'

'I think he will,' Connie said. 'We don't all feel the same about it, about the past. Roland wasn't even born when he walked out on us. But he knows there won't be any come-back. If that's what he wants. He's old enough to decide for himself.'

'He's been a lot more relaxed,' Patrick added.

She nodded.

There was a pause. I looked at them. My stomach lurched. I took a breath. Felt the room sway a little. 'I found out what happened to Miriam. I'm so sorry, Connie, it's a terrible thing.' I held her gaze, my hands clamped tight on the chair arms. My heart skipping beats and trying to get away. 'She didn't jump, it wasn't suicide. It was Eddie Cliff,' I said.

Connie stared at me, her eyes wary, her mouth tightening. 'Eddie?'

'He did it, Eddie, he killed her.'

What? Her mouth formed the word but she made no sound. She turned to Patrick then back to me. Her eyes beginning to dart here and there, head shaking, denying it. Not admitting.

'He tried to shut me up,' I felt an eddy of fear at the thought. I spoke over it. 'Eddie killed her. I'm so sorry.'

She raised her arms, fists balled, as though she would fight the truth. Patrick caught at her. She hit him, his chest, crying out, 'No, no, oh, God, no.' He pulled her closer, ignoring the blows, holding her in her grief, his own face creased with emotion.

241

I stared at the lights on the tree, the stars of light blurring and streaking as my eyes filled up.

Some time later she spoke again. Turned her eyes full with pain to mine.

'Why?' She said thickly. 'But why?'

I leant forward in my chair and began to explain.

CHAPTER FORTY-NINE

Nana 'Tello had insisted on the Queen's speech. This didn't make much sense as she is a raving republican. However, Nana's passion for the gee-gees means she feels an affinity with Lizzie and knows exactly what animals she has in training, in stud and in the running on any given day. Lizzie is a fellow horse fancier rather than a Queen. So Nana 'Tello was glued to the telly. She was probably hoping for a tip for the Boxing Day meet at Newmarket.

Laura and Ray were loading the dishwasher. I never got my vegetarian feast. Ended up with all the trimmings and no turkey. It was fine. I was a little hurt that Ray hadn't treated me to a cashew roast or chestnut and stilton roulade but he couldn't do that without dropping the wall of disapproval he was lugging about. I'd not got him a CD anyway or anything else, nor Laura. Hadn't had chance. He'd bought me a book on water gardens, a nice one with lots of design ideas. I was touched, I'd been planning a pond for years and not getting very far. He accepted my thanks gruffly with a nod rather than a smile.

I couldn't quite get away with telling the kids I'd fallen down the hill especially when they'd been party to Laura's 999 call and the ensuing drama. So it was a 'bad man' who had pushed me and the police had got him locked up. They seemed to accept it with only a few whys and wherefores.

They were playing on the computer. Frogger Two had gone down a treat, 'Si-i-i-ck,' they'd chorused, 'so si-i-ick.' They were happy negotiating the cartoon creatures through the violent threats posed by relentless lawnmowers and aggressive bumble bees.

I went outside, wandered round the garden. It was almost dark. Someone was letting fireworks off, a series of bangs and shrieks. I glimpsed a few fleeting star bursts.

Diane would be in the thick of it in her winter wonderland. I tried to imagine the northern lights flickering over a snow-draped landscape. Bright and beautiful unlike this dull, damp, grey one.

A great tit swung on the seed feeder followed by its mate. Beneath the tree a sliver of green caught my eye. I moved closer. Two tiny sword-like leaves, the green striped with white. I bent, grimaced at my aching muscles, touched the tightly rolled bud with the tip of my finger, stroked the length of the leaves between thumb and forefinger.

The first snowdrop. So early. A promise of things to come. I slowly straightened up. Turned to face the house, windows aglow.

Maddie came out, she had her slippers on. I thought about it but decided to say nothing.

'Why didn't it snow?' She sat on the swing and tilted herself back.

'Well, it doesn't usually, not in Manchester. It's not cold enough.'

'It always has snow in pictures.'

'Yes. Like it's always sunny in the summer.'

She sat upright and narrowed her eyes. 'But it is.'

'Do you think so?'

She frowned. 'Yes.'

Can't be bad, a child who remembers all her summers like that.

'Are you going to make any New Year's Revolutions?'

I laughed. 'Resolutions.'

'What are they?'

'Things you want to do, things you want to change.'

244

'What like?'

'Well, some people stop smoking or start going to the gym.'

'What can I do?'

'You don't have to do anything.'

'If I wanted to, though?'

'Okay. What would you like to do next year that you haven't done this year?'

'Get a kitten?'

I raised my eyebrows, kittens aren't an option.

'I don't know really,' she said. 'Are you doing any?'

I considered the question.

'Oh!' She flew off the swing and darted into the house and returned a couple of minutes later with an envelope. 'I did this.' She thrust it at me. It said Mummy on the front in a big red heart.

Inside was a green card with a cotton wool snowman and a red robin stuck on the front. Inside Maddie had drawn a picture of our house with a face at each window, all smiling. 'There's you and Tom,' I said. 'That's Ray with the 'tache and beard. Is that Laura?'

'Yes, and Digger,' she pointed.

'And that's me.'

'Your nose is a bit big but it went wrong there.'

She had written *Happy Christmas and New Year.* The rest of the card was covered with kisses and I love yous.

'That is lovely, come here.'

She screwed up her nose, anticipating a kiss. I gave her one and a hug. 'And I love you, you know.'

She nodded and returned to the swing.

'Would you, then? Make a resolution?' She swung up, her toes pointing skyward, hair falling towards the ground behind her.

'I don't think so. I like things pretty much as they are. Maybe my resolution will be to remember that more often.'

She gave a grunt which signalled I was talking rubbish

again and swung higher. I watched her for a while, drinking in the sight. When she slowed and stopped I walked over to her. 'Come on then,' I said. 'My turn. Give us a push.'

I watched the tree rock above me and the warm lighted windows of the house dip in and out of view, and felt Maddie's small hands press on my back and her giggles ring round the garden. And I swung higher and higher.